Loving

Vengeance

Georgia Rose

1st Edition Published by Three Shires Publishing

ISBN: 978-1-9164669-2-0 (paperback)

Loving Vengeance copyright © 2019 Georgia Rose

Georgia Rose asserts the right to be identified as the author of this work in accordance with the Copyright Designs and Patents Act 1988. All rights reserved.

No part of this publication can be reproduced or transmitted in any form or by any means, electronic, mechanical or otherwise, without the express written permission of Georgia Rose.

www.georgiarosebooks.com

Edited by Mark Barry
www.greenwizardpublishing.blogspot.co.uk

Proofread by Julia Gibbs
juliaproofreader@gmail.com

Cover design by Simon Emery
siemery2012@gmail.com

All characters appearing in this work are fictitious. Any resemblance to real persons, living or dead, is purely coincidental.

British Library Cataloguing in Publication Data
A CIP catalogue record for this book is available from the British Library

<u>Authors Note</u>

Thank you for choosing to read this book but please note, if you haven't already, that *Loving Vengeance* is the second book in a duology. I strongly advise you to read *Parallel Lies*, which is the first, before you get stuck into this. While *Loving Vengeance* is a complete story in itself I have not rehashed a lot of back story from *Parallel Lies* and you'll miss many of the reasons why characters are where they are or behave as they do. If you go to find *Parallel Lies*, and find it is not at a price that encourages you to buy it please contact me (details at the back of this book) and I'll be delighted to get a copy to you. I only want you to get the best experience of reading *Loving Vengeance* that you can.

Thank you

Georgia

Loving Vengeance is dedicated to all those who wanted more when *Parallel Lies* ended.
If that is not you, read no further.

It is also dedicated to someone who has come into my life recently and turned it upside down. Oliver, you are a delight and I look forward to spending the rest of my life getting to know you.

There is nothing like returning to a place that remains unchanged to find the ways in which you yourself have altered.

Nelson Mandela

Chapter 1

He stands in the doorway. A silhouette cast against the golden remnants of an autumnal sun in a sky so clear as to guarantee an overnight frost. I hide my disappointment, but inside my heart sinks, because I don't know the man who's come to visit.

But he knows me.

"Hello, Madeleine." He holds up his warrant card and gives me a moment to process it. The acidic contents of my stomach turn over as I do so. "I'm Detective Inspector James Lambert." I look from the card back to him as he adds, "From the—" but I cut him off with a raised hand.

"I know where you're from." I pause and he remains silent as I deliberate on how to proceed, then considering he's come a long way, I decide I might as well find out why. "Come in," I say, as I turn my back to him and return to my place on the sofa, my sore and aching body grateful for its softness as I ease myself back into it. He follows me in and I indicate towards the armchair I want him to sit in. He does so and we study each other. He doesn't look like police. That had been my first impression, and further scrutiny changes nothing. Crisp white shirt, dark grey well-cut trousers, shiny shoes, smart haircut. Nice lips. I keep my face passive, but my mind is whirling with a hundred questions, none of which I ask, wanting him to show his hand first.

He clears his throat, looks directly at me. "I'm

sorry for what happened to you last night." He hesitates for only a fraction when I fail to respond. I don't because my throat tightens and I'm not sure how to reply or even if I can. I nod instead. Even before he introduced himself I knew he was already aware of what had happened to me. He didn't flinch, not in the slightest, when he first looked at my face, and you would, if you didn't already know what to expect. "I've been asked to come out and follow up with you." I allow myself a small smile. "What?" he frowns, clearly not expecting that reaction. I shrug and he persists. "May I ask you some questions?"

"Only if you tell me why you're here." He tilts his head as he appraises me.

"We have some follow—" I hold my hand up again.

"The truth." I glare at him, daring him to utter one more word of nonsense. He seems indecisive about what he should say next so, to nudge things along a little I tell him what I know, counting the points off on my fingers. "I answered more than enough questions with the police earlier. You've turned up out of the blue, on a Sunday, on your own and you're from the Metropolitan Police, not the local force. I know who you are, Detective Inspector James Lambert, so what do you want?"

It's his turn to smile, which looks good on him, blue eyes sparkling as he holds his hands up admitting defeat. "Okay, you got me." I wait, patient once more, but pull my sleeves down over my hands as I bury them in my lap. "You can call me James, and you're right I am from the Met. I'm here on a Sunday because I needed to speak to you before anyone else does." *Why?* Although even as I think this I realise it is the fact he is from the Met that is more alarming to me. There is only one reason someone from the London force would turn up. There's a long silence that I leave him to fill, and eventually he does.

"I know who you are too, Scarlet." It comes as no surprise that he knows my real name. But brittle like crisp leaves that crumble to the touch, I'm powerless to do anything other than accept whatever past sins he's scraped together and is about to arrest me for. And weary, I wish he'd get to the point.

"What do you want?" There's a note of exasperation in my voice but as I finish speaking I hear another car outside; he does too, glancing at the window, and for whatever reason he gets up and looks like he's about to leave.

I'm annoyed by the distraction, frustrated at potentially now not discovering what it is James is here for. To give him credit, he at least gives me something.

"I think we can help each other out. I have a proposition for you and in return I'm going to do you a favour." Okay. I am intrigued. However, as I suspected it looks like the sound of the car and another person's arrival is going to prevent him from saying anything further. Or, it might just be that he simply wants to fully bait that appetising hook but leave it dangling, so as to build up the anticipation and possibly smooth the way to me agreeing to whatever it is he's touting as mutually beneficial.

"You're not going to tell me now?" I try to sound as though I'm not remotely bothered even though he has sufficiently raised my levels of curiosity to make that difficult.

"No, it sounds like you're about to have company, I'll leave you in peace and now I know where I can find you we'll catch up another time." He is now as nonchalant as I am, and I wonder who, in this game of cat and mouse, is playing which part.

I push myself off the sofa once more and follow him to the door, like any good hostess would, although I realise I never so much as offered him a cup of tea. I open it to let him out, managing to maintain my air of indifference, while all the time enduring the frantic itch of curiosity that scratches at my brain, and it's all I can do to resist the urge to demand he tell me now.

He smiles at me as he passes, then pauses as he's about to leave and turns back, "You know, over the years I've often wondered how I would feel when I saw you again," he says, and on that note he walks away. I can't deny it, that rocks me, which is, I suspect, exactly what he wants. *He knows me?* He doesn't just know *about* me. He actually knows me. So how come I'd swear I'd never seen him before?

It's Dan who's my next visitor. The one I'd wanted in the first place, but never honestly expected. He passes James at the gate and they take a moment to look each other up and down. He doesn't look happy, which is no surprise and I brace myself for the lecture I suspect I'll receive for going directly against his specific wishes to stay away from Tag. Given the fact I didn't think I'd see him here again, however, I find I don't mind that prospect. I haven't moved so he meets me at the door.

"Hello," he says, and I reply with the same. It feels stilted and I try to add a smile, feeling the split in my lip start to open again as I do. I bring the back of my hand up to dab it, to test it's not bleeding. He looks tired and I can empathise with that. The shadows under his eyes accentuate the darkness in them, his hair, a mess, like fingers have been drawn through it repeatedly, and perhaps they have. I watch him check out the state of my face, the quick frown of concern puckering his forehead but I'm pleased he says nothing about it, simply asking, "May I come in?" Again I turn and walk into my cottage but this time I go straight through to the kitchen. I hear him close the door behind us and while I wanted him to come, I'm not sure I'm strong enough to deal with the fallout from the previous night yet, so I stall.

"Do you want something to eat?" I call back over my shoulder. The arrival of DI James Lambert has not only piqued my curiosity but also reawakened my appetite. My stomach rumbles and there's a pang of hunger like it's trying to digest itself and I need to feed it regardless of whether Dan is joining me or not. But, as I load up a tray with cheese and crackers then reach for a jar of chutney he gets the plates and knives, so I guess that's a yes, and we make our way back to the sofa where we sit and eat picnic style. It seems he's as hungry as I am, and also not wanting to talk. I eat slowly, taking small bites, but with each mouthful I can feel the punishment Tag meted out to my face. The movement hurts my jaw, cheek and lips. A dull throbbing builds around my eye and temple and I know I need more pills. We eat in silence but it feels fine, not awkward, or loaded, just comfortable. Which is strange because I hadn't imagined us being able to be like this again, like we were before the rape, before the row.

Eventually we've eaten enough and we clear away. I pour us each a large whisky and as he digs out the ice for his I use a good slug of mine to wash down the pills, and we wander back through to the sitting room and take up our previous places on the sofa.

"Should we talk?" he says, the words tentative.

"Do we have to?" His smile as weak as I feel.

"I think so, I need to say I'm sorry."

"What for?" My surprise shows in my question; an apology was the last thing I was expecting.

"For not being there, when you needed me." I stare at him for a moment. I can sense his pain but beyond that there's something else.

"What happened is down to me, Dan, not you."

"But if I'd been more... accepting, perhaps you would have opened up. Told me what was going on. I could have helped, or at least been involved. I could have protected you." I smile, and try not to laugh. I know he means well but he has no idea. He frowns and I realise it looks like I'm mocking him, and his efforts, then I feel it again, that definite something, deep down inside of him. I shake my head, which hurts.

"The last thing I would have ever done is tell you what was going on, Dan. Tag was threatening to tell you all about my past and that is the last thing I ever want you, or anyone else, to know about. As it is I'm going to have difficulty keeping my anonymity through all this." I sound as exasperated as I feel and would give anything to have things return to how they were. All I want is to have my quiet life in the village back again but at the moment that feels unlikely to ever happen. "Look." I turn in my seat to see him better, easing my body round carefully as I do, and he leans slightly towards me. "I didn't set out to deceive you. There was nothing going on between me and Tag. He brought certain pressure to bear and I played along hoping he would get what he came for and disappear out of my life again."

"Do you think that was a realistic plan?" He's right to call me out on my naivety. Although I'd tried to put something cohesive together, ultimately I'd been hanging a good outcome in all of this on a wing and a prayer, and Tag's good nature, of which there was none.

However, I say, "It's not ended that badly," feeling I need to argue my case and although he looks incredulous I carry on regardless, counting the points off on my fingers, again. "I protected the collection. I called the police. Tag got locked up."

"You got attacked." That stops me in my tracks

and I go quiet. I notice he can't use the word rape.

"That was unlucky," I mutter.

"Unlucky! That's an understatement. It's just as well Tag *is* locked away. He needs to be for his own safety." And in that moment, in that precise second, I know what it is I've been sensing in him. Rage. Burning away deep inside like a furnace. He wants to punch something, or preferably someone, a particular someone. He exhales loudly, dragging his fingers through his hair once more then he rubs his hands down his unshaven face as he adds, "I'm sorry." He looks over at me and in a softer voice asks, "Are you, you know, all right?" I assume he's asking specifically about what Tag did to me.

"I will be," I say, and I reach out and lay my hand on top of his as if for reassurance. His, not mine. To be honest I've had worse things happen to me but Dan definitely doesn't need to know about any of that. I'd hoped he'd take my hand in his but he doesn't so I withdraw mine and look at my watch. It's still only early evening but I'm exhausted. However, there's something I have to do before I can go to bed. "I'm going to go and run a bath. Do you want to top up the drinks?" He nods.

I know I've already had one bath but my body aches all over and when I lower it gingerly into the hot water, like earlier, the cuts and scrapes sting initially, but then the warmth does its work in making my muscles relax and I gradually become more comfortable. I scrub myself, again, my skin turning pink under the brush I use. In some places I've made myself sore I've scrubbed so hard, and I vow this is to be the last time I do this. I wash my hair and give myself some time to think about Dan as I lie in the water staring at the tiled wall in front of me. Having thought it was unlikely I'd ever see him again, a thought that had made me sad, I'm relieved he has come round and that he hasn't lectured me much, at least not so far. I wonder if he's planning on staying or not and I'm not sure what to do about that because I don't know what I want and I hate being this indecisive.

I put clean dressings on the worst wounds, and pull on fresh pyjamas, easing them over the sore patches of skin. I dry my hair and wrap myself in a cosy dressing gown before going back downstairs. Dan has refreshed my glass and I down half of it, seeking the sweet relief of the numbness it brings. The television is on, a nature programme showing, and, grateful he leaves me to my own thoughts, we sit staring at the screen from our opposite ends of the sofa while we drink. I don't take in the details but merely watch the images flicker before my eyes as anxieties start to mount about the complications that have hit my work and home life. Although I know the night to come is unlikely to be restful I still crave the oblivion of sleep to calm my thoughts and hopefully bring much needed perspective by the morning.

"Feeling better?" Dan asks as the credits roll.

"Yes, but I'm exhausted. Do you mind if I go to bed?" I turn to look at him.

"Of course not." But he doesn't make any move to go.

Not quite sure where we stand or what's going to happen next I say, "Um, what are you going to do?"

"I'm going to be staying right here," he says, and he indicates the sofa, his tone brooking no opposition to his decision.

"Okay then," I reply in agreement and with relief that he's been decisive because that works for me too. I didn't want him to leave, but neither did I want him in my bed so I go to get him a pillow and a couple of blankets.

He arranges his bedding and from the bottom of the stairs I say goodnight. He looks over at me as if coming to a decision about something, then asks if I mind if he touches me. I shake my head, wondering what it is he's about to do, but then he simply wraps his arms around me giving me a hug. I reciprocate, loving the feel of his body close to mine, his strong back, his broad shoulders. Him holding me feels so good, but it's only as I relax into him that I realise how tense I am. And, weakening me like the incoming tide washing away a sandcastle, I feel myself starting to go, to crumble, the defences coming down, the tears welling, and I don't want that, not now, not in front of him. I hold everything together then feel him kiss the top of my head; his touch is gentle but I know I need to go. I release my arms from around him and that is the signal for him to do the same. We smile at each other, both a little awkward, and I look away quickly and head upstairs.

A short while later I crawl into bed, grateful to reach my safe place, and as I curl up the final layer of my protective wall collapses, as do I, and as tears flow in much needed release I sob into my pillow, crying until sleep finally claims me.

Chapter 2

I wake exhausted after a night heavily punctuated with flashes of violence and startled awakenings. From experience I know there is nothing I can do about this. However well I manage to block unwanted thoughts and images while awake, my horrors are always waiting for the weakness sleep brings. I've never been able to protect myself from what is unleashed in my dreams, and now Tag has added a whole new layer of Hell into the mix of what disturbs my nights. I lie in bed, my head aching and eyes scratchy. The working week stretches before me and I give myself a few minutes to ponder how much has changed in such a short period of time. I don't allow myself to include the rape in what's gone so wrong, that's in a completely different class, so putting that to one side I consider that only a few weeks ago my life was ordered and under control. I had clear lines drawn between my home, gym and work lives and they never crossed. Now everything is muddled, and I don't like it.

I run through the issues to try and clarify things in my mind.

One thing is certain, my gym life is over. Well, my previous gym life is over. I need to continue going to a gym but not *that* one. I shall have to do some research and find out what the alternatives are and, as I'm not going anywhere today, I resolve to make that a task for my to-do list.

My work life? That feels like it's hanging in the

balance. Dan didn't say anything last night but there are bound to be repercussions. Cubby said we would meet to discuss what happened so there is little I can do until I see how the land lies. I do have to write up my notes though. Needed for the report to go to the Trustees of Danewright House they are probably another job for today.

My home life? I've done all I can to ensure my anonymity as far as the rape is concerned. I don't want my friends to find out about it, I'm not sure I could stand the pity. Other than that, my modest lifestyle means that as long as I have some income I can stay in my cottage. Therefore, if I lose my current job I shall need to find something else but it doesn't have to be anything fancy (which is just as well given my lack of qualifications or experience in any sector of lawful employment). I'm relieved to find that once examined in the fresh light of the morning my home life does feel considerably more comfortable than it did last night.

Dan? I appreciate him coming round and staying over, that was kind of him, but I don't know whether there is a future for us, not anymore. I feel he's seen way too much of the dark side of me now, my past coming far too close to our present. I know he didn't understand the hold Tag had over me, or appreciate the way I pushed him into the background while I tried to sort things out. The harsh truth is that I don't think he is strong enough to handle everything I have got going on and much as it's a shame I can't blame him for that, he's not had the upbringing I have. I wonder at what point he will realise it too. Or perhaps he has already done so and is even now just doing his duty as Cubby would expect him to.

DI James Lambert? It irks me that the ball is totally in his court as to when I get to see him again and, as I don't know where to start in thinking about him or what he wants, I decide not to. Although even as I decide this I know my curiosity about whatever deal it is he has in mind will mean he will, in fact, be at the forefront of my thoughts until I know what's going on. Which is irritating.

I can smell bacon.

There is nothing quite like that scent permeating the air for getting the salivary glands working. I ease myself carefully off the bed and my muscles, which have seized up as though atrophied overnight, complain bitterly as I force them to move and totter to the bathroom in pain as I try to get my body loosened up and working.

I check out my face in the mirror as I take some painkillers. My lip is puffy and weeping, my bruises developing so I have a black eye I'm struggling to open, and one side of my face and along my jaw are shadowed in dramatic shades of dark purple. Heavy makeup will take care of the worst of it, if I have to go out, but for now my stomach is rumbling so I pull on my dressing gown, tying it around me as go down stairs.

"Ah, just in time! Good morning," says Dan, who appears to be remarkably perky as he tips eggs out of the pan and onto two plates. If he's shocked by my face he doesn't show it, for which I'm grateful.

"Something smells delicious." I see he's already laid my tiny kitchen table and as he tells me to sit he places a plate in front of me. He has gone to town. It is laden with toast, eggs, sausages, bacon, tomatoes and beans.

"I couldn't find any mushrooms but I think I've remembered everything else," he says, grinning at me as he takes the seat opposite.

"I don't like mushrooms."

"Just as well there weren't any then," he says brightly, tucking into his plateful. I don't usually eat much for breakfast but today I find I'm ravenous and appreciate every flavoursome mouthful, savouring each small forkful as I chew slowly, my jaw aching.

"Thank you for cooking this," I say inelegantly, my mouth still full.

"You're welcome." He looks over at me, then hesitates in taking his next mouthful, the food poised on his fork. "Can I ask? Who was that man yesterday?" I knew that question would be coming and am only surprised he's managed to hold off asking it until now.

"Police."

"Oh!" I can sense his relief. "Haven't they already asked enough questions?"

"That's what I told him."

"I bet you did." He smiles at me, then changes the subject, clearly believing that to be the end of the mystery. "Any plans for today?"

"I'm going to see if I can find a local gym to go to. A new start, and all that." He nods, in approval or perhaps further relief. He seems in a good mood, certainly more relaxed than last night.

"That would be good." It then occurs to me that I can't go out until my face improves so I'm not sure how far I'll get in finding anywhere. When I voice this thought to Dan, he says, "I'll leave you with my laptop if you like so you can do some research. It's about time you came into the twenty-first century." He chuckles and I pull a face at him, which I instantly regret, wincing with pain.

"What about you?" I say.

"I have to go to work. There are things that need attending to after the weekend." Then he frowns as though he's had an afterthought, and looks across at me, "Will you be okay here, on your own?"

I try to give him a reassuring smile but feel it's distorted somewhat by my fat lip, saying, "I'll be fine, thanks," but it's thoughtful of him to ask. Before I take another mouthful I end with, "Cubby said something about coming in for a meeting?"

"We'll discuss that today and set something up. I'll let you know."

"Okay." We both concentrate on finishing our breakfast, washing it down with mugs of strong tea.

It is already after office opening hours by the time Dan starts making moves to go, having folded up his bedding, leaving it in a pile at the end of the sofa. As he is about to leave he says, "I'll stay in touch and if you want me to come and sleep here tonight," and he points to the sofa, "or until you're feeling okay about being on your own again, that's fine, I'll be happy to."

"Oh, okay, thanks, I'd appreciate that." I had felt safer having him in the cottage last night which made no sense at all because it wasn't as if Tag could come and get me from where he was now anyway. I suppose it was simply that I felt generally insecure and wary after the assault. However, Dan did make it sound like it was a temporary arrangement and that he'd then be on his way. Perhaps he has already come to the same conclusion as I have and decided he couldn't deal with everything a relationship with me would involve. Acknowledging this fills me with more disappointment than I'd anticipated.

Before he leaves he brings his laptop in from the car and sets it up for me. I had queried whether he'd need it that day but he said he could always use one in the office if necessary. At least it gives him another reason to come back, I think, for that if nothing else.

After Dan has left I go to have another bath thinking that would be more soothing than a shower. I dress in soft, stretchy comfortable clothing and then clear up the kitchen before going to the laptop to start my research. I don't have to look too far. It turns out there is a gym down at the private school in Oakton, and it is open to the public at certain times, mainly before and after school, and in the holidays. Oakton is only a few miles away, which makes it handy and, as I like to get my exercise done in the morning it should suit me. It would mean an earlier start than I'm used to, to fit it in, but that might work well if I have to get a proper job too, though goodness knows what one of those might look like.

It will certainly be worth trying that gym out before I look any further anyway but there is no point in me going down there to join until my bruising has gone. I note how little time the research has taken and it crosses my mind that now Tag, and the police, have found me I no longer have the need to hide my existence to the extent I once did and perhaps I could consider getting my own laptop and venturing online more often.

There's a knock at the door. Damn it. I hadn't anticipated visitors and therefore I've done nothing to cover the damage to my face. I wonder if I can ignore it and realise that will depend on who it is. I creep over to the sitting room window and peer out of it sideways straining to see who has come visiting. It's Diane, and I can't ignore her. She'll have seen my car's here and will know I'm at home. If I don't answer she'll worry, and keep knocking, eventually letting herself in with the spare key she keeps for emergencies. I know I shall have to face her questions so brace myself as I open the door.

Her face drops the moment she catches sight of me.

"What the bloody hell has happened to you?"

"You'd better come in." I ask if she wants a coffee as I walk ahead of her and fill the kettle before flicking it on.

While it comes to a boil Diane takes my face in her hands. She peers at the damage, gently touches my swollen lip, and tuts. More than once.

"I'll bring you over something to help the healing process later," she says, as she lets go of me. I make the coffee then carry the mugs over to the table where Diane is now sitting. I open a packet of chocolate biscuits, my favourites. Shake them out onto a plate. They sit between us untouched as Diane patiently waits for me to settle.

"Are you all right?" she asks when I eventually do. I shrug.

"Not at the moment, no. But I will be."

"Do you want to talk about it?"

I don't but feel it wouldn't be fair to her if I didn't so I tell her the bare minimum. That I got myself into a situation that allowed Tag to attack and rape me. She flinches when I say *that* word. She might have suspected but the confirmation hits harder.

So much for managing to keep it from my friends.

"I saw Dan's car here," she states.

"He's been staying over, being a friend."

"Just a friend?" I nod again in resignation.

"I think so. It all got rather complicated, and he doesn't need that in his life. So I think whatever we might have had is over."

"That's a shame. Still, it's good of him to be looking after you." She's right, it is. I wonder how long he'll keep it up for and when he'll feel he's done his duty and can slope off into pastures new.

I want to change the subject so say, "How are you, anyway? What's been happening?" I reach for a biscuit.

"I'm fine, not much changes. I told you about the kerfuffle between Ben and Letitia, didn't I?"

"Well, you told me she'd locked him out when he came round and he found all his stuff on the lawn."

"They had a hell of a row apparently. He put what he could in his car but then had to hire a van for the rest and she still wouldn't come out of the house when he came back with that. Didn't want to chance it, I suppose. Mrs Tompkins could hear the shouting from her garden." She looks at me over the rim of her mug as she takes a sip, then keeps her eye on me as she says, "Your name came up."

"What?" That takes me by surprise. She nods.

"Mrs Tompkins couldn't hear the detail but he was yelling something about you having told Letitia."

"And did she happen to hear Letitia's response?"

"Not clearly. But judging by whatever Ben said next she seemed to be denying it."

"Oh." I nod thoughtfully, wondering if this is going to be a problem. I didn't think so. There was no evidence linking Letitia finding out to me. Ben was just jumping to that conclusion because he knew I was the one person who had definitely seen him and Purity together. Ben's accusation would have come as a complete surprise to Letitia though.

"So, did you?"

"Did I what?" Brought abruptly back to the here and now, I'd forgotten Diane was even there, my automatic response a stalling tactic.

"Did you tell Letitia, about Ben?"

"No," I deny categorically, "how could I possibly have known anything about him and Purity anyway?" Her eyebrows rise, in a silent 'Aha' at my intentional slip.

"How did you know her name?"

"Er, you must have told me."

"I didn't know it."

"Ah." There is nothing left for me to say to that so I try to look as innocent as possible as I attempt a smile, take another biscuit, and concentrate on emptying my mug as I search for a subject to divert the conversation onto. "Seen much of Joe recently?"

"Nice change." Which makes me smile again, then I wince as my lip splits. This distracts Diane sufficiently into finishing her coffee quickly so she can go home to prepare me a little something.

When she leaves I know I don't have to ask her to keep what's happened to me to herself. There's news she will spread and news she won't, and mine is definitely the latter. She pops back a little while later with ointments to soothe the bruising to my face and to apply to my various cuts and abrasions, telling me to be lavish with them. There's also a small vial of a fiery liquid to dab onto my lip. Its initial touch stings like anything but then there's an immediate numbness, which feels odd, like when a dentist's anaesthetic is wearing off.

There isn't much left for me to do after Diane's second visit other than write up my notes for the report. I approach this clinically, not allowing myself to dwell on anything other than the facts. It doesn't take long and I'm glad once I've got it all down. It can be fleshed out following the meeting with any other details Cubby and Dan deem relevant for the Trustees to have.

Kourtney is due in the morning to do the cleaning so there's no point in me doing any of that and, having been told at the hospital to give myself plenty of recovery time, I decide to spend what remains of the day resting and reading instead. I'm surprisingly tired and I only manage to get through a couple of pages before I feel myself nodding off and, after dragging one of Dan's blankets over me, I sleep a good part of the day away.

Dan is back in the evening. After appearing to be so bright this morning though, he now seems subdued and says little about his day other than telling me Cubby wants me to come in the following morning, if I'm up to it. That's fine with me, I say, but I decide to wait until the meeting to share my notes with him in an attempt to keep what's happened away from my home. Having said that, though, as far as I'm concerned the sooner we can get all of this done, dusted and relegated to the past, the better, as I want to put it behind me.

I don't know what to do about his mood. I don't know him well enough to know if this is normal, and he likes to be left alone when on a downer, or if I should be trying to jolly him out of it. Though I'm hardly well placed to be doing that at present as I'm low too, which is perhaps not surprising.

We eat and watch television together, our conversation sparse and only covering necessities, and
we sleep, separately.

<u>**Chapter 3**</u>

I'm up early the next morning, after a slightly better night, and manage to spend a decent length of time applying make up to cover the worst, after smoothing on copious amounts of Diane's various ointments of course. Although I'm pleased to have something to focus on today, I'm feeling down and dress accordingly. Dark jeans, ankle boots, long-sleeved black top. I leave my hair loose.

I hear no movement from Dan and when I come downstairs he's fast asleep. His dirty blond hair is tousled, his face looking more relaxed than it has for a while, and I briefly ponder what he dreams about. He starts to stir, as though he can feel my gaze resting upon him, and I go into the kitchen.

I prepare breakfast, a simpler one than he made yesterday as time is getting on. I hear him moving next door and when I turn around from filling the kettle he's in the doorway, stretching, and wearing nothing but his boxers, and a smile. It's difficult not to think back to our, too few, intimate moments, his warmth, his scent, his body toned and moving against mine and I drag my thoughts away from that dangerous territory and simply smile back at him. I then regret having to move closer to get the bread, the big sleepy male scent of him only adding to the attraction the nearer I get, and he yawns as he says good morning.

"Didn't you sleep well?" I ask, selfishly concerned that if he didn't it may put him off coming round.

"I slept fine, once I got to sleep. I stupidly started watching a late film so didn't turn in as early as I should have done." I see him glance at the clock, register the time and turn to go and have a shower while I finish getting the breakfast together.

We leave for Hartleigh a short while later, Kourtney arriving as I'm getting into my car. We merely exchange greetings as I explain we're off to a meeting. But I'm glad I only see her fleetingly, I didn't want her getting too close a look at my face.

Dan and I drive separately as he's staying at the office after the meeting. He didn't say anything this morning so I don't want to assume he's coming back tonight. I'd ask but I also don't want to appear needy.

There are no spaces left on the road near the office so we both drive into the Market Square to park. I'm reminded of the last time I'd parked there. When Dan had seen me leave the pub with Tag and of his fury, of our row and of him telling me to keep away from Tag. If only I had been able to. I risk a quick peek over at him now and wonder if he is thinking of the same things as me. His face gives nothing away.

I'm reminded, as I walk up past the entrance to The Cromwell, that it was here I'd seen Ben and Purity together. It was then I'd obtained the hotel receipt and decided to covertly tip Letitia off by leaving it in Ben's pocket for her to find. I realise now that even if Letitia is unaware that it was me that spilled the beans, if she tells Ben that's how she found out it won't take him long to put two and two together and for that to confirm his suspicions about me. Still, I think as I stride out towards the office, I can't worry about that now, what's done is done, and I'll have to deal with the repercussions as, when, and, hopefully if, any arise.

Dan and I haven't exchanged a word since parking up and our silence is maintained as we walk. We greet Helen, the receptionist, as we enter and when she tells us Cubby is already expecting us we head straight for his office, although I make a slight detour to make a photocopy of my notes.

Cubby gives me a big hug when he sees me then holds me at arm's length to take a good look, "You okay?" he asks, his voice gruff.

"I'm fine," I reassure him and he hugs me again. When he lets me go this time I take a seat next to Dan in front of Cubby's desk and he makes his way round to the other side and takes up his usual place. He's taking a gradual approach to retirement, I know that, a party being planned for a couple of months' time, but although he's winding down I briefly wonder how often Dan gets to sit in that seat in what is now meant to be his office. I hand the copy of my notes to Dan, who's sitting back in his chair, his legs stretched out in front of him and crossed at the ankles, and place the folder containing the originals on the desk, sliding it across to Cubby. As Dan is already reading his set Cubby opens the file and scans through the pages, running his finger down the lines as he quickly assimilates the information. Dan finishes first and adjusts his position sitting up and leaning forward. Once Cubby reaches the end he closes the file and looks at us.

"Okay, so," he says, and he leans on his elbows, his fingers meeting in a point as he studies me. "That's comprehensive but I think we need to verbally run through what happened, what you told the police, what they asked. That sort of thing. All right?"

"That's fine," I reply and I lay out the whole night for him and Dan, sparing no detail while keeping everything in line with what I told the police. They both ask questions along the way, prompting, clarifying and getting me to go over various points so that it is clear to all of us. However, when I get to the end I also know I can't leave it there and that I need to let Cubby know the real issue. I lean forward.

"The thing is, it probably won't take the police long to find out that Tag and I know each other, from way back. That might be a problem."

To my surprise Cubby seems unperturbed by this information, almost as if he already knows it. I glance over at Dan as he could have told him about the Tag connection, but he appears to be as surprised as me.

"I grant you it's not an ideal situation but I don't think it will come to anything."

"You don't?" How could he not think this was an issue? He clears his throat and gives me a confident smile that even manages to put a twinkle in his eyes.

Before I get to ask anything further there's a

knock at the door and he shouts, "Come," over our heads. I turn to see Detective Inspector James Lambert closing the door behind himself.

"What are you doing here?" my less than friendly greeting.

"Cubby invited me to join the meeting." I maintain eye contact but remain silent as the seconds tick by, my mind trying to process what this means. He's obviously already met Cubby and is on first name terms with him and I wonder if he's revealed to Cubby his reason for being here. I also wonder if Dan had already met him too and had kept that from me. That would not please me at all. Was that why he was so quiet last night? I don't like being on the back foot and eventually break the eye contact to look back at Cubby, raising a questioning eyebrow.

"James came to see me last night, after Dan had left for the day. He tells me he has a proposition to put forward, that would be helpful to you, and I thought we should at least give him the courtesy of hearing it."

"I thought this was just going to be a debrief of what happened on Saturday night?" and I hear Dan murmur his agreement with my question.

"We'll cover anything else we need to, don't worry, but for now, Daniel, I don't think you've met? This is Detective Inspector James Lambert. He has already had a few words with Madeleine on Sunday, but I understand you weren't present." Dan and James shake hands and James tells Dan to call him James, like we're all friends here.

"We passed each other, that's all," Dan says,

his attitude dismissive and decidedly unfriendly.

"Okay then. Everyone take a seat." Cubby sits again as we pull up another chair so we're in an arc in front of him, with me in between Dan and James. Once we're settled, he says, "I suggest we let James tell us why he is here, and what he wants." Cubby speaks directly to Dan and me and we both, equally reluctantly, agree and I become increasingly uneasy about what is going to be revealed.

James clears his throat, "I'll keep this brief, and get straight to the point. I am the officer responsible for getting Tag locked up in the first place. I had been working on building a case against him for several years and eventually it all came together." He glances at me as he takes a breath and gathers his thoughts. But I immediately know that if he has pulled together enough incriminating evidence to lock Tag away he will also have enough to do the same to me, should he want to, and I feel my stomach clench with nerves as to what's coming. "I kept tabs on Tag when he was released until he disappeared off my radar, much like you did, Madeleine, several years ago now." He looks pointedly at me and in that moment I know that this is about me, and not Tag. It is not him he has any interest in, not anymore. He continues, "Because of my ongoing, and registered, connection with Tag I was alerted as soon as his name showed up on the system early on Sunday morning. I was sent through the details and, once the photos followed, I knew I'd found Scarlet too."

"Scarlet?" Cubby asked.

"My former name," I admit, feeling dreadful for having lied to Cubby, again. He, bless him, merely nods and tells James to continue.

He turns to me. "Do you remember Craig?" I do, I murmur. A flash of clenched and bloodied fists causes an involuntary shudder to run through me at the unwelcome reminder. "You may well shudder, Madeleine. Since Tag left the scene, at my doing, what Craig has unleashed on the estate is considerably worse." That doesn't surprise me. Craig was Tag's second in command. A vicious piece of work. Tag had reined him in, as best he could, kept him as merely a threat. But he had always been straining at that leash and, while I hadn't given any thought as to what would have followed in Tag's absence, it made perfect sense that it would have been him that stepped into the void.

"What is it you want?" I need to cut to the chase, I already think I know what he's after, but I need him to say it. To ask what he is here to ask. James inclines his head to me and there's a pause that's filled with way too much drama for my liking before he speaks.

"I want Craig, and as many of his accomplices as I can. Ninety-nine per cent of crime is carried out by one per cent of the population, and on my patch they are that one per cent. I want to remove them from the estate. I made an error last time. I only took out the top man and left a space to be filled. I won't be making that mistake again."

"And what does that have to do with Maddy?" Dan's voice is quiet. Again I know the answer, but he needs to hear it, as does Cubby. James speaks to me, although he is answering Dan's question.

"I want Maddy to bring them down, from the inside." I can't help but smile. His request appears so simple when you say it like that. It is anything but.

"No! You can't put yourself at risk like that!" This comes from behind me as Dan makes his objection clear, just as I thought he would, and while I appreciate his interjection I know it is pointless. I turn to him though and give him a rueful smile. I reach out my hand more in hope than expectation, but my spirits lift as he takes it and threads his fingers through mine.

"I appreciate your concern, Dan," James says, but I know he's merely paying lip service to him because I watch as this sympathetic James disappears, only to be replaced by one considerably more ambitious. "If there was another way I'd take it, but there is no other option, and I know if Madeleine gives it enough thought she will agree with me."

"What if I say no?" Fruitless though it maybe I might as well check out my options, for Dan and Cubby's benefit if not for my own.

"I think you know the answer to that." The direct path to jail then. But even with this confirmation I'm not beyond at least trying to make a bad situation better.

"What's in it for me then?" You can take the girl out of the gang, but…

"Well, it won't take the local police long to make the connection between you and Tag. That will result in many more questions. Questions which I can make go away."

I ponder his words in silence as the seconds tick by, all eyes upon me. I try to think through the limited alternatives that lie before me and feel Dan's hand tighten around mine.

James sweetens the pot. "I would also arrange for you to be granted amnesty from all your past misdemeanours, if you do this." I'm surprised. This encouragement has come far quicker than my brief hesitation warranted. I had already been on the brink of saying yes. Because I have no other choice, I know that, I never did have. But this additional extra certainly makes the risk that much more worth it.

"What do you have in mind?" This is as close as I can get to saying yes. I hear Dan's frustration in his exhaled breath but see the relief cross James's face. I ask the question because I assume he has an idea, a plan for dealing with the problem he wants dispatching. But it appears on this I have overestimated his abilities as, with a name change to confirm my return to the dark side, he says, "That, Scarlet, is for you to work out, not me."

I sigh, bowing to the inevitable; of course it is.

Chapter 4

The meeting had ended shortly thereafter. Dan, furious, had rounded on James for requesting this of me when he couldn't even manage to come up with a half decent plan himself. I didn't blame James. He had clearly been getting nowhere so it would seem sensible to him to bring in someone else; someone who could bring fresh eyes to the situation. I had resurfaced at just the right time.

I felt calm. Resigned to the situation, you might say. It's as if I've always known that one day my past would catch up with me. And I don't mean in the way that Tag had found me but in the fact that authority would eventually get to have its say.

Karma, and all that.

It's almost a relief for it to have finally happened.

I tell James I've heard enough and that he should leave. We'd talk another time. I didn't want unnecessary aggravation between him and Dan, who I could feel bristling beside me, and without any further argument James hands each of us his card then walks out leaving us with much to think about.

As the door closes behind him I turn back to Cubby and Dan. "I realise that for whatever reason James felt it necessary to come to this meeting and involve you in this situation, but this is nothing to do with Watson and Grove so I shall deal with this on my own from now on."

Cubby inclines his head before replying, "I appreciate you saying that, Maddy, but I, and most probably, we," and he nods at Dan, "consider you part of the team here. I have no idea how we can help you but if there is anything we can do, then we will do it." I feel Dan's hand rest lightly in the small of my back and as he smiles gently at me my eyes ache as tears well behind them.

"Thank you," is all I can muster.

"He has a bloody nerve though," Cubby then mutters.

"What makes you say that?"

"What right does he have to ask you to do this?" I'm surprised this comes from Cubby and not Dan, who after his initial burst of fury against James has remained remarkably quiet.

"Unfortunately, I suspect James has plenty he could use against me, should he choose to. I'm sorry it has come to this, and that he has chosen to involve you, but due to the stupidity of the decisions I've made in the past he will have all the leverage he needs."

"I knew you were no angel when I took you on, Maddy, but even so."

"I'm sorry to have let you down," I say, and I truly am, I would do anything not to have him think badly of me.

"You haven't," he says, his manner brusque, as if all of this is of no matter, but I feel his disappointment nonetheless.

"Do you have any ideas?" Dan asks, breaking the silence that has fallen, and I shake my head.

"None at all." I feel drained. The intensity of

the meeting has taken its toll in my current state and I know that I need some quiet time to recover and think this through. After I've voiced these thoughts I suggest we finish off our discussion about what happened at the weekend so that we are all on the same page.

"I think it's clear what happened," says Dan. He shifts in his chair to turn slightly towards me, my notes now clasped in one hand.

"It is?" I'm surprised he isn't wanting to continue the third degree about every moment of Saturday night, Sunday morning.

"Yes. From what I understand, on your previous reconnaissance you became aware that someone else was watching Danewright House. You realised it was someone you once knew, met up with them and teamed up in order to keep an eye on what they were up to. You put a call into the police to let them know what was going to happen and when. Then, knowing what Tag was after, you protected the necklace by substituting a fake for the real thing and allowed the theft to proceed in order for Tag to be caught.

"On leaving the house it had been your intention to separate from Tag and leave him to be apprehended by the police while you left via the other side of the estate. Unfortunately, that's where the plan went wrong as Tag didn't take too kindly to being left, and... er... he, um... he attacked you and kept you with him, probably intending on abducting you, until the police arrested you both. Does that about sum it up?"

He's focused, direct and solid in his delivery.

Goodness, I think with some surprise, someone has been giving it a lot of thought. "Yes," I say with relief, "Yes, I think that does just about sum it up."

"Good, so that is what we will stick to should there be any further meetings with the police, or anyone else. I assume that will be in line with what you have said to them anyway?" He's looking at me sternly, and I nod in agreement. This side of Dan has come as something of a revelation and to be honest it's not a moment too soon. He has taken charge of the situation at a time when I am struggling to be strong enough to do so and I have to say I rather like it, particularly because it's taken the weight off me. I glance at Cubby, who is smiling somewhat benevolently at his nephew, and he confirms he is happy with Dan's statement as well.

I rise from my chair, pleased this is over and keen to get going.

Dan stands. "I hope it goes without saying, Maddy, that if you need any support, or counselling, or anything over what has happened we are here to help with that or to arrange anything else that you need. There'll be a court case in the future which is going to be tough for you but we're here to support you through it." This feels terribly formal but I suppose that's him just doing his company bit.

"Thank you, and I know. I'm going to be dealing with all that one day at a time." I certainly can't be thinking about all the court stuff yet and have pushed it right to the back of my mind.

"Okay, well don't forget we're here." That

takes me aback. All right then, I get it. So they, meaning him, are going to be here, dealing with it as a company then, and not with me dealing with it personally. It sounds final and as I say my good-byes I leave feeling deflated.

As I'm driving out of Hartleigh I see a new piece of paper in the window of Sidney's shop. I pull over. It's the notice of his funeral. A simple card, outlined in black. Judging by the shabby quality of the previous note in this window I suspect the funeral directors will have placed this one. The funeral is on Thursday and for reasons unknown to me I think I might go.

Before I drive off I receive a text from Kourtney telling me that a DI James Lambert had called round while she was cleaning this morning. He'd told her he'd catch up with me later. Well he'd certainly done that.

I leave for home, making a detour for groceries on the way and arrive at a cottage left spotless in the wake of Kourtney. As I put the shopping away I binge eat sugary junk food and have nothing sensible at all for lunch.

Then I sit down to think.

Usually, when I need to come up with a plan I have a definite goal. Something that I can aim for. Take a house I need to break into, for example. That's relatively simple. I can research the house, how to get to it, the security that surrounds it, options for entry, and so on until a solution presents itself. With this, and no defined goal, it's all a bit woolly and I'm not sure where to start.

James wants Craig, and as many of his accomplices as possible, and he's expecting me to bring them down from the inside. There is my first problem. I can't just rock up after all this time and it not raise a suspicion, particularly with Craig. He and I did not see eye to eye. We never had done, not since Tag had first brought me along to the pub one evening where I met Craig and many of Tag's other 'people' as he called them. I was particularly quiet that evening, taking it all in. I'd hung back and watched the relationships, the interactions, the banter. I worked out the hierarchy among the gang, the who got on with whom and, more importantly, who didn't, and it was quite clear that Craig saw himself as second in command to Tag. He was also his closest friend. Until I came along.

There were two things that doomed any chance of a positive relationship Craig and I might have had. The first being the fact he had to start competing for Tag's attention. Let's face it, for me there was no competition at all as I had charms Craig had no chance of distracting Tag with. The second being the first words I ever said to him.

That evening the pub had been heaving, the atmosphere hot and sticky, and later on I'd needed to get a breath of fresh air. I hadn't realised Craig had followed me outside as I'd walked along the pavement a few metres relishing the cool air on my heated skin but, when I'd turned around, there he was. I'd known immediately that he didn't trust me and had wondered where I was off to. I'd walked back to him, stood toe to toe, and had to look up at him as I'd said, "I don't think I like you very much." The way he'd smiled told me the feeling was mutual.

We had barely spoken since, other than about the occasional bit of business, and I therefore knew he wouldn't be welcoming me back with open arms. I thought through everything I knew about him, looking for some way in. But all I could come up with was that he was mercenary, standard in his line of business, and I knew he liked having people beholden to him. He loved nothing more than being able to call in a favour when he needed to. I wouldn't have thought those two facets of his character would have changed much but I had no idea how to exploit them. Certainly the amount of money I had at my disposal would be of no interest to him at all. And I couldn't think of any reason for me to need anything from him.

However, as I'm thinking all this through one thing does occur to me and I go to retrieve James's card from the side, where I'd left it, before putting in a call to him.

He answers with "Lambert." I have no time for pleasantries or general chit chat.

"I need Tag to be in solitary, with no means of communication to the outside world."

"Already done. I made sure of it as soon as he was back in custody."

"Good." And I end the call.

I go to make myself a mug of tea and seeing that Joe is out in the garden I make one for him too and take it out to him. He is taking a break, filling his pipe with tobacco, jamming it down hard into the bowl before lighting it, the orange glow flaring as he sucks hard. I sit on the bench and am glad I put a thick jumper on. I glance out at the pasture the other side of the wall but disappointingly there is no sign of the horses today. The wind is getting up and has a bite to it that makes me wrap my arms around myself, and I turn my attention back to Joe. It's his green tie today, the colour of evergreen leaves. I ask him what he's doing as I place his tea on the arm of the bench closest to him.

"Clearing up for winter," he says, and I see there's a heap of foliage he's cut down from the back of the wooden garage. I gesticulate towards it.

"You don't want to take too much off that. It might be the only thing holding it up." He chuckles at my feeble joke.

"I keep it in check every year. It's all right on the wood but I don't want it getting a hold on the cottage. Ivy's a bugger for damaging the stonework."

Ivy. I smile as I remember that was what Dan had described himself as on one late summer's afternoon as we'd walked through the sunlit gardens at Danewright House. It feels like months have passed since that day but it was less than two weeks ago. So much has changed.

His tea finished and his pipe gone out, Joe picks up his secateurs and carries on attacking the ivy as I take the mugs back inside.

'Clinging on until the bitter end.' Isn't that how Dan had described the way he'd behaved with his previous girlfriend? Hmm. I somehow doubt I am worth doing that for.

I am heading out of the door when Dan pulls up outside the cottage. I tell him I'm walking up into the village to stretch my legs and he joins me. We ask politely how the other's day has gone and I know he's lying when he tells me his was just the usual office stuff. Nothing out of the ordinary at all. I know he's trying hard to not say what he wants to so I open up the way for him.

"What did you think about the meeting?" I look over at him and see the look of relief that he's going to get to have his say, but he then measures his response.

"I thought our part of the meeting was perfectly fine." I nod along with him and stay silent through the pause that follows. "But, I wasn't happy with Lambert's intrusion."

"No."

"Were you happy with it?"

"Well, obviously I could do without it."

"But?" He stops and turns to look at me. "I sense there's a 'but' coming." I carry on walking and he soon catches up.

"But, I am glad I now know what it is he wants with me."

"And?" I meet his eyes as he glances over and we slow our pace.

"And, it would be nice not to have all my past indiscretions hanging over me any longer." He tilts his head in thought then gives a quick nod as if he can see my point.

"Do you think you can trust him to give you the amnesty he's offering though? Has he got the authority to do that?" I give this some consideration before replying.

"I'm sure he won't be working in isolation and that his superiors will have agreed on the points he can bargain over. But I do think in these situations there has to be a certain amount of trust."

"So you trust him. What else do you think about him?" He's searching, I sense it.

"He seems nice enough. Genuine, you know."

"You don't think he's a bit...over friendly? All that, 'call me James' stuff."

"Can anyone be over friendly? Especially a policeman. I would have thought that was a good thing, for me anyway."

"You know what I mean." I'm not sure I do but clearly Dan has seen something I haven't so I tell him what I suspect.

"Look, I think he knows me, from my days back in London which might have something to do with it but why do you think he's being too friendly?"

"He watches you, I think he likes you. What makes you think he knows you, wouldn't you recognise him if you'd met before?" I shake my head as I respond, because I think he's reading too much into things.

"You'd think so but I don't. It was just something he said."

"Did you have anything to do with the police back then?"

"Nothing if we could help it, obviously." My memory strays to a moment during that time when there had been police involvement and I'm distracted as he says,

"And if you couldn't?"

"Couldn't what?" I try to focus on the image that has come into my mind but which is now hovering frustratingly out of reach on the periphery.

"Help it."

"What?" I know my exasperation shows but I no longer have any idea what he's talking about. "I don't know any police from back then, all right!"

"All right." His hands rise in a defensive 'calm down' gesture that does nothing to alleviate my irritation. "Slow down a minute. Do you want to go for a drink?" I look round to see that we're outside the Snipe and Partridge.

"Not yet," I say, and I excuse my reticence by gesturing towards my face.

"You look fine," he says in reassurance and physically I know I do. I've put enough makeup on to assure myself of that. I'm just not ready to go somewhere public with him, where people will know me and wonder who he is and what we are. How can I face all that when I don't even know what we are myself? So I use my battered face as the excuse, ignore what he just said and walk on by the pub.

He continues to walk with me, remaining silent until we're half way up the high street, during which time I try and recapture the memory that briefly flitted across my consciousness a few moments ago. Then, presumably thinking he'd left enough time for me to have moved on from my previous annoyance, he interrupts my thoughts again and returns to the issue. "What about his proposition then? What are you going to do about that?"

"I don't see how I can refuse it."

"You could simply say no."

"And then he could stir up a load of trouble for me. He could charge me with exactly what he charged Tag with, more or less, and look where he ended up."

"Well, just for the record I need you to know that I don't want you to do it."

"Tell me something that isn't a surprise." It's my turn to stop this time, in irritation. I turn towards him. "It's not exactly something I'd choose to do either, Dan. But sometimes we don't get to do what we want to do."

We're at the village hall and Dan points to a bench positioned against the wall of the building. "I understand that. Sit down." I'm not sure I care for his tone and I stay exactly where I am. He wraps his hand around my elbow encouraging me to move, and reluctantly I do so. I sit down heavily on the bench and lean back, crossing my arms. "Why don't you tell me a bit about this Craig?"

"What do you want to know?" I sound sulky.

"What's he like? How well do you know him? Did you get on? I don't know, Maddy, I just thought maybe if you spoke to someone about him it might help with your scheming. I'm new to this, remember, I'm just trying to help."

I nod, "Okay." *Try to be nice*, I think. "What can I tell you?" I look up to the sky for a moment to gather my thoughts. "Well, he's a lot bigger and tougher than Tag. The only reason he wasn't in charge before was because Tag had a loyal following and he was outnumbered.

"Tag lived by…" and I hesitate, searching for the right description, "well for want of a better word, a code when it came to business, and never set out to ruin anyone's life. Craig, by comparison, has no morals, and wouldn't think twice about dealing to kids, or beating up little old ladies who'd borrowed money from him and were unable to pay it back. And I know he'll have expanded the business into such areas because that's where the big money is, and he's greedy.

"Oh," and I have an afterthought, "he hates me. There is that." He's silent for a moment as he ponders what I've told him.

"Ah, I hadn't quite expected to be left wishing Tag was back in charge."

"No," I say, and I pick at a ragged edge of nail. "He would certainly have been more straightforward to deal with."

"So, any weak spots?" There's more hope than expectation in his voice and I have no easy answers for him.

"None. But, as well as his passion for collecting money he loves nothing more than having someone in his debt. That, I think, is my only way in. I need to have him help me for some reason. I need to be beholden to him. That is the problem I have to solve." Without saying anything further I get up and start retracing my steps. He remains silent as we wander towards home, and again I try to let my thoughts drift, until we're half way back down the high street.

"So, any idea what you could need him for?"

"No, I've been thinking about it ever since I left the meeting and I've come up with nothing. It's why I needed to get out and clear my head a bit."

"Sorry, I've not exactly helped you do that. All these interruptions." I shrug. It doesn't matter, it's hardly going to be far from my thoughts until I come up with a solution. Then he surprises me by going off on a tangent. "Tell you what, I'll give you a massage when we get back, that'll relax you and might help release the blockage in your strategizing." As I eye him with suspicion he grins over at me and I can't help but smile back.

"You know how to give a massage?"

"I had a summer job at a spa once, while at uni, I'd help out when they were short-staffed." He looks a little sheepish as I laugh.

"I'm sure the ladies loved you."

"They did!" His indignation is obvious. "There's nothing a lady likes more than a firm massage. I've been told I have exceptionally strong fingers and they're able to reach right int..." I hold my hands up as I interrupt him.

"Enough, I don't want to hear any more about where your fingers can reach right into." I can't help laughing as he tries to defend his position, and I love it. The release of laughter, of his joining mine as we head back home. It helps break through the tension that has been there, hovering like an invisible wall between us since, and I was going to say Sunday but it was longer than that, it was since the row in the Market Square. Which felt like eons ago.

Our laughter dies but we're closer now, walking closer, and as our arms touch I link mine though his at the elbow and he accepts it, squeezing my arm against his side.

"What shall we have for dinner?"

"I don't know. I'll see if I have anything in the freezer." That has him laughing again.

"You could feed the whole village with what's in that freezer."

"Well," I say, all knowing. "It's at times like this that you should be thankful for that foresight of mine."

We end up with bowls of chilli and rice and don't talk any further about my plans, or rather lack of them, for tackling Craig that evening, because we get far too busy with the massage. I feel awkward at the thought of stripping off in front of him, although I find I can't tell him that, and I also don't want him seeing any of the grazes and bruises that will remind him of what I've been through. However, fortunately, when I suggest limiting it to a neck and shoulder massage he's totally fine with it.

He sits on the sofa and I take my place on the floor between his legs, boosting myself up to a suitable height on some cushions. I undo a couple of buttons on my shirt to open up the collar while he goes to get a tube of body lotion from the bathroom.

As he settles back in behind me I brace myself, expecting to feel the chill of cold cream on my skin, but I don't. Instead the first touch is of his warm hands, soft and well-oiled with the lotion already at body temperature as he smooths it across the skin of my neck and the top of my shoulders. After the violence brought by the hands of the last man to touch me, I appreciate how gentle he is being, his hands moving across my collarbones and stroking up my neck in long soothing motions. My neck arches with the pleasure of his hands on me as they continue sweeping around and down again across my chest and the top of my breasts. My breath catches and eyes close as his hands move in large circles, and as I relax his hands glide up and over my shoulders again with no interruption to the hypnotic rhythm. The pressure of his fingers increases as he goes to work on my shoulders and I feel his thumbs rotating on each side of my spine, massaging the muscles and paying particular attention to those that hold so much tension at the top. He finds knots that he applies increased pressure over to break them down and continues working his fingers into all the muscles of my shoulders. While I'm enjoying every minute and don't want this to end, I'm sure by now he must have had enough, but it seems he's not content to simply leave it once he's finished on my shoulders as his fingers continue to travel up my neck and start to massage my scalp, applying and releasing pressure at certain points like he knows what he is doing.

Eventually he works his way back down my neck and with a final sweep of my shoulders he presses slightly harder, and then as the pressure lightens he lifts his hands away from me and I know it's finished. But I don't move, I'm still, relaxed and calm, like I'm in a trance.

I feel him bend towards me then whisper, "We're done," close to my ear, his soft breath against my skin doing nothing to lessen the desire the massage has aroused. I open my eyes, appreciating just how relaxed I am and how close to falling asleep. It turns out that Dan was right, he is surprisingly good at it.

"That was wonderful, thank you," I say, then I realise my shirt is gaping open, and conscious of this I pull the edges together, pulling my bra straps back up over my shoulders, although I hadn't even noticed them slip off. I gather the material across my chest as I fumble with the buttons. There are far more open than when we started and I have no idea how that happened.

"You're welcome."

"You were absolutely right about your fingers, they really are quite skilled." I have to clear my throat as I turn to look at him.

"I'm surprised you hadn't noticed before," he says, and grins mischievously at me, and realising he's referring to our nights together I find myself blushing, which is quite out of character.

"Oh I don't like to boost your ego too much." I try to lighten the moment then meet his eyes but when I do I can see he's enjoying my discomfort which only serves to make me feel even more awkward. "I am absolutely shattered now though; do you mind if I go to bed?"

"Of course not, I'll be right here." I hesitate.

"You are okay with that?"

"Absolutely, there's nowhere I'd rather be," and I know he's teasing me so roll my eyes at him before I head for the stairs but then I hear his chuckle behind me and can't help smiling.

Chapter 5

What on earth made you think giving her a massage would be a good idea? No sooner were the words out of your mouth than you started regretting them and now here you are, physically having to do it, and it's proving to be every bit as tortuous as you imagined. You look down on her, her shoulders bare, her skin pale, unblemished and soft and you can't help but enjoy the feel of it as your hands, slick with lotion, glide smoothly across it. Her neck arches sensually as you make long sweeping strokes up it, and as her eyes close you realise you've forgotten to breathe and carefully have to let out your held breath so she doesn't notice. You avoid gazing at the curve of her breasts, all too obvious from your vantage point and it's all you can do not to lean forward and kiss her forehead. In an attempt to quash the building desire, making itself only too obvious in another part of your body, you try to distract yourself with other thoughts...

Which isn't difficult because there are plenty of them. You're not sure how she feels about you for starters and you have to admit that has been playing on your mind. It was bad enough when you saw that Tag had hit her but after finding out everything else she'd been through at his hands, you were not only nervous as to how she'd be with you, but furious when you arrived at her place on Sunday, although you tried to hide it. All you wanted to do was hold her tight but you weren't sure what her reaction would have been to that and you'd been told at the Centre she'd been taken to that you should ask first before touching her.

It didn't help either that you were suspicious of the bloke who was leaving as you arrived and you'd wanted to question her about him straight away. But you bit your tongue, and managed not to show her your anger, or your misgivings over her visitor. Instead you said what you needed to in order to get out, that you were sorry, that you felt you had let her down. She was having none of it though, taking full responsibility. Typical of her. But it hasn't stopped you feeling guilty, and you know you need to be much stronger, and become someone she deserves to have any chance of a future with her.

Cubby has already told you that of course. He's realised what has been going on between you and told you in no uncertain terms that you need to do more, much more, to be worthy of her. Which is difficult when she won't confide in you or let you in on her life. You know he has a soft spot for her, he might well be your uncle but seriously, he is totally on her side.

At least you managed to ask if she was all right when you got here and she'd said she was fine, or that she would be. But how could she be? The worst of it is that you have a horrible feeling she's been through worse. Your trip to London taught you as much and that thought has done nothing to ease your anger.

Because you hate her past. Hate it. Everything

about it from how she lived with that no-good mother of hers, and you suspect you barely scratched the surface on what you know about that, to those she mixed with. Tag was bad enough but now you know that Craig's worse, much worse. She's filled you in a bit but you could tell by her initial reaction, that shudder. It doesn't look good, does it.

You were patient though, staying to eat and drink, waiting while she had a bath and then being decisive over staying. You don't think she was expecting that but she seemed to appreciate it. You got to hug her then and unusually she felt fragile, delicate like some precious flower as you'd wrapped your arms around her. You'd smiled, remembering one warm sunny day when you'd told her about the language of flowers, and that she was like a freesia. Free-spirited. She is certainly that. But that day feels, at the moment, as if it belongs to another lifetime.

You sit on the sofa after she's gone to bed and turn down the television so as not to disturb her but then you hear her crying and have to fight the urge to go to her. If she'd wanted to cry in front of you she'd had plenty of opportunity so you know she wants her privacy and you remain where you are, your frustration building as you're left with the flickering screen and your thoughts which you can't keep from dwelling on her.

Overall she seems friendly enough, happy for you to sleep on the sofa anyway, but nothing more, which is not surprising, given what's happened, and you guess you should be pleased she's not blaming you for failing to protect her. Not that she'd ever expect you to, you know that, she's one tough cookie. Independent too, you've never known anyone more so but then she's had to be. But it's only natural that you should want to try to look after her now. Isn't it?

Your thoughts pick over the facts of your relationship and particularly the row you'd had after such a brief period of time together. It wasn't a relationship ending row but, after what's happened since, you don't know how she feels about it. Does it mean that what you had was just a fling and now you're only friends? You hope not because it meant far more to you than that.

You do know you are resigned to being on sofa sentry for as long as she allows you to be here because you don't want to push the relationship at all. You've decided the way forward is that you're going to make sure to be there when she wants you, whenever she wants you, that's how you're going to play it. It's not so bad, comfort-wise, the sofa that is. It's just that you're struggling to manage to get to sleep with her so close, and yet not close enough, and even when you do eventually drift off you don't get the restful sleep you need and find yourself waking frequently. The fury that's been boiling through your veins manifesting itself as violence in your dreams. It was only just getting light when you woke and, despite still being exhausted, you knew you wouldn't be able to get back to sleep again so you decided to get up and cook breakfast. At least you can make sure she eats before you leave for the day.

You were shocked by the sight of her face that morning. It looked worse than the day before and you'd felt your anger ignite once again at this stark reminder. But you don't show it, continuing to serve up breakfast as if everything was perfectly normal and as she seems okay you ask her who the mystery man from the previous afternoon was. Police, she says, which puts your mind at ease straight away. Stands to reason they'd be all over this.

She tells you she's going to research a new gym to join which delights you as you never want her to go back to the one in Hartleigh, and it seems a positive step that she wants to move away from the life she had there too. You happily leave her with your laptop and tentatively offer to come back to sleep there that night if she wants but you don't push it, or sound too eager, however she says yes which pleases you.

It was a long and tiring day at work made more so for coming on top of a sleepless night. You spend some of the day going over the details of what happened to Maddy with Cubby which you find depressing. You're in poor form by the time you get back to Maddy's place and are pleased she seems as content as you are to have a quiet, and early, night.

But, even following a night of no sleep it had gone three before you finally nodded off. That's why you were still asleep when she came downstairs this morning. You think you made a mistake then, appearing in her kitchen in just your boxers, as you got the distinct impression it made her uncomfortable and you could kick yourself for your thoughtlessness. Of course she wouldn't want to have a near naked man around her, why would she? Fortunately, you're late up so excuse yourself quickly to go and shower.

You thought the meeting at the office later was going well until he showed up. Detective Inspector James Lambert. The man she said was just police. Yeah, right. You took against him immediately and even more so when he made it clear why he was there. Angry, you took a back seat and left Cubby to direct the meeting but you couldn't help but blurt out your objection then felt foolish for having done so. Maddy was sweet though and when she offered you her hand you gladly took it, happy to have that connection and, if you're being totally honest, deep down wanting James to see it too.

All you want to do is take her away from everything to do with her past, but now James is wanting to send her right back to where she came from, and you couldn't help but have a go at him after he revealed he didn't even have a plan. All that pent up frustration you didn't get to vent on Tag threatened to boil over with him instead, but Maddy told him to go and kept a firm grip on your hand in the process. After that though you think you did yourself some good. You took charge. And felt proud for having done so. You came up with exactly what happened at Danewright House on Saturday night/Sunday morning which everyone agreed with and which solved that particular problem. You liked the way she'd looked at you then, like she valued your input. That felt good and you went on to offer the company's support to her; however, you're not sure why but you felt like that didn't go down quite so well and she left soon after.

You get home just in time to join her for a walk and you have the chance to talk but you can tell she's distracted. She has a lot on her mind with the task James Lambert has set her, of course, and while you wish she'd turned him down you understand her reasons for not doing so. A clean slate and all that. You have no idea how she's going to achieve what she needs to but you do know one thing; whatever happens, you're going to make sure you are with her, every step of the way. You haven't always supported the way she's done things but that is going to change from here on in. She probably won't like it, that damned independent streak of hers, but somehow you're going to make yourself useful so she has no option but to involve you. It's all part of becoming stronger for her although, in truth, you have absolutely no idea how to go about making yourself indispensable.

As for that James Lambert, you don't like him. Not one little bit. He's far too smooth for your liking, and good looking, and you hate the way he looks at her. You're damn sure she knew him way back when too. He's certainly given her the impression they've met before and you're sure she's remembered when, but she's clammed up tight on that one.

Is he competition for her affections? That wouldn't be very professional of him, would it?

But you suspect he's not one for the rules, just look at what he's asked her to do, that's not right, is it? Therefore, you doubt he'd worry too much about blurring the lines of professional etiquette. Which is another reason to stay close to her.

If course, there is also the issue of work but you discussed that with Cubby today and, for the duration of getting whatever this situation entails sorted out he's happy to come back into the office to cover when needed. He's barely left anyway, finding it far harder to retire than he ever expected.

You're glad you managed to make her laugh on the walk earlier. You felt that brought you closer, but it's also how you've ended up in this position. You gaze back down at her now, your fingers aching because you've been massaging her for so long but she appears to be totally absorbed, which makes you smile, and you wonder for a moment if she has fallen asleep. She needs it, you know that, she needs some relaxation. Unsurprisingly she's been tense and distant and you hope this might help close that gap. She's flustered when she comes round and you say nothing as she straightens her clothes and you hope you've not overstepped the mark, but then you manage to end the evening on a good note. There's a little banter which feels chilled and you smile, enjoying seeing the colour rise in her cheeks as she excuses herself and goes to bed and you know she's had a good time, and at your hands too.

<u>Chapter 6</u>

I have been diligent in applying Diane's concoctions to my battered body and face and, more concerned with the wounds that are visible and, considering it's only Wednesday, I'm impressed with how quickly my lip is healing and the bruising reducing. Maybe she really is a witch, and I ponder this as I tend to covering the bruises I see in the mirror. I definitely still need makeup, and plenty of it, but after applying that I decide I'm going out for a walk. So when Dan has gone to work, after joking that as long as I don't think he's moving in surreptitiously he'll be back in the evening, I wrap up against the distinct chill in the air and leave the cottage. I walk up the lane, past the pub and along the high street. I see quite a few people out and about, and exchange greetings and views on the weather. Hasn't it turned cold, I'm told repeatedly, yes, I reply and I huddle further down into my coat, the wind whipping my cheeks, as I bury my hands deep in the pockets. It's nice. It's normal, and it's nice to feel normal even if it does only last as long as the walk.

I come up with no answers to my Craig predicament. No reason why I could possible need him has come to mind and of course there's not just Craig to consider, there's the rest of the gang too. I can't see me finding a friendly face among any of them. Those once loyal to Tag will hate me for having left him. Craig's men, well they'll just hate me. Nothing about having to return to the gang is appealing.

I walk each street of the village in turn, not that there are that many, eventually ending up back at the shop. It's not yet lunchtime but I pop in to see if I can be tempted into something delicious. I don't disappoint myself, walking out a few minutes later with a fresh-from-the-oven and still warm sausage roll, that I start eating as I walk, and a double chocolate with chocolate chunks muffin to enjoy after. I head back down the lane towards home.

I'm surprised when I see Ben's car parked outside Diane's cottage. I notice it's crammed with black bags and I've only just got past it when he comes striding along the pathway from around the rear of her cottage, flinging the gate back on its hinges aggressively. *Uh oh.* He sees me, his face twisting with rage, and jabs a finger in my direction as he shouts, "This is your doing, this is, you little bitch." I freeze, fear weakening my legs, but I set my face and make no response, simply stand and stare back at him. He stops and glares at me and in those few moments where I'm not sure what he's going to do next I feel my heartbeat rise, anxiety tightening my breathing, afraid he's about to come over. I'm alone and, acutely aware of my isolation, tense in readiness but then let out a held breath when he abruptly turns away, gets in his car and slams the door, his tyres spinning as he speeds off. As I'm left shaking.

Being more gentle with Diane's gate than he

was, I walk round to the back of her cottage concerned by what I might find. Diane is sitting at her kitchen table, her head in her hands, when I first catch a glimpse of her through the window but by the time I'm at the door she has risen. Although she has turned away from me I can see she is using the heels of her hands to dry her eyes and I know she heard me coming.

"Oh! Hi, Maddy, come on in," she cries, her voice unnaturally high and falsely bright. She turns and forces a smile and I see her eyes are red-rimmed, the blue of them sparkling with unshed tears. I place the muffin on the table and am relieved to sit, my legs still wobbly.

I know Diane doesn't like a lot of fuss so I get straight to the point. "Let's share this," I say, "while you tell me what's going on. Sorry there's only one. I wasn't planning on stopping." Cat jumps onto my lap as Diane gets a couple of plates out but while she gets a knife and proceeds to cut the cake in half she brushes my concern away saying everything is fine. My fingers automatically knead their way into Cat's fur as I respond, I'm direct and tell Diane that it clearly isn't, and I'm not leaving until she tells me the truth so she might as well get on with it.

Cat's purr is so deep I feel its rumble against my thighs but, because I'm anxious about Diane, he is nowhere near as calming as he has been in the past. Diane sighs, and tries to distract me by checking out my face. I allow her a brief discussion on its improvement and lavish praise on how great her potions are, which briefly cheers her up, but then I get back to the point of my unscheduled visit.

"Well?" And I fix my gaze on her.

"It's Ben."

"Yes," I say, trying not to sound impatient.

"He's putting up my rent." She looks down at her hands and when she lifts her head up again I see her eyes have filled with new tears, her voice miserable as she finishes, "and I'm in trouble." This is completely new information. I had no idea she rented her cottage.

"He's your landlord?" She nods, and sniffs, wiping away at her eyes again. "But I thought you owned this cottage. That's why you sold the other one to me." She shakes her head.

"I owned yours but couldn't afford to do it up and make it habitable. So I was renting this one off the Smithsons at mate's rates, because me and Ted go way back." She sighs and I fear a fresh wave of tears is about to engulf her but she shakes her head again, blinking them away before she continues. "Ted got into financial difficulties a few years back and Ben offered to help him out and got this cottage as part of the deal. Ted made him keep me on as a tenant which he agreed to do as long as I paid the rent but he keeps raising it and now, after what's happened, he's done it again." She sobs and although I know what's coming I leave her to say it anyway. "And I can't afford it anymore."

The Smithsons farm all the land around here but there are several branches of the family and consequently it's a complicated set-up. It is no secret that Ted, the head of one of the branches, is a gambler and it doesn't take much to work out how he'd got into financial difficulties. But something in what she said sets off those tiny jangling bells of alarm. I'm almost afraid to ask, but know I have to.

"After *what's* happened?" There's a silence while *this is your doing this is, you little bitch* runs over and over through my thoughts.

She sniffs again, "I'm sorry but he says you're to blame, that it's all your fault he's taken this action."

"Letitia?" She nods. "Because he thinks I told her?" She nods again, and it all becomes clear. "But he has no leverage against me so he's taking it out on you instead because you're my friend. That's outrageous!"

"Is it?" She looks at me and I can see her desperation. She's right, we know what he's like, maybe not first-hand but there have been enough rumours over the years to know he's not averse to ruthless business practices. So perhaps it's not surprising he'd behave in exactly the same way privately. But still, I find it unacceptable. I take in a deep breath, inhaling the heady mix of herby aromas that makes my friend's kitchen such a welcoming place to be, but like Cat it doesn't have its usual calming effect on me today.

"Yes, it is. Attacking my friend is a low blow, Diane, even for him, and he has no proof I did anything anyway. He's just leapt to that conclusion." I feel terrible that my actions have caused this massive problem for Diane, and silence descends for a few moments. She gets up to remove a boiling pan from the stove, peering into it and giving the contents a stir, before returning to her seat. I think through the state of my finances and wonder if I can make up the shortfall. I probably can for a little while, as long as I keep my job, but not long term, and it's not a solution to the problem anyway. He'd only put the rent up again. I know I need to put this right somehow but at the moment I have absolutely no idea how I'm going to do that, and I can't help feeling that my life has just become a whole lot more complicated, although the change from the constant, and increasingly violent, thoughts of Craig comes as something of a relief.

The halves of muffin lie untouched on the plates between us and absentmindedly I reach for mine now and take a bite. My thoughts wander to Letitia and dwell on her for a bit. I wonder how she's faring through the breakup. Much as it goes against the grain, I think I'm going to have to go and see her, at least to find out what Ben knows, or thinks he knows. She might be a useful source of information on him as well, and I think I'm going to need some. I couldn't see any other alternative before me anyway so would have to start somewhere.

Diane brings me out of my thoughts as she murmurs, "I suppose I could go and live with Joe." I look at the plate and realise my bit of the muffin has gone but that I didn't taste one crumb of it.

"Do you want to do that?"

"Not really. Although we, er," she looks at me a little sheepishly, "we, um, have a sort of thing going on."

"You don't say," I say, though I realise she probably doesn't appreciate my sarcasm right now.

"Oh, is it that obvious? Does everyone know?" This concern seems to, temporarily at least, distract her from the main issue. I shake my head.

"As far as I'm aware no one knows, I just guessed." She shrugs.

"Oh, okay."

"So do you want to live with him?" She stares out of the window for a moment, deep in thought.

"He's offered in the past but I value my independence too much. Still, I might have to take him up on the offer now." This galvanises me into telling her of my intention.

"Hold on for the moment, Diane. Don't make any rush decisions. I'm going to deal with Ben."

"You're going to deal with Ben! How are you going to do that?" Her voice rises with her question but I ignore the look of disbelief that comes across her face. She doesn't know who I am or just how devious I can be so I can hardly blame her for lacking faith in my ability to do anything to help her. In addition, the only words I can offer are not exactly convincing.

"I've no idea at the moment, but something will come to me. It always does." However, I'm hoping they're enough to satisfy Diane for the time being.

I leave a little while later, telling her not to

worry, though I realise she's unlikely to do anything else.

That evening, when Dan arrives, I suggest we take
a walk up to the village again and on the way I tell
him what Ben has done. That then involves me
telling him how I tipped off Letitia.

"You do use your powers for good then, as well
as evil?" I know he's only winding me up, and
throw him a look which tells him as much.

"I try to help people where I can, Dan. I don't
like Letitia but that doesn't mean I want to see her
being treated badly. Although frankly why she
should expect any better of him when it's how she
came to be the current Mrs Pritchard I'll never
know."

"What are you going to do then?"

"I'm not sure at the moment, but something
will come to me." I know I keep saying that but
not a thing has materialised by way of an answer
as yet, however when I tell him the Ben issue has
come as something of a welcome relief to having
my thoughts constantly dwelling on Craig, he
looks at me, shaking his head, like I'm ever so
slightly mad.

Dan offers me a drink again when we get to the
pub and this time I relent, because I could certainly
use one. Josh greets us when we enter and I introduce Dan as a friend of mine. There are only a few
in at this time of an evening so Josh is free to serve
us immediately. A beer for Dan, a cider for me.
We take our drinks and go through to sit at a table

away from the bar area. There is only one other couple in there, chatting away in one of the booths.

We're catching up on each other's day when Kourtney appears behind the bar looking irate. While she is keeping her voice low for the sake of the customers, she has her phone in one hand and the way she is gesticulating to and with it clearly shows that she is not happy. Josh is trying to pacify her but then a group of four walk in and as he has to get back to work she shrugs and walks off again, leaving him to serve them.

She is back moments later with food for the couple in the booth, and once she has delivered it to them she comes over to us, pulling her order pad out of the pocket in her apron at the same time and flicking it open to a clean page.

"Hi, are you eating?" She is not her usual self at all, a frown fixed to her forehead.

"No, we're not," Dan says.

"What's wrong, Kourtney?" I ask, after quickly introducing her to Dan as she's only seen him in passing before.

Her shoulders heave with a sigh of frustration before she answers, "I've 'ad five clients cancel today. Five!"

"Why have they done that? Did they give a reason?"

"I didn't fink to ask the first two, but then when I asked the others they said they'd heard I wasn't to be trusted. I'd stolen something from when I was cleaning another 'ouse. Can you believe it!"

She is understandably angry and I feel a tickle of discomfort cross my scalp, her next sentence confirming my fears. "It's that Ben Pritchard spreading the lies, an' I don't even clean for 'im! Bastard!"

"One of them told you it was Ben?" Dan asks, saving me from having to.

"Yeah! Then I asked the last one too and they didn't deny it. All big 'ouses too, all my biggest jobs."

"Okay, okay." I raise my hand in a calming gesture, "I know what's going on, Kourtney, and you're not going to like it but I think it's my fault this has happened."

"Why is he takin' it out on me then! What 'ave you done to 'im?" Her frown lines deepen across her forehead. I'm tempted to say, 'nothing yet but watch this space', but I don't, replying more equably instead.

"I can't tell you here. Can I see you tomorrow?"

"Yeah. I'll come round at nine if that suits, it turns out I won't be cleaning then after all."

"Sorry about that," I say, and I grimace. "I will sort it out though, I can promise you that."

She looks at me and nods, probably more out of good manners than belief, then mutters, "I look forward to hearing how," and heads back to the kitchen.

"You shouldn't promise something you don't know you can deliver," Dan warns me.

I glare at him, "Oh, I will be delivering, you don't have to worry about that. I can't let everyone else suffer for something I did." His eyebrows rise though he remains silent, lifting his glass to his mouth instead of offering any other words of wisdom. My course is determined, of that I am certain, because if Diane has been the catalyst for my decision to seek vengeance on Ben, then Kourtney has only strengthened my resolve.

I can't settle when we're back home. Dan offers to make us a stir fry but rather than leave him to get on with it I'm restless, so hang around the kitchen and, as I watch him slice onions like a pro, I have to ask, "Where did you learn to do that?"

"I had a short stint in a professional kitchen a few years back..."

"Of course you did," I interrupt with glee and he looks up from his rapid chopping and can't help but grin at me before he continues.

"But mainly at home, mum is a fantastic cook but she made each of us responsible for feeding the family one night a week, and it used to get competitive."

"How old were you when you started doing that?"

"Oh, about ten I think. Mum was keen on us being useful, as well as independent. We always had lists of chores we had to do. My older brother was a complete slacker though and used to find any excuse not to do his share. He's married now and I don't suppose his wife gets a lot of help around the house." He considers this for a moment. "Although I guess as he's a lawyer he probably pays for help." I smile.

"Ah, well it might be useful knowing a lawyer." He looks up from slicing the peppers and raises one eyebrow at me when he sees me grinning about the predicament I could potentially find myself in.

"I don't think he's the sort that would be of any help to you, he's in corporate law or something."

I don't understand what that means so ask, "What do you need to have to use his services then?"

"You need to have a lot of money, I know that," and the way he says this makes me laugh.

"Well that counts me out then," he smiles and nods in acknowledgement. I find I'm becoming intrigued by his family and am keen to know more but wary of looking like I'm interrogating him I continue along the same vein. "So did you always eat as a family?" He's finished his preparation and scoops all the vegetables into the pan to join the chicken.

"Always, Dad would come home from work at six and dinner would be on the table at six-thirty. It was like a ritual in our house, everyone sharing their news, both good and bad, help, advice, rows, bickering, tears and laughter, it all happened over that table." He looks wistful for a moment, pausing from stirring the contents of the pan.

"I can see you miss that." I set the table then lay two plates out on the worktop ready for him.

"Yeah, I do. But life moves on and we've all grown up and gone our own way." He tips our dinner out onto the plates and we carry them over to the table and sit. My first taste confirms his mother taught him well. "And you never know, maybe one day I'll have my own family and we can do the same." He catches my eye then and I briefly wonder if he might consider building that family with me but then banish that thought from my head, because while I think about how nice that would be, it is so far off into the future it seems an impossible dream. We continue chatting as we eat and he lets me into the secrets of creating a good stir fry when I praise him for this one. I enjoy listening to him, and although he reciprocates with the questions I soon turn the conversation round again, pleased to let him talk and me be able to absorb the smallest detail of his life.

Eating and chatting with Dan has been a good distraction, but once we sit down to watch a bit of television my mind wanders back onto the growing number of problems I have facing me. I haven't heard anything from James but suspect it won't be long before I do, and if he's expecting me to have come up with a solution he's going to be disappointed. I know he didn't give a time frame so that's in my favour, but I also know I can't hang around on this as I'll be unable to concentrate on anything else until it's resolved. And I now have the Ben stuff to be turning my attention to as well, as if one predicament were not enough.

I struggle to get to sleep when I go to bed, tossing and turning in a bid to get comfortable. My body is healing quickly, thanks to Diane, but it feels underused which is not helping when it comes to sleeping well, and I'm impatient to get back to working out in the gym next week. All this resting is doing it no good at all.

<u>**Chapter 7**</u>

I eventually sleep in fits and starts, waking in the morning feeling decidedly ragged. Dan doesn't look any more rested than me and we are quiet around each other as we get ready for the day. I've noticed he doesn't touch me, not since that first time when he asked if he could give me a hug. There was the massage of course but other than that it's always been me making the first move and reaching for him. He's accepted the gesture each time but not responded with anything further, and I can't help but wonder about that. It's like he's distancing himself. He leaves for work and I'd have liked to have given him a peck on the cheek as he did so but I don't, simply clearing up from breakfast instead and then finishing my coffee on the bench outside, keen for some fresh air before Kourtney's arrival.

She's bang on time and I usher her in and take her through to the kitchen. I make us more coffee, and as I do I realise that with my mind elsewhere I haven't replenished my supply of biscuits and have none to offer Kourtney. Irritated, I'm then surprised to find there are two packets in the cupboard when I open the door. I take one out and gaze at it a moment, wondering if I did go shopping after all and not remembered doing so but then it occurs to me there is a simpler explanation, it must have been Dan, and I smile to myself. That was a kind thing for him to do and I turn my attention back to Kourtney.

We sit at the table as I tell her what I did for Letitia, what Ben suspects and that as he can take no action against me he's picking on my friends instead. I explain that Ben has already got to Diane but don't give her the details, those she doesn't need to know.

Throughout my explanation she remains quiet, a serious expression on her face. I apologise for the trouble I have brought her but at this she stops me.

"Don't worry about it," she says, "Ben's the one who's bein' a dick. I'm glad yer did what yer did for Letitia. Though I didn't know you cared about 'er so much." She grins at me, which releases the tension in her face, and I smile back.

"I think you know she's not my favourite person, but at the time it felt like the right thing to do."

"I think it was too. Though it's a shame we're all payin' for it now."

"I will put this right, Kourtney, I meant it when I said that last night," I tell her, in as reassuring a manner as I can.

She nods, her ponytail bobbing as she does so, "I know you will, bu' if there is anythin' I can do to 'elp, let me know." She clearly has more faith in my abilities than Diane and I know I cannot let her down. I would hate for her burgeoning business to be brought to its knees before it's even fully up and running, all because of me.

"I will, thanks." I'm sure I won't be taking her up on her offer but it's nice to know I have her support, and I'm pleased to be able to change the subject. "How's the driving going?"

"Not too badly, I've put in for my theory already and will apply for my test as soon as I've got that."

"That's terrific news, well done." Her eyes sparkle as she smiles and it's nice to see her so positive and eager.

"Thanks. I need to get a lot of driving in and Chris has offered to take me out for some practice."

"That's good of him." I then feel a little awkward. "I'd, er, offer to take you out too, but I think I'm going to be a bit busy over the next little while." I hope she doesn't mind.

"Don't be ridiculous! It's only because of you I'm able to be doin' this at all!" That's a fair point and, reassured I've done my bit, we finish our coffees while Kourtney tells me her other plans for the business. I'm pleased to see Ben's interference hasn't entirely dampened her enthusiasm and she leaves a short while later, off to her first client of the day.

After an early lunch I head towards Hartleigh. It's Thursday and Sidney's funeral is at two. The weather is suitably bleak with low, iron grey clouds that threaten rain. The service, if you can call it that, is basic. Nothing in a church or chapel, just a few words said at the graveside. There are few to hear them. One man, dark suited with a smart navy overcoat, and me, considerably less formal but still sombrely dressed. A small group of grey-haired men from the funeral director's stand a short distance away and once the vicar has said what he has to say, they come and lower Sidney into the ground. And that is it. A sad and lonely departure.

The man turns to me after the vicar has left us, and asks who I am.

"Nobody," I say, "well not a relative or anything. I used to go into the shop." The man studies me with some curiosity, no doubt wondering why I am here. I would have no answer for him if he asks so I'm glad he doesn't question me further. I enquire who he is.

"Sidney's solicitor," he explains, and passes me his card. "He left instructions with me to deal with his estate."

I nod, unsure of what to say to that but wary he might think I'm after something I say, "I hope you manage to get it all sorted without a problem then." We say our goodbyes and I watch as he walks off across the graveyard. I'd noticed Sidney's plot was right next to another and I am curious to look at the inscription. As I move closer I can see it reads – 'Margery Cooper and Emily. Beloved wife and daughter of Sidney Cooper, taken too young and never forgotten. Rest in Peace'. Their dates are listed. Margery had been twenty-three, their daughter, three. They'd died more than fifty years ago, and on the same day. I am filled with sadness for a story that is nothing to do with me but the tragedy of which I can't help but reflect on. What a terribly lonely life Sidney had lived. It has always fascinated me, the human spirit and the many forms it takes. How one person can spend a life mourning the loss of a family, while another can walk away from theirs without a backward glance. I only hope Sidney is now reunited with his. Yet that thought in itself opens up a whole world of imponderables I have no time to dwell on right now.

I wander round the graveyard for a while. It's an old one, with gaps like missing teeth in the haphazard rows of gravestones. I enjoy the peace and tranquillity of looking at headstones and imagining the stories behind them, and am engrossed in deciphering the worn words on one when a voice makes me jump.

"Hello." I spin round, my hand on my chest, and see James standing a few feet away, one palm raised towards me. "Sorry, I didn't mean to startle you."

"Then you shouldn't creep up on people like that."

"I didn't creep, but point taken, I'll make more noise next time."

"What do you want, and how did you know I was here?"

"That's what I like about you, Maddy, no small talk." I scowl at him until he continues. "I saw your car in passing so thought I'd have a quick catch up. I am intrigued though. Why are you at this funeral?"

"You saw my car in passing?" I cock an eyebrow at him in disbelief. "I think you're following me."

"And I think you're good enough to know if I was." I don't break the eye contact we have. He has a point, I am.

"It's Sidney's funeral, I used to buy my paper from him." It seems a perfectly valid reason to attend a funeral to me but I can see James is sceptical.

"Right," he says slowly. Then clearly deciding it isn't an avenue worth pursuing he changes the subject, "So, the catch up. How are you getting on?"

"Not well. I haven't come up with a solution to your problem yet."

"Our problem." I ignore the correction and decide to change the subject myself.

"How do you know me?" This question has been one of many rattling around in my head. I can only think of one time when any police were involved in my life and although I don't remember him specifically I assume it comes from then. But I want confirmation.

He indicates a bench, "Shall we take a seat?" I follow him over and once seated leave him to answer my question.

"I was there, the day you found your mother dead. I was the one stationed at your flat until everyone had done what they needed to."

My assumption was right. I still didn't remember him. But I did recall a young constable who wouldn't take any tea. Who was sent to watch over the scene. Who gazed down on the body of my mother dispassionately, and who carried out his duties quietly, thereby disappearing into the background while watching all the drama an unexpected death entails unfold in front of him.

"You made an impact on me that day," he continues, leaning back on the bench and stretching his arm along the top of it.

"In what way?" I sit on the edge, hunched, my knees together, hands either side gripping the seat but I turn my head to watch him and he shrugs.

"The way you were living. I felt sorry for you."

"I didn't need your pity."

"No, maybe not. Let's say you got my interest then. I was curious so went out of my way to find out more."

"You've climbed a long way up the career ladder since then."

"I was fast-tracked. Through you I made the connection to Tag, and putting him away did me a lot of good." I sit up then, forcing myself to let go of the seat and making myself lean back.

"I'm glad to have been of service to you." He can't have missed the sarcastic edge to my response, but he ignores it.

"I've been looking for you ever since."

"What, so you can put me away too?"

"Not necessarily. Like I said, you affected me, unexpectedly. So I started trying to find you."

"You weren't alone."

"No," he says as he tilts his head. "You did a good job of disappearing."

"Thank you. It's a shame I didn't make a better fist of it, if I had I might still be enjoying my quiet life in the great British countryside." He smiles then there's a long pause. I wonder if that's it and if it's appropriate for me to get up and leave, but then he breaks the silence.

"I meant it, I have been looking for you."

"I heard you the first, and second, time and I'm still not sure how to respond to that." Then he abruptly changes the subject.

"What's the score between you and Dan?"

Something else I have no answer to, so I mutter a feeble, "We're together." It feels safer to say that but why it's any of his business I have no idea.

"Together, but not sleeping together." I turn to look at him sharply.

"What the hell's that got to do with you? And how do you know that anyway?" My mind immediately goes into overdrive trying to puzzle it out.

"I'm a detective, it's what I do. Sorry." He looks uncomfortable, as well he should. But then the answer comes to me. Kourtney, I think. Kourtney's text. She'd told me he'd called round. He must have seen the pillows and blankets on the sofa. Two and two, and all that. Satisfied I know the answer, I continue.

"He's giving me some space." Which only seems reasonable after being raped I think, although I don't know why I feel the need to explain anything to James.

"Of course. Sorry. Again." I decide that with everything being in the mess it is, and my head a confused muddle of things I have to sort out, I need to stop dancing round the subject and know what's what. Like he said, I don't do small talk, so I ask him bluntly.

"Are you trying to tell me you're interested in me? And not just on a professional level."

His eyebrows rise in surprise at my candour and he smiles as he says, "Yes, Maddy, yes I am." Okay then, at least I know what I'm dealing with, though what direction I take with that information I have no idea.

As I get to my car I receive a call from Chris, saying "Pub?" his often made greeting. Unfortunately, I can't reply in my customary fashion so I have to say, "Yes, but I'm only just leaving Hartleigh, can you wait that long?"

"I'll see you there, Madeleine," he says, and he's gone. He does make me smile but as quickly as this comes to mind another thought replaces it. *What if Ben has got to him too?* Anxiety builds on the drive home as I dream up ever increasingly dire scenarios of what it is that Ben has done to him. I park outside the front of the pub and rush in.

"Steady on," says Chris, who is propping up the bar as I enter. "Don't worry, Madeleine, they haven't run out of your favourite tipple yet." I manage a smile and hope it looks more convincing than it feels on my face, my tension hard to dispel. "You must have broken a few limits on the way back, I've only just got here myself." Chris then looks at me more closely, the corners of his eyes creasing as he does so, "Are you all right?"

"Yeah, yeah, absolutely fine. Just, you know, the stresses of work." And now I'm here I take a deep breath, let it out and try to appear calm and collected.

"Okay, well in a change to our usual pattern as I'm at the bar, what can I get you to drink?"

"I'll have a half of cider please. Excuse me, I'm just going to pop to the ladies."

"No problem, I'll get us a table."

I check my face in the mirror, and touch up my makeup. It's still heavier than how I would usually wear it but it's hopefully not too obvious that it's there to cover anything up. I go back out to the bar and join Chris in the booth he's got for us. He's already half way down his pint.

"Thirsty?"

"This one will barely touch the sides," he says, and smiles at me as he downs the rest and goes straight back to the bar for a top-up. I take the opportunity to send Dan a quick text to let him know I'm with Chris and to invite him to call in to meet him if my car is still outside the pub when he returns. It's a spur of the moment decision and I hit send before I change my mind, then ponder for a moment on my motives for integrating him further into my life here. Maybe if he likes my friends he'll hang around a bit longer? It seems a pitiful stretch when I view it like that, and I sigh and try to put him out of my mind.

Chris is soon back. "I'm not getting in the way of anything, am I?"

"No, why would you think you are?"

"You're all dolled up," he says as he waves vaguely in the direction of my face.

"Ah, no, I had some meetings today that's all. Wanted to look my best."

"Aha." He stares at me for a long moment like he doesn't quite believe me, and I hold the stare and refuse to back down. Eventually, he says, "So, Madeleine, do you fancy a bite to eat?"

"I do, Christopher." He frowns at my full use of his name which I like to throw in now and then to wind him up. "I'll put the order in." I go and do just that with Josh and get a refill of both of our drinks at the same time.

I re-join Chris, place the glasses down on beer-mats and slide into the booth. I then decide to get straight to the nub of what was worrying me all the way home, and plunge in without thinking it through.

"Is everything all right with you, Chris?"

"Yes," he replies, sounding suspicious, "why, shouldn't it be?"

"Yes. Good, yes, it should be, absolutely." His frown deepens and I wish that for once I'd been subtler, but then rather than stopping I choose to flounder on, for some reason needing to be absolutely sure. "It's just, well I was thinking, well wondering if, well you know, if anyone has been causing you any problems recently?" He shakes his head.

"Nope, not that I can think of," he says, and he reaches for his glass again.

My relief is clear as I say, "Excellent, good, good." Then I take a long draught of my cider, as if that is the end of the matter. If only. Chris is looking at me, bemused.

"What's going on?" It only dawns on me then that perhaps I don't want Chris to know all about the issues I have going on. Having one place where normality reigns might be quite nice, however I rather think it's too late for that, although I still give it a go.

"Oh nothing, nothing at all."

He raises one eyebrow in question at me and says, "Tell me." I know I'm going to have to but groan at my stupidity for being so obvious. Fortunately, I am bought a little time by our food arriving, delivered, as always, by Kourtney.

"How's your day been, Kourtney?" Chris asks.

"I've 'ad better," she replies.

"Oh, what's happened?" This question and answer session takes place while we get ourselves set up with cutlery and sauces.

"You'd better ask Maddy, she'll fill you in." I grimace as she then turns to me and says, "One more gone today."

"Sorry, Kourtney. You do know I am absolutely going to sort it out."

"I know." She still sounds considerably more confident in my abilities than I feel is perhaps warranted, but it feels good to have her in my corner. "I can't stop an' chat as chef needs some 'elp in the kitchen, we've got a large party comin' in later," and with that she turns on her heels and goes back to work.

I turn my attention to the steak and chips in front of me. We exchange the usual accompaniments and I reach for an early onion ring.

"Fill me in then," Chris says, after we've had an initial nibble at the contents of our plates. The interruption has bought me enough time to get my thoughts in order. I know I don't want to tell him too much, particularly of other people's business, but also with regard to the wider scope of what I get up to because, rather like Diane, he thinks I work in insurance, doing admin or something similar I imagine.

When I ask he already knows that Letitia has thrown Ben out, but doesn't know why, being generally out of the loop on the detail of village gossip. I explain what has happened and that it appears Ben blames me for telling her and is now taking it out on my friends as he has no way of causing me grief directly. I explain what he's done to Kourtney which I can tell riles Chris up no end, his face darkening as I fill him in.

"That's why you were asking those questions earlier?"

"Yes, I wondered if he'd got to you too."

"Who else has he got to then?" This is where it gets a little awkward.

"I don't think I can say, I might be betraying a confidence." He mulls this over for a minute.

"If I guess, I don't think you're betraying anything."

"We can give that a go."

"Is it Diane?"

"Yes." I have few friends, so this lucky first guess wasn't much of a stretch.

"Okay." He ponders this for a moment, thinking out loud, "Okay, so a link between Diane and Ben." He carries on eating as he thinks, as do I, although I'm not enjoying my steak and chips as much as I would do usually. Then with his fork fully loaded and on the way to his mouth he pauses it in mid-air and says, "Ah. He's her landlord."

That was the bit of information I was wary of revealing so I'm pleased he already knows about it, but I merely mumble a confirmatory, "Hmm," as my mouth is full, and let him carry on.

"So, I guess the most obvious thing is that he's put the rent up? He hasn't served her notice, has he?" This afterthought clearly alarms him, the frown lines deepening between his eyes as soon as it comes to mind.

"No, no," I say, clearing my mouth, "It is the rent."

"And, you going to sort that out too." I nod, though sense the change in tone, the question and possible disbelief, when he says, "along with Kourtney's client issue?" I nod again.

"How are you intending on doing that?" He's put down his knife and fork so he can give me his full concentration.

"I've absolutely no idea, but I've told them both I will." I grimace and he smiles in sympathy, I think, or despair, and we both lapse into silence again as he picks up his cutlery and we finish eating. Pushing away his plate before screwing up his napkin and placing it on the table, he looks at me carefully.

"Well I have every faith in you, you know that." I didn't, particularly, but it's good to know and I thank him before he continues, "and if you need any help you know where to come. Although I think I'm going to have to completely revisit that manuscript I've been working on. There's more challenge and tension in your life at the moment than there ever has been in my heroine's." I can't help but laugh at that; he's quite possibly right, I wouldn't know, but then I dwell on the fact that he's only aware of half of what's going on, and if he knew about Craig he might be thinking quite differently about my abilities.

Kourtney comes back a few minutes later and clears our table just as Dan arrives. I introduce him to Chris and as they formally shake hands he asks if Chris and I want a drink. I don't but Chris is keen for another pint so Dan goes to get that, and one for himself, returning a few minutes later and joining me on my side of the booth.

"Madeleine has just been filling me in on the trouble Ben has been causing for Diane and Kourtney."

"I hope you haven't had any problems with him?" Chris shakes his head at that and I reassure Dan.

"No, it was the first thing I checked with him. Do you want anything to eat? As you saw, we've already done so but I'm happy to stay if you fancy something."

"No, don't worry. I'll get something back at home." Home. He called my place home. That sounds promising, or perhaps it is only a figure of speech. I don't allow myself to dwell on the implications of his use of that word as there probably aren't any and instead I focus on the conversation.

I smile when I hear the first question Chris asks Dan. "Do you read?" It was the first thing he ever asked me and I suspect is his opener with any new acquaintance. He'd once told me he wasn't quite sure he'd ever be able to fully trust someone who didn't. I am therefore pleased when Dan and he are able to enter into a lengthy conversation about books. Taking a backseat for a while allows me to think back to my encounter with James that afternoon.

"I have a boyfriend," I'd told him, feeling the need to make the situation crystal.

"Do you?" he'd questioned, again, and I'd told him I definitely did although feared it came across like I was trying to convince myself as much as him. Then, as I'd opened the door to this direction of conversation, he'd made his interest quite clear, telling me as he reached out to capture a stray lock of my hair, that he wanted me. I only had to want him too.

The old Maddy would have taken James by the hand at that point and led him down into her dirty world. She wouldn't have thought twice about it, and sitting on that bench earlier it had certainly crossed her mind. He's attractive and has those lips. Kissable lips that it would be so easy to lean towards. But I'd said no, I'd said I wasn't interested and he'd nodded and gone on his way. Just like that.

I thought back to the point Diane had made that if things didn't work out with Dan I could always return to my old ways. As I watch Dan chatting with Chris now I wonder if I am kidding myself. If it is in fact all over. And I'm curious as to whether James has seen those doubts in me and I hope he isn't going to make trouble.

Because there's another issue with James, one that makes me extremely uneasy. He has all the power in what passes for our relationship and I wonder if he's above abusing that.

I look at Dan now. The messy edges of his dark blond hair hang over his eyes and he drags a hand through it to lift it back off his face. I enjoy watching him, enthusiastic and animated in his discussion with Chris, and I like the fact he takes an interest in and seems to care about my friends. He turns to look at me, his grey eyes crinkling at the corners as he smiles, and I realise he and Chris are sharing a joke about my passion for thriller reading and I leap in to defend the authors I love, adding that Dan is hardly in a position to judge, his reading choices no more literary than mine. I also tell him that Chris is writing a book, news he looks suitably impressed by, though Chris downplays it in his usual introverted way. The banter continues, it feels good and I resolve to banish all thoughts of James from my mind. I've known Dan for such a short period of time and yet it feels like he's always been here, something comfortable in my life, and because of that I still think it's something worth exploring further and maybe if I do Dan's interest will reignite towards me.

Dan excuses himself a short while later to take a trip to the gents and Chris finishes his drink.

"He seems like a decent man," he says as he puts his glass down.

"I think he is," I reply.

I get Chris's questioning eyebrow rising at me again, "You think?"

"It's complicated." I leave it at that. For some reason it feels wrong to talk to Chris about Dan, like it's disloyal or something, but he seems to recognise this and asks no more.

He reaches out and places his hand over mine, giving it a squeeze, "Well, I'm happy for you. Don't let complications get in the way."

"I'll try not to." I turn my hand in his and squeeze it back.

Dan returns soon after and we're all ready to leave. Chris hugs me once we're out on the road, and shaking Dan's hand again he says his good-byes and walks off up the high street. We both drive our cars the short distance down to my cottage, and returning to my place in darkness I'm pleased to get inside, draw the curtains and turn some lights on to make my home cosy and warm again.

"I'm surprised James Lambert hasn't been in touch by now," Dan says later as he's demolishing a pizza lovingly prepared by my own fair hands, or at least lovingly transferred from the freezer to the oven by my own fair hands.

"He has. I saw him today."

"You didn't say." I might be imagining it but I sense accusation in his tone, which I don't appreciate.

"At what point have I had the chance to do so. I could hardly bring him up in front of Chris, could I? I gave him enough to think about as it is."

"Fair point. Where did you see him?"

"After Sidney's funeral." His brow furrows

with confusion.

"You went to Sidney's funeral?"

"Yes." As if it was the most normal thing in the world.

"Many there?" And I wish I could have said yes and removed that trace of doubt in his voice.

"No. Just me and his solicitor." He stares at me a moment, his final piece of pizza poised right before entry to his mouth.

"You are probably the most intriguing person I think I've ever met," he says, then he bites into the slice.

"Thank you, it was the least I could do for all those papers he provided me with," and I smile at him.

"You do know you can read the papers another way now, don't you?" He brushes his hands together to get rid of the crumbs and reaches for his laptop while I mumble something incomprehensible under my breath. He taps a few keys then passes it over to me, and there on the screen is the local rag and on its front page the announcement that Ben is running for mayor, his smug face staring out of the screen at me. Oh joy. I am deeply engrossed in reading the piece when Dan speaks next.

"So, what did he have to say?"

"Who?" I reply, distracted by my reading.

"James." *Oh, we're still on that, are we?*

"Not much."

"So, what? He was just catching up?"

"Yeah, I guess so."

"You're being evasive." I sigh.

"I'm not. I just don't think you would be that interested in what he said."

"Try me."

"I asked him where he knew me from, and he told me." I hesitate, framing what I tell him next. "It was from the day my mother died." I'm looking directly at Dan as I say this and it takes a moment for him to react. A long moment.

Then it's like he blinks and says, "Oh, I'm sorry, Maddy. I had no idea." I shrug.

"There's no reason why you should have. We've never discussed the detail of our families. But for the record I am the only child of an absent father and dead mother."

"When did you last see your dad?"

"When I was eight." I want to deflect the conversation away from this area so given the opportunity to find out more, I ask after his family.

"I am the middle child of five. I have older, and younger, brothers and sisters, all of whom are highly accomplished in everything they do. My father is a doctor, my mother a florist." He smiles as my face lights up, this bit of information reminding me of the day we spent at Danewright House together.

"Ah, the flower knowledge."

"Absolutely. I used to work in the shop after school and weekends."

"So, your parents. Are they still together?"

"Yes."

"And you get on with and see all your brothers and sisters?"

"Yes, and frequently."

"I know one's a lawyer, what do the others do?"

"My other brother is a doctor, like Dad, my older sister is a vet and the other one is a teacher."

"Oh."

"I know what you're thinking."

"You do?"

"Uh ha, you are wondering why I'm so flaky when they are all so damned driven and disciplined."

"I wasn't exactly thinking that." He raises his eyebrows in disbelief. "I was just thinking you must be more of a free spirit, not willing to be hemmed in by the constraints of an everyday career, or something," I'm not even sure where I am going with this so stop talking.

"I don't seem to be able to settle, it's true. As I told you before my parents sent me here because they'd had enough of me not sticking at anything. I guess I do feel a bit like the odd one out but, to be fair to the family, they don't treat me like that."

"Well we definitely couldn't have come from more different backgrounds anyway." I'm not sure I've ever come across anyone from such a stable family before, or such a supportive one.

"No. But you know what they say?"

"No, what do they say?"

"Opposites attract?" He's grinning as he says this but the minute the words are out of his mouth his smile fades. Ridiculously I blush as though I'm some timid virgin but it's because this pleases me, it's a declaration of sorts, and I think, all hope is not lost for this relationship after all. But then he's immediately scrabbling to take his words, and their meaning, back. "I'm sorry," he says. "I didn't mean anything by that, I don't want you to think I'm making a move, or anything." I didn't, I think, uncomfortable with how quickly he's back-tracked, I just thought he was being nice. But now he looks about as embarrassed as I feel.

"It's fine," I say, and brush his apology away and try to ignore the sudden awkwardness be-tween us. I think back to our, too few, nights to-gether. We were at ease with each other then and didn't suffer this tension and worry about saying or doing the wrong thing all the time. Maybe we need to get back to that? But I know I'm not ready, not yet, and I know Dan isn't, he just said so. *I don't want you to think I'm making a move, or an-ything.* Oh, okay, then.

I try to get past this difficult moment by return-ing to where this all started.

"So, I was telling you about James."

"Of course." Dan looks equally delighted to be able to move on to safer conversational ground, saying, "how did he feature in, er, what hap-pened?"

"When there's a death at home the police attend and usually someone is stationed in the property while everything is sorted out. He was the consta-ble at the time, apparently. I didn't remember him but then I had other things on my mind."

"Of course you did." He pauses for a moment. "Do you mind if I ask how your mother died?"

"Drugs overdose. Not an accidental one." I don't feel I need to spell it out any further other than to add one final thing. "It was my eighteenth birthday."

"Oh God, Maddy. That's terrible. It's like she planned it."

"I know. She was a mess but there was no sign she was ever going to do that. However, she must have been counting the days." Then I'm surprised by how quickly he joins the dots.

"I guess you being an adult though, it at least meant you didn't get taken into care or anything." It's amazing he's even thought of that angle. It's not like it's a part of society that would have ever touched his life.

"True."

"Did you have anyone to help you?"

"Well there was Tag, of course, and the couple who owned the flat, and also ran the fish and chip shop below it, were nice." He reaches out a hand to me and I take it, grateful he's made the first move this time.

"You've done well for yourself, I hope you realise that, Maddy. You should be proud." His kind words take me by surprise and I unexpectedly find myself blinking back tears.

"Thank you. I appreciate that coming from you because I know how disapproving you are of the work I've been doing for your uncle."

"Well, I'm in charge now and I'm going to do everything I can to keep you on the straight and narrow from now on." He grins at me before adding, "after you've dealt with Craig, of course, and Ben. I have a feeling you're going to have to bend some rules there."

Ah, yes indeed, with the conversation we've been having I'd almost forgotten about them, but he was right, there was more than a fair chance I would be needing to stray over to the dark side again.

<u>**Chapter 8**</u>

Friday morning, I wake early and know I need to take some action. I've been sitting on the issues I have in front of me for getting on a week and I'm no further forward.

I stare at my face in the mirror as I apply Diane's potions. My lip has healed, the swelling reduced completely and my bruises have faded to mere shadows. My jaw is still tender so I know the bruising is there lingering underneath but to anyone else it's barely noticeable. I do still look like I have a black eye but when I wear eye makeup it's always dark, so the amount I have to apply to cover it up isn't unusual. I do what's needed to pass casual inspection after I shower then go downstairs for breakfast.

While I'm ready to face the day Dan is anything but, and I have to edge round him, his body dominating the kitchen as he makes coffee, and plenty of it, he tells me. At least he is wearing long shorts and a tee shirt, instead of the boxers, but I'm still pleased when he has gone for a shower and I can relax. I indulge myself by having toasted hot cross buns, with butter, and prepare some for when Dan reappears. When he does he looks brighter, but still tired.

I thank him for the biscuits as I'd forgotten to do so the day before.

"You're welcome," he says, "I noticed you'd run out. They are your favourites aren't they?"

96

"Yes."

"Well, there you go then." He shrugs like it's nothing but I don't think he has any idea this is probably the nicest thing a man has ever done for me.

I ask him again if he's getting enough sleep on the sofa, anxious about both alternatives if the answer is no; the thought of him leaving and the thought of inviting him back into my bed, just to get him to stay. But he assures me the sofa is perfectly adequate, which was not quite what I asked.

He leaves for work after wolfing down the breakfast I made and pouring himself another coffee to take with him.

I decide I'm going to tackle Letitia and plan what I want to say to her on the way. This is not as easy as it sounds as my thoughts are frequently interrupted by greetings from the villagers I pass. The conversations generally follow the same pattern.

Them: Morning.

Me: Morning, you all right?

Them: Yeah, you?

Me: Yeah.

And that's it. Unless there's some requirement to mention the weather which can extend the exchange like so.

Them: Cold, today.

Me: Yeah. Bitter wind.

Them: Not even winter yet.

Me: No.

These exchanges don't require, or expect, a slowdown in my pace. No one's wanting a full on conversation.

Too soon I find myself at her door and I wonder what kind of greeting I'm about to get, all the while half hoping she'll be out. Although I hear the jangle of the bell when I ring it, and the barking of the dogs in response, there is no sign of Letitia and I'm on the brink of turning away, inwardly cheering as I do so, when the door opens a crack and a much reduced form of Letitia peers through the gap. She says nothing.

"Hi, Letitia. May I come in?" She nods, casting her eyes downward, the door opens wider and I step into the hall. The dogs greet me with their usual boundless enthusiasm which couldn't be more stark in contrast to the state of their mistress.

She looks a mess.

Straggly hair that could do with a wash, or at least a hairbrush through it, hangs limply down each side of a pale and pasty face. Her eyes are swollen and reddened from crying and she's still in her pyjamas. Nice pyjamas, but pyjamas none-theless. She smells, and I wonder when she last changed out of them, or showered. The wow has definitely gone out of her and all of this annoys me.

"Seriously! He's worth this?" I hold my hands out, palms up, making it clear I'm talking about her directly and not the general state of the house. Also a mess. There's a fetid smell of dog and I wonder when they last went out.

"I'm losing it all," she says, her voice cracking and barely above a whisper.

"Well you will do, won't you? With that attitude." I don't quite *tsk*, but I could well have done, I'm that disappointed. I have to admit, from what I'd heard, I was expecting more. Maybe she'd used up all the strength she'd had chucking his stuff out and dealing with the confrontations that had caused already. I get a waft of something else from her, and lean closer to check again, "Have you been drinking? It's ten in the morning for Christ's sake!" I see her cheeks pink up and know I've hit home. "Okay, Letitia, this was going to be a quick pop in to see how you were doing visit. Let's now call it an intervention." She stares at me wide-eyed. "Go and get yourself in the shower, wash your hair and put some clean clothes on." She remains exactly where she is and makes no move to go anywhere. "Do it, or I will put you in the shower myself." The threat in the tone of my voice does the trick and she moves off, heading for the stairs though travelling far too slowly for my liking. "Hurry up! We have a lot to do." She glances back at me and speeds up, marginally, using the banister to help her.

All of this exchange has taken place in the hall and I now head into the kitchen, the dogs eagerly following. I unlock the back door and let them out, the grateful pair heading straight for the lawn to do their business. The utility room stinks. I don't even have pets but I know that you have to keep on top of pet spaces, they become rank if left untended for any length of time.

I pull my phone out of my pocket and call Kourtney. "Have you got any free hours today?"

"Due to my cancellations, unfortunately yes."

"Excellent. Come round to Letitia's as quickly as you can, and bring your brother, if he's available. There's a garden that needs tidying up as well."

"Are you sure? I'm not exactly a favourite of Letitia's." She sounds doubtful but I plough on.

"She's in no state to arrange anything so leave that with me. I'm here now."

"Okay, I'll see you in a bit." I hang up, then as it isn't raining I drag the dogs' beds outside for an airing.

Turning back to the kitchen I take a look at the coffee machine, decide that due to its complexity I have no idea how to get it working, so fill the kettle instead. While that is coming to the boil I clear the surfaces, piling up the dirty plates, cups and glasses by the sink. I make a large mug of black coffee for Letitia and leave it on the side for when she returns.

I am just checking through the contents of the fridge, throwing out everything with mould on it, when I hear the doorbell. The dogs race barking through the house and beat me to the door where I'm delighted to see Kourtney and her brother, who she introduces as Gaz (full name Gascoigne; his father, now mostly absent, a football fanatic, apparently).

I invite them in, tell Kourtney the whole house needs a once over, starting with the kitchen, and point Gaz in the direction of the garden. "You'll need to clear up after the dogs before you tackle the lawn," I say, though that doesn't seem to bother him. They both get to work.

There is no sight or sound of Letitia so I go up-stairs. Progress has been made. She's showered and dressed but has come to a halt in front of the mirror of her dressing table. Her wet hair hangs down her back creating a damp patch on her top. I grab the hairdryer and, turning it on, start to briskly dry her hair. She makes no move to stop me or take over the drying herself so I carry on. Thankfully the noise from the dryer prevents further conversation.

Once her hair is dry enough I turn the hairdryer off and place it back on the dressing table. I stand behind her and meet her puffy eyes in the mirror. "You and I are going to take the dogs out now. You can decide if you want to put any makeup on or not but be downstairs in five minutes, or I'll be back up here." I see a flicker of something pass across her eyes. I'm hoping it is alarm at the thought of going outside, with the possibility of seeing other people, and that it will stir a little pride in her.

Sure enough when she comes downstairs a few minutes later she has made some effort. Mascara highlights her eyes, a little blusher giving her some colour. She glances at Kourtney, a frown wrinkling her smooth brow. Before she has the chance to object I tell her what I've arranged for Kourtney and Gaz to do and she merely nods.

I push the mug of coffee towards her, "Drink that."

She picks it up, wrapping two hands around it, and takes a sip. Once she knows it won't scald her she finishes it quickly.

I lift the dogs' leads from the hooks where they hang, hand one to her and slip the collars over their heads as they come and sit obediently in front of us. Letitia puts on her coat and we leave by the back door. I don't know where people generally walk their dogs around here, not being an owner myself, but as I only have my ankle boots on I have no intention of traipsing across the fields so opt for sticking to the tarmac. There is little traffic down here as it's a no through road ending eventually at a farm. Once we are past the remaining few houses and are out of the village Letitia lets her dog off the lead, so after checking it's all right for me to do the same they are both soon running freely over the verges, sniffing and scenting as they do. So far we haven't spoken but now I look across at Letitia and say, "Do you want to talk?"

She shrugs. "I'm not sure what to say."

"Why don't you tell me why you're so upset?"

"Isn't it obvious?"

"Not to me. I didn't like him so it wouldn't bother me at all if he disappeared out of my life."

"Well it does bother me!" She stops and is on the brink of saying something else but then doesn't and I give her another prompt.

"Go on then, tell me." And she does, at length. I hear all about how she'd gone to work in his office. How he'd confided in her that his then wife hadn't understood him. *Original*. How their marriage was already over. *Of course it was*. How he'd seduced her and set her up as his mistress, just until the divorce was finalised, he'd said. *Whoever said romance was dead?* How that time had dragged until his wife found the earring Letitia had 'accidentally' left in the poor woman's bed while she'd been having sex her husband. *Classy. I added the "poor woman" bit. Letitia was not that sympathetic, even now.*

I hear how he'd introduced her to a whole new world of wealth and possessions. How she likes the life she leads, the activities she does, the people she mixes with. How she likes the privilege; it's not how she was brought up. How she likes the status money gives her. How she likes being Mrs Ben Pritchard because of his place in the local business world and how she was looking forward to him becoming the mayor and all the extra power and prestige that will bring. She has no doubt that he will win the election either, such is her confidence in him.

But at no point does she tell me she loves him, or even likes him. At no point does she say she misses him, that she can't live without him, or that her heart is breaking. Interesting, although to me hardly surprising.

"So why did you throw him out?" I'm pleased she has, because so many women in her situation will put up with the infidelity and turn a blind eye, all in order to keep the comfortable life, to keep what they have grown accustomed to. I had half expected Letitia to be one of those women and was delighted to hear she'd had more respect for herself, and shown some gumption.

"I was so angry," she says. "It was my automatic reaction. I threw out everything I could find of his and bolted myself in the house. I screamed at him when he returned."

"I heard."

"He was so angry with me and we rowed terribly. Yelling awful things at each other." She shakes her head as if that would remove the memory.

"That's understandable, I think," and I try to sound sympathetic.

"He wanted me to come out of the house but I was afraid of what he might do if I did."

"It was probably wise of you to stay put. Has he ever been violent to you?"

"Not really. But sometimes, when he's angry, I've felt like he's been on the brink, like he's having to hold himself back."

She stops and turns to me, bringing me to a halt too. She says what she says next like she's only just remembered. "He said it was your fault. He told me I shouldn't have listened to you. That you were lying. I didn't know what he meant. You hadn't said a thing to me," I knew this conversation would eventually lead to this point and now she stands staring at me, waiting for some response.

"How did you find out?"

"I was getting his jacket ready to go to the dry cleaners and found a hotel receipt in the pocket."

"Did you tell him that?"

"No. I didn't get the chance. He was ranting about you and I had no opportunity to say anything further." She looks at me curiously. "Was it you?" By the expression on her face I'm concerned she may not appreciate what I have to tell her. She may have preferred not to have known and to have remained ignorant. That is a distinct possibility in which case what I'm about to say will not go down well at all. But I can't back away now.

"It was me." Her mouth drops open a little. "I planted the receipt."

"How? Why?"

We turn back towards the village, calling the dogs to come closer to us.

"I'd seen him with her, in Hartleigh. Once from a distance and I couldn't be sure it was him. But last Friday I bumped into them, just outside The Cromwell. I waited until they'd gone in then I went and booked a room so I could get a receipt."

"Why didn't you just tell me?"

"I wasn't sure how you'd take it. I thought at least this way you could choose to ignore it if you wanted to and you'd never realise that anyone else knew." She goes quiet, mulling this over as we continue to walk back towards the village.

"That was a thoughtful, if expensive, thing to do."

"It was a bit pricey, but I had no other option." I glance across at her as we walk, "They don't exactly book rooms out by the hour at The Cromwell."

She remains silent and I fear she's imagining what was going on in that room so I'm surprised when she says, "He wouldn't have needed an hour," and we both burst out laughing and have to stop walking for a minute to gather ourselves.

I'm glad she doesn't ask anything further about

it, or about how I got the receipt into his pocket. I don't want to have to explain the detail, I don't think she'd like it.

She looks brighter again, more her old self though quieter and, dare I say it, humbler. I do hope so; I may grow to like her more if she is. She says, "Thank you. I didn't realise you cared to be honest. In fact, I've always had the distinct impression you didn't like me much, however friendly I tried to be."

"We're very different people, Letitia. That doesn't mean I should stand by while a wrong is being done."

We're back at her house a couple of minutes later. Gaz is driving the ride-on lawnmower and looks like he's having the time of his life, and when we enter through the back door the utility area is all in order and the kitchen looks spotless again. There's no sign of Kourtney but I can hear the sound of a vacuum going somewhere in the house. The dogs quench their thirst from the water bowl and when Letitia tells them to go to their beds, they do, fussing about for a few moments before finally settling down.

Letitia says, "Do you want something to eat? I've barely eaten all week and now I'm famished."

"Yes please, if you have enough. Shall I stick the kettle on?" She nods and goes to the fridge. When she comes back she has a loaf of frozen sliced bread and breaks some slices apart using a knife before putting them in the toaster. A short while later we're perching on the bar stools at her island enjoying buttered toast and smooth pâté, and as I eat I try to work out how to tackle the next part of the conversation I need to have with Letitia.

Eventually, I say, "What are you going to do next?"

"I don't know."

"Are you going to take him back?"

"No!" she says adamantly, but then pauses and softens it with, "I don't think so."

I want to make sure of where her loyalties, and interests, lie before I proceed with the questions I want to ask and I'm not keen on her unconvincing stance here. "What do you think I should do?" she eventually asks.

"I can't answer that for you but I will tell you what I heard when you were talking on the walk."

"Go on."

"I heard how much you love your home and lifestyle but nothing about loving Ben, or even liking him for that matter, or that you're missing him."

"Oh!" This appears to have come as something of a revelation to her and as she considers it her eyebrows draw together in a frown. Eventually she nods. "I think you're right. It is all this that I will miss, not him, not especially," and as she says that she looks round her kitchen in appreciation of what's important to her. I take a deep breath and let it out slowly; this is what I was hoping for.

"You're talking as if you've already lost it." She sighs.

"Well I will do, won't I? If I divorce him I'll end up with something, but nothing like this, he's already told me that." I bet he has, I can see him laying on the threats already. Horrible man.

"Perhaps."

"What do you mean by that? He told me the only way I get to keep all this is by taking him back, but you're a divorce expert all of a sudden?" Her voice has risen so she's sounding almost confrontational.

"No, but I do have an interest in seeing that you get what you want, while at the same time trying to help out some friends of mine that Ben has caused some trouble for." There, it's out there.

I see definite interest flicker across her eyes, as she leans forward and says, "Tell me more."

So, I do. I tell her about the trouble he has brought to both Diane and Kourtney and she does falter a little. "I can't believe he would do that."

"Can't you? You don't know much about his business affairs at all then, Letitia. There have always been rumours of the way he does things."

"But why would he do this to Diane and Kourtney, what's it got to do with them?"

"It's because of me. He thinks I told you about the affair and as he has no hold over me he's gone after my friends."

"That's a bit shitty."

"Indeed it is, Letitia. Indeed, it is, and I have to sort it out."

"How are you going to do that?"

"Well I'm hoping that's where you come in." She looks unconvinced that she'll be able to provide any help, but I'm hoping I'm about to show her that with some careful thought and considered imagination we shall find just what I'm looking for. Then she tries to take me off course.

"Shall we have a drink? Is it too early for a drink? I'm thinking a glass of wine would go down well."

"It is too early for a glass of wine, Letitia. It's lunchtime, and this is still an intervention, remember? You can make us both a coffee, or tea if you'd prefer."

She looks sullen, pouting at me for withholding the alcohol which makes me wonder when she usually starts. She might need more help than I was anticipating. However, she gets down from her stool and makes us tea, opening up a packet of posh looking biscuits at the same time.

"I get these in especially for Ben but I guess he won't be needing them now, will he!" She appears almost gleeful and I hope I can get for her what she wants out of all this. She's certainly perked up from the pathetic creature she was when I arrived. It's amazing what a little hope can do to someone's spirits.

Once she's settled down again, and I've munched my way through three of Ben's special biscuits, and delicious they are too, Gaz pops his head in to say he's finished for now, and could we let Kourtney know when we next see her. I reassure him we will and send him on his way. I then turn back to Letitia ready to crack on with finding out what I need.

"Okay. Now I want you to concentrate and tell me everything you know about Ben, his business and his finances."

This turns out to be a shorter conversation than I had been expecting, because it appears she knows bugger all, which comes as something of a disappointment as I was hoping that this was where I would find that chink in his armour. She doesn't deal with any of their finances, and shockingly, she has no money of her own. None at all. Ben simply puts money into a joint account each month and she spends it. This is the sum total of the financial knowledge she has of her situation, and I can't believe she has been so naïve as to not have set up her own account somewhere with a security fund in it in case of, well, exactly what's happened now.

She thinks I'm being ridiculous when I say this. "He wouldn't do that," she says, "he wouldn't stop my money. He's always looked after me. He's always been so generous." It's all I can do not to roll my eyes.

Chapter 9

I have a tearful, though furiously texting, Letitia on my doorstep the next morning. Her card has been declined at the village shop, she is mortified and letting Ben know all about it. He, it turns out, is not responding. It doesn't surprise me at all and I bet he is delighted it's causing her such misery. He's putting the pressure on. Letting her see what life's like without him and his money.

I sit her down at my kitchen table and pass her the tissues. Dan has gone out but left his laptop, so rather than fuss over her I bring that into the kitchen and open up a bank account for her online. By the time that's done she has finished blubbing and is in a more practical frame of mind. As soon as the new account is approved and I have the number I tell her I'll transfer a grand from my account into hers. Then I give her fifty quid to tide her over until her bank card gets here. That is all the cash I have, and she's made a big hole in my bank account too.

She thanks me, staring pitifully at the notes in her hand and no doubt wondering how it has all come to this.

I suspect Ben has simply transferred the joint account over to another bank to cut off her access to it but he will probably carry on making the monthly payments for the house. He's unlikely to want to fall into arrears and mess up his credit rating. I tell Letitia all of this and warn her that she may start getting bill reminders and such like if that's not what he's done and she's going to have to deal with those and not simply ignore them. She nods but has a glazed expression on her face and I'm not sure what, if anything, she's taking in.

Once all the computer stuff is done I get up to make us both a coffee. While I'm doing that she receives a text. Judging by her expletive it's not good news.

"Ben?" I question as I return to the table with the mugs.

"No. He's ignoring me. This is a friend telling me riding has been cancelled tomorrow. I'm being dropped." There's a whiny edge to her voice I could do without.

"Dropped?"

"Uh huh. First it was the tennis, now riding. I'm no longer, 'In'," and she even does the air quotes, "so I'm being dropped."

"And these are your friends?" She nods, and I detect the merest quiver of her bottom lip. "Some friends," I add, thinking I'm glad I don't mix in the same circles. She remains quiet as she lifts her mug and sips tentatively at the still too hot coffee, so I give her a verbal nudge.

"I think you should still go, show your friends you're not putting up with being dropped."

"Hmm." She thinks about this for minute, doubt registering on her face.

"Come on, Letitia. Stand up for what you want to do. You enjoy riding so don't let them put you off," I say, and at my tiny motivational push, she does sit up a little straighter and I see that chin of hers jut out again. However, although I do feel sympathy for her I'm not aware how I've managed to transmit this, but I clearly have because she senses that tiniest chink of weakness in my tough outer shell and pounces, surprising me all over again.

"Ooh, you could come with me."

"What! No. No I couldn't. I can't ride."

"Then this is a perfect time to learn." *In exactly what realm is this a perfect time?*

"I don't have anything to wear." *Oh listen to me.*

"That's no problem." She looks me up and down. "We're roughly the same size although you *are* a little broader in the backside." *Charming.* "But jodhpurs are stretchy so you'll be able to squeeze into a pair of mine." I'm about to object to her comment then find myself doing a sneaky comparison before I shake myself out of it as she continues. "Come round this afternoon and I'll sort something out for you." Before I even have a chance to protest and take back my previous encouragement by suggesting that perhaps in her new situation she should maybe think twice before spending her, correction, my money on riding, she sends another text, telling me at the same time that she's confirmed the booking at the riding centre and told them now she's bringing a newbie. I have been railroaded, and there's that unwelcome glimpse of the old Letitia back again. However, I put that aside for the moment knowing I'll have to deal with it tomorrow, but for now I simply need to get her back on track.

"Can we get back to business? Your money? Or rather, my money?"

Without hesitation she tells me she'll pay me back. Which brings me on to the next point to be covered. Because I'm not entirely sure she's thought that through.

"With what?"

"With, um, money," she says, like that's sooooo obvious.

"Which you're going to get from?" and I raise my hands as if a gift from above is about to drop into them.

"Well, this situation with my money," and she waves her useless debit card in the air, "is bound to get sorted …" but her response peters out as, I hope, she pauses to consider the actual likelihood of that happening and the limited number of options before her. When she says nothing further, I prompt.

"You do know what comes next, don't you?"

"I have a horrible feeling you're about to tell me."

"You need to get yourself a job."

"What!" I was right, she's not thought that far ahead.

"You just said you'll pay me back and for that, and so much more, you need to get some money coming in, and working is the best way of doing that." Her face falls as she realises the free ride she was having courtesy of Ben Pritchard has come to an end. Unless, of course, she takes him back. I float this idea past her again, but she says no, he can't be trusted.

At least she's learned something through this experience.

She gives a big sigh, then says, with reluctance in every syllable, "I'll go and sign on with some agencies this afternoon then."

"Well done. It'll take time for your finances to be worked out with Ben so you need to keep some money coming in in the meantime, especially if you want to keep that big house of yours. By the way, did you give any more thought to what I asked about yesterday?"

"The business and his finances? Not really. Although from what I remember when I worked for him, anything important he put in the safe, so it might be worth looking in there."

It might indeed, Letitia, thank you, I think. A safe, of course.

For the first time since James Lambert and the Craig predicament arrived in my life I feel the tiniest frisson, the hairs standing up on the back of my neck in response, and I know instantly that here it is, here is my opportunity.

"Where is the safe?"

"In his office." Of course it is. It couldn't be situated handily at home, could it.

"What sort of safe it is?" She shrugs.

"I don't know, it's just a safe." *Let's start off slower*, I think, as I take a deep breath.

"What does it look like? And don't say a safe. I need some details." She gazes up at the ceiling for a moment or two, and I sit patiently, ever hopeful she's gathering her thoughts.

"It's grey, it's quite old, at least it looks it. It's

all scratched up.”

“One or two door?”

“One.”

“Shape and size?”

“Square, it comes up to my mid-thigh.”

“Does it have a push button or dial lock?”

“Neither.” I frown.

“It opens using a key?”

“Yes, and it has a handle you turn, it has three spokes to it.”

It is definitely an old style of safe then, but that works in our favour. “Have you ever opened it?”

“No,” she says, and she shakes her head, but then she brightens, “but I’ve seen in it.”

“What? When Ben’s opened it?”

“Yes. There’s only files and piles of paper in there.”

“Do you know where the key’s kept?”

“No,” she shakes her head again. “Why do you want to know all this?” I’m deep in thought when she speaks and I stop.

It’s a reasonable question and I’m not quite sure what to tell her, eventually coming up with, “I may have just come up with the solution to all the problems,” which seems a bit of a stretch but ever hopeful I ask a few questions about the offices themselves, the staff, the layout, the access. But I’m distracted now and know I need to go and have a look for myself. There’s a pulse of excitement running through my veins, my blood pumping because something is happening at last and I know there’s no time like the present.

I tell Letitia she needs to go and get on with her

job-hunting as I have something I have to do, and I try not to appear rude as I practically eject her from the house. I check my look in the mirror, write a note for Dan and leave not long after she does.

As I drive to the city I think through my strategy. I don't think it's unreasonable, or out of character, for me to pay a little visit to Ben. I'm sure he would be expecting it given the trouble he's caused for my friends, and because of that I don't even need to come up with an excuse. I do need to get my timing right though or the trip may not be as productive as I want it to be.

There is something, however, a tiny tickly something in the back of my mind that's itching away right in that place you can't quite reach that is telling me that this is all very well but if Letitia changes her mind by even one degree, by so much as an iota, this plan is doomed. Because if she weakens and decides to take Ben back then the first thing she will do is tell him all about my interest in his safe. Although of course if she takes him back he may just reverse the damage he's done to Diane and Kourtney so at least that will solve those problems, but I won't be holding my breath on that one.

A little over forty minutes later I'm standing back in the shadows of a doorway on the opposite side of the road to Pritchard Estate Agents (agents just love the use of their own names, don't they), and at a diagonal angle to its plate glass frontage. I can see those inside. Or at least those bits of them that aren't behind the 'Houses for Sale' displays.

Tim is at his desk fiddling with his tie as he leans back in his chair. Purity is at hers, perched like the perfect plastic doll she is, if such dolls were available in their own range of slapper gear, and the pair of them are gazing in adoration at something between them. This, I see, is a pacing Ben. I imagine he's giving them a splendid performance-enhancing, motivational speech to get the afternoon's selling off to a good start so as to give Purity something to type up. When he's done he strides to the rear of the shop floor space and disappears through one of the two doors along the back wall.

I give it two minutes to ensure he's not about to make a quick return trip and then cross the road. I'm in through the front door before either of them have spotted me.

Tim looks horrified when he looks up and recognition dawns, his mouth dropping open, as he starts to stand. I hold my hand up. "Don't worry, Tim, I'm not here for you." His relief is obvious as, caught mid-rise, he collapses back into his seat again.

I'm still moving as I turn to Purity, "He's back there, is he?" as I indicate to the door I'm marching towards. Not sure what else to do she nods, staring wide-eyed, as she watches me go.

Those two are sitting in the front set of desks. There are two more pairs, currently unoccupied, for me to pass before I reach Ben's exit point.

I don't knock, choosing the surprise approach of bowling on through the door instead. I wasn't sure what I'd find beyond but it takes me directly into Ben's office. He looks up from whatever he's reading and I'm delighted to see a flicker of fear cross his face before it's replaced by an expression considerably smarmier.

"Madeleine! Do come in. Oh, I see you already are. Here, take a seat," he says as he gestures expansively towards the chair but I've come to a stop in front of his desk and I choose to remain there.

"I won't bother, thank you. I'm not going to be here for long."

"Oh, what a shame. What can I help you with? Are you thinking of selling?" He grins, all teeth and tan, which makes me long to wipe it off his face and while I'd like to do that physically, I'm a lady, so I won't. Besides there's more than one way to achieve my goal and I'm all about playing the long game.

"I'm here to tell you to leave my friends alone. If you have a problem with me at least be a man and deal with me directly, not by hurting them."

His hands are up, his eyes wide like he's so innocent. "*Moi!*" (Pretentious tosser.) "Now why would I have a problem with you?" I remain silent and let him continue, his face twisting as he does so. "Could it be that I don't appreciate you spreading lies about me?"

"Lies? Is that the best you've got? I haven't spread any lies."

"You told Letitia about the affair."

"Technically that is a truth, not a lie, and no, I didn't, not directly anyway. I just gave her a clue which confirmed the suspicions she was already having about you."

"I don't believe you."

"You should. You messed up your own marriage, Ben. Don't blame me for that."

"Oh, but I do. Without you she wouldn't know, even if you didn't tell her directly."

"Me, or someone else. It was only ever a matter of time."

"I still prefer to do these things on my own timescale."

"Oh I bet you do. So you can screw her over before you move the next one in, I imagine. You have form for it. Purity? Is that who you're lining up?" He looks away in avoidance. *Interesting*.

He doesn't appear to have anything to say in response to that and I lean across the desk. "I'm going to make sure you pay for what you've done, Ben. Letitia. Diane. Kourtney. You will regret messing with them, and me."

Big words, Maddy. Big words. But I can't stop them coming out of my mouth and hope I don't end up looking a fool.

"And I shall enjoy watching you scrabble about trying." The grin is back again. I ignore it. I have all I came for so turn and walk away. I leave his office door open as I cross to the exit.

Tim and Purity turn to watch me; I don't know if they heard any of my exchange with Ben so for good measure I call back over my shoulder.

"Letitia said chucking you out was the best decision she's ever made." I see Purity's face fall. "Oh, sorry, didn't you know, Purity? Yes, she threw him out a week ago." I stop and glance back at Ben now standing in the doorway to his office.

"Naughty, naughty, Ben, shame on you for not telling your girlfriend you're single again." I look back at her, it's difficult to tell but she does appear to be a little perturbed by this news, a pout coming to those painted lips, so I leave her with something else to think about. "You never know, Purity, you might be in line for a promotion, you lucky girl you." With that I consider my work is done and I walk out.

I got what I came for, and in addition, had the pleasure of stirring things up, which was an added bonus, and I think through the facts as I return to my car. The access points are at the front and rear of the property. Though access via the front is obviously a no-no as it's so exposed. There's a basic alarm system, I could see that, nothing too fancy though as there is nothing to steal in a unit like that, other than what the safe protects, so it's there more as a deterrent.

The safe is tucked away in the corner of his office. It's an old fashioned type as Letitia recalled and quite large. He probably inherited it from somewhere else. It won't be bolted to the floor because it's far too heavy to consider taking away and opening elsewhere, at least not without some serious machinery. Besides I might not want him to notice anyone has been in it, depending on what is found in there. It has basic key entry rather than any code being required but that doesn't help much as I still can't get into it without that key. However, that very issue might just provide another opener for me.

I'd parked in the multi-storey but when I get

back in my car I drive up rather than down until I'm on the top floor. I park up again, and taking a small pair of binoculars from my glove compartment I walk to the edge that overlooks the majority of the city. It's blustery up here and I can feel the rain coming on the wind, the first few drops hitting me as I choose where best to stand.

From my vantage point I can see estate agents row, as they have mostly congregated in one short stretch of road. There's a small dead-end alley that runs behind all the shops to give them access for deliveries. I pinpoint where Pritchard's is and work out where the rear door is situated in the back road. There's not much to see. The road is too narrow for there to be any parking, there only being a small area at the end for vehicles to turn around in.

I lift my binoculars and scan the buildings each side of the access road. I can't spot any CCTV cameras although that doesn't mean there aren't any. However, I do know the frontage is covered by them, which rules that out as an entry point.

Once I'm satisfied there is little else I can check I return to my car, stow away the binoculars and head off home.

I'm on autopilot for the drive. My mind is racing with the plan forming in my head. When I get back to the village I drive straight round to Letitia's, as she asked, to pick up the riding clothes. She welcomes me in and, as usual, we go through to the kitchen. I'm pleased to see she has her laptop open and that she is on the site of a local recruitment agency.

"How's the job hunting been going?"

"Not too badly. There are a few administration jobs I can apply for but I'm not sure how successful I'll be. I have few qualifications, less experience and zero chance of getting a reference from the only employer I've ever had."

"All you can do is apply. You never know, there may be someone out there desperate enough to take you on." I grin at her to let her know I'm only joking and fortunately she laughs.

"It's that or the supermarkets. I may be a shelf stacker yet! My mother will be so proud." It's my turn to laugh, though only to make her feel better. Personally I'd far rather be a shelf stacker than reliant on a man to keep me. That aside, I'm pleased with the improvement in her attitude from when I found her yesterday. "Come on upstairs," she continues, "and I'll get those jodhpurs out for you."

I'd only been in her bedroom yesterday and the change between then and now was extreme. Kourtney had done a good job of clearing up and Letitia had managed to maintain it. The carpet was clear of abandoned clothes, the tell-tale rings from glasses and bottles on the bedside table were gone, the unmade bed a thing of the past. Letitia starts opening drawers and cupboards in her dressing room, which, when I peek in, I see is roughly the size of my whole bedroom. While she is rummaging for her spare jodhpurs I look round the beautifully decorated room. Now, looking like it should, it could feature in one of the glossy magazines. The bed is so prettily dressed it would be a shame to disrupt the display by sleeping in it. The blue hues of the room are soothing, even blending with the pictures on the walls. I know little about art, but I know what I like.

"Lovely paintings," I comment as Letitia appears holding a pair of navy jodhpurs out towards me.

"Yes," she replies, gazing around the room as if with fresh eyes. "One of Ben's passions, the art. He's a bit of a collector."

"I didn't know that."

"No, well, he tends to keep it quiet. No point advertising the fact he has hundreds of thousands of pounds hanging on the walls is it?"

"Bloody hell! Is that what they're worth?"

She gesticulates around the room, and is dismissive as she says, "These aren't worth that much. A few thousand each, probably." My eyes widen with surprise as I take a second look at them. "He likes to speculate so he buys up work from a variety of artists while they're relatively unknown, spending only a few hundred or a couple of thousand on them. You never know if that artist is going to become popular and then you could be the owner of something special. At least that's what he tells me."

"And is he?"

"Is he what?"

"The owner of something special?" The idea of spending a couple of thousand on a picture was more than enough, but I was interested to know if his speculation had paid off.

"Oh yes. I'll show you." She heads back downstairs and I follow. As we walk she tells me more. "The paintings were the reason I wouldn't let him in when I first found out about the affair. I could see him taking them and I wasn't having that. I was furious then and fuelled by anger, I suppose," and she glances across at me, a rueful smile on her face. "I had the energy to get the locks changed, and the alarm code. That was before it all became too much for me and I succumbed to, well, the state you found me in." I see her bottom lip tremble and reach out to place a hand on her shoulder.

"I think you did well to think of that in the first place." I try to be reassuring and her smile is brighter towards me this time.

There is much of this house I haven't seen before, and she leads me down a passage and opens the door at the end into what I assume is Ben's office, should he ever need to work at home. Although it is the massive mahogany desk that gives it away rather than any signs of paperwork. I think then how any indication of any work being done in there would immediately ruin the aesthetic. The room is beautiful and masculine, panelled in dark oak, a burgundy carpet adding to the richness.

"I wasn't allowed to touch this room when I redecorated," Letitia remarks, tutting as though this was a dreadful oversight, "It's far too gloomy for my liking." She flicks on a switch, and a couple of brass picture lamps come on to light up the art they hover over. In both cases the paintings look to be fairly traditional, and old, with large and ornate gilt frames, which looked splendid in here but don't quite fit with the up and coming artists Letitia had mentioned.

I indicate to one of them, a dark picture of a

horse being shod, and rather hesitatingly say, "Is this it?"

"Oh good grief, no, these are worth twenty grand apiece at most. It's over there," and she points to one side of the fireplace where there's a recess in the wall. There, dwarfed and inconspicuous by comparison with the others in the room, hangs a small unlit painting. The frame is black and plain, the artwork itself a riot of many shades of red swirls and patterns which I found attractive but it wasn't a picture *of* anything, as far as I could tell.

"This is worth a lot?" I sound doubtful.

"Hmm, surprising isn't it? It's a Ramboult. The artist died tragically young, that's always a plus because it adds value."

I'm shocked by her total lack of awareness at what she just said, and murmur, "How terribly convenient."

The look she throws in my direction manages to make me feel like I'm the one being admonished. "A similar painting by the same artist went for nearly a million recently," she tells me, as if that somehow justifies her previous remark and I wonder if she can hear the things she says sometimes.

"Wow. I'm surprised the insurers are happy with this being here."

Letitia turns off the lights again and guides me out of the room. "Oh, they've had their say on the alarm and general security and are happy it's safe."

*And yet I managed to get in without much diffi-
culty, Letitia.*

We walk back to the kitchen and, placing the
jodhpurs on the granite of the island, I take a seat
on one of the bar stools then, as she does the same
I turn to face her. "While I'm here, I'm after some
information."

"I thought you might be."

"I've been to scout out Pritchard's this afternoon." Her eyebrows rise in surprise.

"Did you see Ben?" I nod, concerned at how
eagerly she asks this question.

"Better than that, I went in to speak to him."

"How was he?" And a spear of alarm goes
through me.

"He was fine. Apparently unaltered by his recent experience." I watch her carefully and can see
she still cares. This is no good.

"Oh." She wilts a little.

"You're not having second thoughts, are you?"

"No, not really." Which doesn't convince me at
all and I feel I have to be direct.

"Look, Letitia, I need to know if you're considering taking him back. I can't carry on with what
I want to do if you are." She takes a deep breath
and straightens her spine, that chin of hers jutting
out a little as if in defiance.

"No, you're all right. I may be a bit soft over
him but I only have to think about what he's done
with that woman and I know I won't be taking him
back."

"Okay then," I say with some relief, "let's carry

on. Like I said, I went to the offices this afternoon."

"What for?"

"To have a look at the set-up and the safe."

"You were in his actual office?"

"Yes, I needed to see the safe. I went in to see
him and we had words."

"What sort of words?"

"Harsh ones, Letitia, as I'm sure you can imagine." Other than this brief explanation I wave
away her enquiry as I don't want to rehash it all,
and fortunately she accepts that. "What was said
was largely irrelevant to my reason for being there
anyway."

"Which was?"

"Which was to study the layout and access
points, and this is where you come in." She nods
and looks eager to help, which is encouraging. "I
want to take a look in that safe, preferably without
Ben being aware that I have. I need access in
through the rear of the shop and I need you to tell
me everything you can about the back door, the
locks on it and the alarm." She smiles like she's
lost a quid and found a tenner.

"I think I can do better than that." I'm intrigued
and watch as she hops down from her stool and
crosses the room to a beautiful old oak dresser.
Pulling open a drawer she rummages around in its
contents, reaching right towards the back of it before apparently finding what she's looking for and
announcing her success with an, "Aha!" She turns
back towards me, one hand held out in front, her
index finger and thumb pinched together and

swinging below where they join a set of keys. Bingo!

"Whose are those?"

"Mine, from when I worked there. There's never been a need for me to give them back but I haven't used them in years, and I'm sure Ben will have forgotten I even have them by now."

"And they unlock the back door too?" She nods. "That does still leave the alarm though. Any chance you know the code for that?"

"No, I'm afraid not, but it doesn't matter because this fob will turn it off anyway. It can all be controlled from these two buttons on here." She comes closer and shows me through the rudimentary buttons on the fob. I look up, her smile reflecting mine.

Dan will be pleased; for once I don't have to break in. Though of course I do still have to get into the safe. I ask Letitia again if she's had any thoughts on where the key may be kept but she hasn't. I can't think of any other information I need from her at the moment so after she finds me a pair of her old riding boots I send her back to her task of looking for jobs. I watch her for a moment as she takes the seat in front of the screen. A niggling concern that's been lingering from the previous day won't leave me.

"Everything else all right with you, Letitia?"

"Yes, well other than the obvious." She looks up at me then frowns, "why do you ask?"

"I'm just a bit, you know, er, well, concerned, about your drinking." Her cheeks blush as she places her hands flat down on the table to each side of the laptop.

"After what you said yesterday I did have a think about that and decided I had been overdoing it." I nod encouragingly.

"Oh, good. I was worried."

"You had every reason but there's no need to be now. I've stopped." She pauses. "Well, probably not for forever but until I feel back in control of it again."

"Okay then, I'm pleased to hear that and relieved. I'll leave you in peace and I'll see you tomorrow." I turn to go.

"Yes, see you tomorrow… and thank you." I'm crossing the hall by the time she says this and don't respond any further.

I call in on Diane on my way home to see if she is all right. She's brewing something in a huge black pan; I wish I could say it was a cauldron but sadly it is not, however it smells noxious, my eyes watering the moment I step into the kitchen. Diane somehow appears unaffected by it and tells me to breathe through my mouth, which does improve things. Cat winds himself around my legs and I bend to pick him up, giving him a little cuddle as Diane examines my face and seems to approve, asking after the rest of me which I confirm is now nearly all healed up.

She looks okay, a little distracted perhaps, and not many minutes have passed before she asks vaguely how things are going when I know what she wants to know is if I've made any headway with Ben. I tell her that everything is in hand and reiterate that she is not to worry. "I'm not," she reassures me, "I'm keeping myself busy," and she throws what looks like a handful of wood chips into the steaming pan.

"I'm surprised you have need of my help anyway," I say, "couldn't you just brew up something that would turn him into a frog?" She casts me a sideways look.

"You need a wand for that sort of magic, Maddy. Sadly, mine was confiscated years ago after a minor indiscretion involving the vicar, his wife and a bag of sherbet lemons… ask no more." I smile as she chuckles, pleased to see her in better spirits than she's been of late.

I'd already seen Dan's car outside my home so I don't stay long, reassuring her as I leave that I will keep her up to date with progress.

I'm keen to see Dan when I walk through the door, and I'm sure his face lights up when he sees me too. We've settled into a pattern of living together without intimacy or awkwardness and while comfortable I'm not sure if that in itself is a problem. I wonder if we've become friends, if our chance at being anything more has gone, and it saddens me to think it might have done.

He's cooking a paella which is nothing I've ever attempted, but it's filling my small home with delicious aromas and my stomach growls in anticipation. I ask what he's been up to all day.

"I went home to see my family for a couple of hours," he says. "It was my mum's birthday last week so we were all invited round for lunch."

"That's nice," I say, internally chastising myself for feeling excluded. *Why should I have been invited?* I'm nothing to them, or him, in reality. "Are they all well?"

"Yes, and my younger sister announced she is expecting a baby with her boyfriend."

"Lovely. Was that expected? How did your parents take the news?"

"They were surprised, I think. They are a bit traditional so no doubt would have preferred things to be done in the right order. But they'll get used to it." It must be great to be so confident in the support your family gives you, and to know you have them to fall back on in times of trouble.

"So you're going to be the fun uncle."

"Yeah, I suppose I am," and he says this like it hadn't even crossed his mind before.

Chapter 10

It is Sunday, one week on, but I'm not thinking about any of that because today I am going to get on a horse for the first time, which is turning out to be a great distraction, because I can't help thinking that this is something that you should probably master early on in life, well before you have any fear.

I dress in the skin-tight jodhpurs and slightly too small boots, layer up on top and finish off with a jumper and waterproof jacket so I'm ready when Letitia arrives to collect me. At the same time as having a tingle of either excitement or nerves about the day ahead, I can't help wondering why I'm doing this when I have so much else occupying my thoughts at the moment. I know I didn't put up much of a fight against Letitia's insistence on me joining her this morning and I guess if it keeps her moving forward mentally then that's fine by me. Deep down I also have to admit that I didn't stand my ground against her because I ever so slightly wanted to do this, given my love for the horses in the field next to my cottage and the discussions I've had with Joe, so Letitia's steamroller attitude has forced my hand. I'm now curious to see if I can do it and secretly hoping it's not going to be a one-off.

Plus, it has its advantages, as it occurred to me overnight that Leticia's friends, such as they are, may try to talk her round into taking Ben back. By being close by I can keep an eye on her and make sure she's not wavering, or if she is that I at least know about it.

When we get to the riding school I feel the familiar flutter of nerves taking flight in my stomach, not only because of what I'm about to do but also because of being in such an alien environment. I'm shy when faced with so many people I don't know in a situation where I have no idea what I'm doing, and I find I'm glad I'm not alone. When I get out of the car there's a freshening wind that adds a slight chill to the morning so, taking a deep breath, I inhale and decide I like the smell of the place, it's comforting.

A young, tough-looking girl with a permanent scowl points me in the direction of the selection of riding hats and tells me to choose one. I enlist Letitia's help and she stands close as she selects hats and attempts to squish them onto my head. Apparently it's too big, my head that is, although not any of the hats which mostly turn out to be not big enough until we've nearly been through them all and I'm losing patience with the process. Letitia eventually gives a contented smile when one slides on to her satisfaction and she proceeds to fit and do up the chin strap. I'm not that useless and could probably manage it but it is easier for her to do it for me rather than me do it for myself; plus she appears to be enjoying mothering me. I notice she is fully made up, which I find odd until I remember that this is all about her being *seen* doing the right things rather than throwing herself into the activity itself. Letitia peers back at me then I see her look harder and frown. "Have you got a black eye?" I, never one to wear makeup when doing something likely to make me sweat, am bare faced.

"Only slightly," I reply, "I walked into a door." To which Letitia gives a disbelieving harrumphing sound, not unlike that which came out of the horse I saw over her shoulder only a few moments ago. The slight discolouration around my eye is the only physical sign left of my attack, though my nights are still occasionally broken by startled awakenings from violent dreams. However, I'm adept at pushing those right to the back of my mind during daylight hours, I've been doing similar for as long as I can remember.

Letitia, of course, has her own rather lovely hat that has a cover and a peak to it. Mine, when I get to see myself in the mirror, makes me look as though I'm about to be shot out of a cannon.

I realise, when I'm standing like a spare part in the yard waiting for whatever happens next, that I haven't given a great deal of thought to the actual riding bit. Letitia had assured me on the way over that as a beginner I'd be put on the docile Dolly. That turns out to be pure fabrication on her part because as it happens there is another lady here who is also a beginner and for whatever reason she gets first dibs on the safe choice. I am told I'm going to be on a horse called Stevie and although I saw Letitia's eyebrows rise when we found that out she refuses to tell me why they did so. The good news is that at least my lesson is going to take place within a manège so Stevie, who I'm assuming is wild judging by Letitia's reaction, can only go as far as the fences will allow. Plus, she informs me there's a nice soft landing for when we part company. All of which is terribly reassuring.

Despite the icy reception she receives, Letitia manages to look smug when her friends arrive. I knew who they were immediately, all that *mwah mwah* nonsense, and I can tell she enjoys watching them glance awkwardly among themselves in embarrassment at being caught out in a lie. I'm proud of her when she merely acknowledges them then turns back to me.

She wishes me luck rather than tells me to have a good time, which feels rather ominous, and heads off to her own horse, a splendid grey, which she leads over to a mounting block, gets on and with a few others, including her friends, disappears out of the yard as she'd told me they were going for a ride rather than having a lesson. I notice as they disappear that Letitia has been left at the back of the group and I hope she's not going to be treated as some sort of pariah all morning.

Concentrating now on my own situation, I have been watching the activity around me carefully and taking in all the information I can gather so as to hopefully not look like a complete novice, but none of that helps when I'm presented with Stevie.

The tough-looking girl has tacked him up, led him out of the stable and now looks at me sternly before inclining her head towards the horse. She tells me her name is Sue and she's going to be my instructor. She looks about twelve. I can't tell you how tall Stevie is but when I stand next to him I can't see over his back, so that seems plenty tall enough to me. Sue tells me to get on via the mounting block and talks me through how to do that. While I'm getting used to the feel of the saddle and the strangeness of sitting atop a living animal, Sue moves me into the position I should be sitting in and shows me how to hold the reins. Then we're off, slowly.

While I've been distracted getting onto Stevie, the other lady, who I find out is called Tina, has climbed aboard the docile Dolly. They lead the way and both of us walk our steeds out of the yard and over to the manège.

The following hour whizzes by and, exhilarated by the experience, I love every minute of it. Sue tells us how to make our horses go, stop and turn. We do exercises which help us relax and once we're feeling fairly confident in walk we try a trot. It is at this point that I realise how lucky I was to get Stevie and not Dolly. Tina has to work harder than I do to get Dolly moving. Considerably harder.

Stevie is a more responsive creature altogether, and a nudge with my heels against his side is all it takes. Like Sue told me, I hold his neck strap with one hand before giving the command. I'm surprised by the immediate change of speed and am glad I'm holding on as I'm left behind Stevie's movement. It's tricky, trotting. I'm meant to be rising with the beat but it takes me several attempts before I manage it. However, when I do it feels fantastic like we're moving as one and I can feel the wide grin on my face.

The lesson is over far too quickly, although Stevie might be breathing a sigh of relief, and before I know it we're walking back to the yard and dismounting. My legs feel strangely jelly-like when I land on the ground. I stroke Stevie in thanks, his nose coming round and nuzzling my hand. Sue shows me how to run my stirrups up although as Stevie is going out again he doesn't need untacking. I put on his head collar and he is tied up outside a stable temporarily. Every tiny thing I have done this morning has been something completely new to me and it's been energising.

I catch sight of myself in the mirror as I remove my hat. I'm smiling, my cheeks are pink with exertion and joy and I know I've found something to be passionate about.

As I run my fingers through hair that's been plastered to my scalp I watch Letitia's group walking into the yard. She is still at the back but one of the other women is in conversation with her. I stand back and watch while they sort their horses out, wanting to see whether there's been any thaw between the rest of them. I catch a couple glancing in my direction, curiosity getting the better of them, but they hastily look away again, not recognising one of their own.

"How did you get on?" I ask as soon as we're back in the car.

"Superficially okay."

"Superficially?"

"Well, you know, they chatted to me but only because they wanted the details of the break up so they'd have something to gossip about later."

"Not supportive then." She shakes her head and, feeling her despondence, I try to be kind. "You never know, once a bit of time has passed you may get back in with the crowd." I say this more as a salve for her than anything else because I can't think of one good reason why you'd want to be friends with any of those horrible women. She gives me a look like I'm a child come to play with the adults.

"No, that won't be happening. We're friends because of the connections our husbands have. I no longer have one of those so I'm no longer one of them and they certainly don't want the threat of a single woman in their midst."

"That's sad."

"It's the way the world works."

"Not my world." She raises her eyebrows, briefly nods in acknowledgement and remains thoughtful for a few moments before asking how I'd got on.

I then can't stop telling her all about my lesson and ask her why she'd raised her eyebrows when I was given Stevie because he'd been as good as gold. She said he had a bit of a reputation for being naughty given half a chance so I must have ridden him well if he'd behaved himself. For some reason this puffs me right up, making me feel ridiculously proud of myself.

By the time we're back in Crowthorne I feel like Letitia's mood has lifted again; she's chatty, telling me about the adventures she's had with horses and seems in a much better place than at the beginning of the drive and, from a purely selfish point of view, being with her this morning means I know she's had no change of heart about Ben either, not even after seeing her friends.

I thank her as she drops me off and scoff at her suggestion I might be feeling it tomorrow. I go to the gym, I tell her. I'm fit and a little bit of exercise isn't going to have that much of an impact.

I know I hadn't wanted to take all this time out doing something that was nothing to do with all the problems I'm facing at the moment, but I'm so glad I did. During the afternoon Dan is keen to watch the football so leaving him to it I wrap up warm and go and sit out in the garden to think. I turn my mind back to the problems I have facing me and I do so with a refreshed attitude having taken the time out. Given some distance from the situation I find I'm able to plot my way clearly through the issues having gained some much needed perspective, and by the time evening arrives, I know exactly what actions I'm going to be taking over the next few days.

Chapter 11

The following morning, I ache in places I didn't know I had, physically groaning as I get out of bed and it takes me a while to get moving. I think bitterly on Letitia's parting words and grumble to myself about getting old. So much for my gym fit body being able to cope with the rigours of riding.

I'm up early too as I'd planned on fitting in a workout at my new gym in Oakton and although Dan stayed over I'd said I'd go and do this alone. I tiptoe past him sprawled across the sofa and despite the twinge of envy I feel at him still being fast asleep I resist the urge to go straight back to bed. I leave him a note to remind him where I am and sneak out quietly so as not to disturb him.

I arrive at the gym before seven, sign up and, bearing in mind the aching I already feel, I take it steady on each of the pieces of equipment. It's a small set-up but there's everything I need here and it feels good to be back in the groove of doing some exercise. It's also quiet at that time of the morning and, other than exchanging polite greetings with the couple of other members present, I keep myself to myself.

I'm nearly home by nine having finished with a swim and shower, when I pass Diane walking along our lane and she asks if I'm going into work. When I say I'm not due in until later she invites me for breakfast. I park at my place then walk back to hers meeting at her front gate. She has a fresh

loaf from the shop and my mouth waters in anticipation.

"How are you doing?" I ask as I follow her
along the path to the rear of her cottage.

"Oh, fine, you know," she replies, but I know
her well enough to know she's trying to sound up-
beat.

Once inside, Diane makes coffee and proceeds
to slice the loaf thickly while I gather together
plates, butter (real butter, not some healthy substitute) and a pot of Diane's homemade, and delicious, marmalade. She puts ginger in it, she's told
me before, it adds a real kick. We're soon eating
and that has to be in silence as breakfasts like this
require being in the moment and total concentration to be fully appreciated. I limit myself to the
two slices, I could have eaten more, much more,
but firstly, that would be rude, and secondly, along
with the rest of my often overly indulgent diet, it
would eventually mean that my days of being a
stealthy house breaker would be at an end, and I
might just need those skills again.

As I eat I realise some thing's missing.
"Where's Cat?" I say as I look round the room,
even checking under the table.

"Oh he's out helping someone I imagine, he'll
be back a little later, he usually is. I like the fact
you've missed him though."

"It's not like I care or anything, I just wondered," I reply, although I do know she knows my
attitude to him has changed and I see her eyebrows
rise in recognition of that fact.

Once I finish eating I reach for the mug of coffee and tell Diane I'm making progress on sorting out her problem with Ben. Things are happening this week, I reassure her. She looks up and smiles at me and I see the tension in her face dissipate for the first time.

"I don't know what it is you think you can do to make him back down but I am intrigued to find out."

"I'll tell you everything once it falls into place. But please don't worry, Diane. You won't be having to move from here." I don't use the word promise but I might as well have done, which is perhaps a little reckless in the circumstances, but I know I can't let my friend down. Her face brightens and I know exactly what will cheer her up even further as I say, "Oh, and you'll never guess what? I've been spending some quality time with Letitia."

"Really? I assume that must be part of the plan, because I can't see you doing it otherwise."

"Ahh, well, yes, it is, but she was in a real mess and needed sorting out. And..." I draw this out in a big build up kind of a way, "I went riding with her yesterday." Diane's eyebrows rise in astonishment. "I know! I could hardly believe it myself."

"What's this I hear? You've bin riding." Joe's voice makes me jump, I hadn't heard him arrive but he sits down at the table sporting a burgundy tie and tweed waistcoat and Diane pours him a coffee and pushes it across to him.

"Hi, Joe. Yup, I took your advice and loved every moment."

"I knew you'd enjoy it."

"Thanks for recommending it to me, I'll definitely be going again." It wasn't exactly his words that had spurred me into action but he was not to know that.

Joe passes on any breakfast, which is probably how he manages to stay as slim as he is, and we chat about his plans for the day in the garden. Diane is going to be out there too, she tells me, picking and drying herbs to top up her supply of ingredients. I see Joe watching her and I wonder if he's noticed the recent change in her demeanour. I don't like to see her so worried, and if he's picked up on it I wonder if she's told him what's going on.

I leave a short while later and Joe follows me out. Once out of earshot he says he'll be keeping her busy in the garden. She'll find connecting with the soil therapeutic at the moment, he tells me. I smile gratefully at him; I guess that tells me all I need to know.

I have called a meeting at the offices in Hartleigh in the early afternoon with Cubby, Dan and James, if he can make it, although I hope he can't as the thought of Dan and James being in the same room together is making me edgy. However, I'm intending on announcing my plan, such as it is, so he ought to be present and I run through it out loud to myself in the car on the way there.

Keep it simple, I tell myself. *The best plans always are.* As I knew it would, right from the moment James Lambert first put forward his deal, it begins with the fact that I have to return to London. And I've been surprised by my reaction to that. My nerves, which build with any thought of Craig, are tinged with an edge of excitement which, considering it is the place I ran from, I wasn't expecting.

When I get to the office the others are already there and waiting for me. Cubby approaches for a hug immediately, followed by Dan who kisses my cheek and fortunately James stays put in his chair and merely says hello, a smile playing on those lips of his.

I lay out my grand plan, starting with, I'm returning to London. The rest of it takes all of thirty seconds and I realise from the looks on their faces that they were expecting more. Whether that be by way of detail or the plan itself I'm not sure, but I have given them all they are going to get.

"I'm going with you," announces Dan, which surprises me.

"Thanks, but I don't need anyone with me and having you hanging around will only put Craig off helping me."

"Then I'll stay in the background but you're not going in there with no support at all."

"I can provide all the support she needs," chips in James.

"Oh that's just what we need, the police trampling all over this," replies Dan.

"We're well equipped, and trained, and certainly have more resources at our disposal than you do."

"You have no idea what I have at my disposal,

so back off." And the two of them carry on sniping as each tries to outdo the other.

I exchange a look with Cubby and think I preferred it when it was just him and me in here working out whatever problem we had without all this competitive male nonsense. He gesticulates towards the pair of them then shrugs, like it's up to me to sort this out. I give them a few more seconds, then...

"Quiet!" They fall silent and I glare at the pair of them. I turn to Dan.

"What do you mean by support?"

"I think I should be tracking you. Then at least I'll know where you are should something go wrong."

"How are you intending on doing that? And what do you know about tracking people? I can't be wearing anything obvious in there, I wouldn't last five minutes."

"I spent some time working for a surveillance company once so I do know a few things. Your phone for example." There's a snorting sound that comes from James along with a muttering of something that sounds suspiciously like, 'amateur', but I add a little ice to the look I give him and his hands come up in silent apology. I nod at Dan to continue. "Your phone for example," he repeats, "frankly you will need an upgrade but then I could track you via that." Another snort of derision comes from James and at this point I have to agree with him that it does all seem a little basic but then what do I know about it. However, because I feel the need to back Dan up and, as I'm perfectly happy going along without any support at all, if whatever Dan has in his toolbox keeps him happy then I'll let him get on with it and I keep my thoughts to myself.

"As long as I can revert to my old phone when I return." He smiles.

"We'll see; you never know, I might convert you yet."

James says, "I'm sorry, but I think I can do a little better than simply offering to track you on a phone." This he says with disdain, which I don't like, instantly protective over Dan and his ideas, but I hope I don't sound too defensive when I reply.

"I think Dan's right, James. We don't want anything too heavy handed on this. Craig is sharp and will be suspicious purely because I've turned up out of the blue. Besides you will need to be ready with whatever support you have available to catch him red-handed." Then, to change the subject, I turn to Cubby. "By the way, are Ben and Letitia clients of yours?" I had been thinking that, if they were, then at some point I should let him know just how easily I got into their place.

He nods, and smiles, "One more reason for you to get this right."

No pressure there then, I think.

"When are you thinking of going?" James asks.

"Tomorrow."

"Tomorrow!" Dan and James chorus, presumably alarmed at the speed I'm now moving. It's the first time they've agreed on anything and I stare at the pair of them, their reactions not budging me an inch.

"Yes. There's no point in delaying. If there are things you need to get in place you'd better get on with them now."

On the journey home I dwell on the fact that Dan kisses me in public but not when we're alone. He's putting on a front by doing so and I wonder whose benefit that is for, Cubby or James.

I stop off for some groceries and bits and pieces for the trip and decide that, once I've dropped the shopping off, I'm going to pop in to see Diane and let her know I'm going to be away, and some of the reason why. Though, when I open my front door to leave, I find James standing there, about to knock.

"What are you doing here?"

"Do you always greet visitors so warmly, or is that special welcome just for me?" I scowl, and without being invited he walks into the cottage and goes through to the kitchen. I follow, wondering what it is he forgot to, or couldn't, say back at the office. He stands looking out of the kitchen window, his hands in the pockets of his suit trousers. I follow his gaze, wishing I could see Joe out there.

"Dan will be back any minute."

"I doubt that, Maddy. I imagine he's going to be working late trying to fathom how he can possibly protect you over the next few days." As I'm quite capable of looking after myself I'm nowhere near as worried about Dan's abilities as James seems to be.

"He'll do just fine."

"You think so?" He turns round to face me. "You have no idea what you're walking back into. You need me there, not some amateur."

"I don't want you there." I feel my pulse rising.

"Why is that, Maddy?" He moves closer, barely an inch or two separating us as he brings his lips to my ear. "Are you concerned about what may happen if we spent any time together?" Heat radiates between us; I shake my head. "Because it seems to me lover boy is still not taking care of business." I curse the fact Dan's pillow and blankets are so obvious.

I turn my head, forcing myself to look him straight in the eye, "That is nothing to do with you."

"No? But it could be." His hand is on my hip. "From what I hear you take a lot of satisfying, Maddy. Not a one-man woman, that's what I've been told." His thumb finds skin, slips into the waistband of my jeans and he pulls me up tight to him, his other hand in the small of my back. "You must be feeling that itch right about now." Hot breath whispers as he trails his lips up my neck and I wonder who he's been talking to.

Despite myself he's pushing all the right buttons. "No," I whisper, the sensation of his thumb caressing my hip hard to ignore. I bring my hands up between us and push back on his chest, to no avail. I'd dearly love to floor him, a knee to the bollocks would do just that, but I fear the repercussions. He has too much over me and, as I dreaded, appears not to mind abusing his position of power. His lips find mine, I give in, kiss back, relax, and feel him do similar, encouraged. His bottom lip, soft, fleshy, my target. I bite. A nip, that's all, taste blood and push back with all my force aided this time by his surprise, he staggers, takes a step away, glares at me as he brings the base of his thumb up to his lip looks at it to check for blood. I stand my ground.

"Bitch."

"I said no."

A nasty smile spreads across his face. "Another time, Maddy." He adjusts his jacket, shirt sleeves just so; I watch him check out the damage to his lip with his tongue. He takes a step towards me, pauses, and I lean away, wary and ready to take further action. "I like it rough though, you might be just what I'm looking for." I leave him to have the last word and watch as he walks out of the front door slamming it behind him. I let out a shudder- ing breath and collapse into the nearest chair. My hands shaking, and heart pounding.

I take a few deep breaths and wait until I feel calm again then, checking James's car is nowhere to be seen, I leave to go and see Diane as planned. On the way I ponder what I should do about him. Report him to his superiors? Would they simply close ranks and protect him? Or support me? I think I know the answer to that and there's no point riling him when no good will come of it. I also need him to give me the amnesty and I can't see that happening if I turn him in so I'm going to have to play this cleverly instead, and hope I don't get burned.

"We're going away for a few days," I tell Diane. "Back to London. Where I originally come from."

"Oh, okay," she says, curiosity momentarily giving her something other than Ben to think about.

"Could you keep an eye on the place? You'll know when we're back because you'll see Dan's car."

"Is this part of the vengeance against Ben thing?"

"Yeah." Then I make a decision and continue, "there's some stuff I need to tell you. Brace yourself though because it might come as a bit of a shock." She squares her shoulders and fixes me with a steely eye. I take a deep breath and let it out slowly.

"Okay, so I need some help with the Ben thing, and London is where I'll find it." She looks confused so I fill her in a little by telling her I'd arrived in Crowthorne after running away, and not just from Tag. I say I'd been in a gang, done some bad things and had wanted to start over. I explain I now have to revisit my past to get the help I needed to tackle Ben. Although her eyebrows rose as I'd told her a potted history of my past she didn't interrupt but as I finish she looks worried.

"I'd rather you didn't tackle Ben if you've got to put yourself in danger, Maddy." I smile.

"That's only part of it, Diane. The police have caught up with me too so I'm doing it to get myself out of trouble there as well. I can't say no."

"All right, is there anything I can do?" I love

the fact there's no judgement from her, just acceptance and an offer of support.

"I don't think so, but thanks. Keeping an eye on my place is enough and I imagine we'll be back soon and all this will be over."

"Let's hope so."

I get ready to leave then hesitate. "Do you think any the worse of me after telling you all this?"

"No, Maddy, I think I know who you are. We're all entitled to start again and you've had to work harder than most to do that." I smile in appreciation of her kindness and leave her to get on with her evening and return to my cottage, noting as I do that Dan is late just as James predicted.

I cook us some dinner. Nothing fancy. Pasta, sauce, and by the time it's ready he's home.

"Hey," I call out as the door opens. "Good timing." He looks tired.

"Something smells good," he says, and I pour us each a beer as he comes through to the kitchen after dumping his stuff on the sofa. I realise he must be finding it difficult to manage his clothes and washing with camping out here and having his own flat too, and wonder if I should invite him back into my bed. Maybe but perhaps not tonight, it might complicate things further just as we're off to tackle Craig, especially if he turns me down.

"So," I say a short while later, "you worked for a surveillance company?"

"Yes, I did," and I notice a slight hesitation, "and I picked up plenty that will help us out over the next few days."

"Did you get training in following people and

suchlike?" He nods.

"Yup, don't you worry about that." Then, and I get the feeling he wants to distract me away from this line, he changes the questioning around. "What time are we heading off tomorrow? I need to go and buy some equipment and get it all set up."

"I thought early evening would be fine. We'll get settled into the hotel and start properly on Wednesday. Does that give you enough time?"

"Yeah, that's fine. We can discuss how best to protect you on the way there."

After dinner Dan is engrossed in his laptop and seems unwilling to engage in conversation so I try to read for a while. My concentration is shot to pieces though, the words floating on the page, and once I realise I've reread the same paragraph three times and still not taken it in, I give up and go for a bath instead.

I'm about ready for bed when I emerge so go downstairs to check everything is locked up. Dan is still on his laptop, the cable trailing across the floor to the plug.

"Night," I say, wishing he'd leave that and come and give me a hug, maybe more, instead. Should I ask him? Is that desperate, too desperate?

"Night," he replies, looking up at me. I smile, try to look encouraging but he doesn't move, simply gazing at me a moment longer and, I real-ise, keen to share something that's obviously been on his mind. "I have to tell you something, I don't like James. I don't trust him."

I nearly tell him then, I so very nearly tell him

what happened earlier but I don't for fear of what
he might do, and what he might jeopardise. "No,"
I reply instead, "I don't like him much either," and
having nothing further to add I turn and go to bed.

Chapter 12

*Who hasn't imagined their life as a spy or, proba-
bly more realistically, a private detective? You
can't be alone in having those fantasies, you know
that, but you've totally outdone yourself this time
by pretending you have experience in a field you
know next to nothing about. It is true that you had
a job with a surveillance company once, but you
were there for all of six weeks and your work experience amounted to little more than answering
the phones and making the tea, not that you were
going to let James know that. But that's why you
said what you did of course, because of him.*

    *'We're well equipped, and trained, and cer-
tainly have more resources at our disposal than
you do.'*

    Smug bugger.

    *God, how you wanted to punch him right there
and then and wipe that stupid smirk off his face.
You don't understand how Maddy doesn't see
what he's after. It's as clear as day to you. And
you don't want him to have the chance to get
closer to her by offering her any protection. No
way. That's going to be up to you to provide and
that's why you're wide awake at three in the morning, disappearing down rabbit hole after rabbit
hole on the net, as you research everything you
can about surveillance and tracking. Your searching has brought up some wild stuff too and you've
had to filter out a lot that quite frankly borders on*

*stalking, rather than any sort of legitimate track-
ing.*

*She backed you though, didn't she? Chose you
over him. That pleased you, and James didn't like
it one bit. Tough.*

*It's hard to believe how much your life has
changed in such a short space of time. Being
around Maddy certainly keeps things interesting,
that's a fact. Usually you'd already be getting
itchy feet right about now but no, yours are warm,
toasty, and perfectly comfortable thank you. Now,
if you could just bring your relationship with
Maddy back to where it was only a couple of weeks
ago, life would be peachy. You know it essentially
amounted to not much more than a couple of
nights together and may never develop further but
you're not ready to give up on the possibility of a
return to intimacy just yet.*

*However, it's difficult to have that as your goal
while maintaining your determination to take a
step back and not be a doormat in this relationship.*

*Over the last few days you've tried to keep it
light, making jokes about what appears to be your
stealthy move in to keep her relaxed about it, because you don't want her chucking you out. It feels
like home already though, her place. It's comfortable and you can relax there. You enjoy walking
with her too, she seems to chill out more then and
you even got her into the pub for a drink but then
it all kicked off with Kourtney. This Ben is a real
piece of work and while you're impressed with the
loyalty she shows to the close group of friends she*

has, you are worried about everything she's taking on, and so soon after she was attacked, and the fact she's promising stuff she may not be able to deliver. In fact she has so much on her mind, what with the pressure James has put her under too, it's hardly surprising she's unsettled and at times a tad testy.

It was a bonus to meet Chris though, he seems like a top bloke. Wanted to talk books though, hardly a specialist subject of yours and you suspect he's not impressed with your choice of reading but he didn't show it and just seemed genuinely pleased to have a chat. You can tell Maddy is proud of him too, wanting to tell you all about him writing a book.

It was surprising that when you brought up the subject of James she'd already met him but didn't tell you about it until you asked, and you wonder if you should read something into that? It led on to a deeper discussion about where he had been a part of her past and about her mother's death and you know it took longer than it should have done for you to realise you weren't already meant to know that piece of information. You hope she didn't notice as you tried to cover.

It turns out that's when James had first met her. That Day. Not that Maddy remembered him, you were pleased to hear. You'd exchanged family histories then and found you couldn't have come from more different backgrounds and when you'd joked that opposites attract it was satisfying to see her blush. Like it had somehow affected her, but you apologised swiftly as you didn't want to appear too forward. It's getting tricky though, being with her so much of the time, as you're finding it difficult to behave naturally when all you want to do is reach out and wrap your arms around her.

You're still struggling to sleep without her near you too and need coffee and a shower to get you going each morning, and you wonder how Cubby would take it if you had a sleep in the office to catch up.

She's out all day Saturday and you're cooking when she gets home. She looks pleased to see you, probably as much as she might do with anyone she likes, you think, and you can't help wondering if this is it, if you are just friends now and the chance to be something more has passed you by. It's sad if that is the case because your heart leapt when she walked in through the door, but how do you get back to what you were? You can hardly push the subject after what she's been through, that would be crass, so you guess you'll have to leave it in her hands to make the first move, if or whenever she's ready, which is frustrating.

After going riding with Letitia she's deep in thought for hours and you watch the match and leave her to it. You could see her from the kitchen window as she sat on the bench staring into the distance, and it's like she's going through some sort of process as she worked it out in her head and you were keen to see what came out of it. By Sunday evening she seemed satisfied and much more settled but she doesn't share, saying she's not ready to do so; she simply calls her meeting instead.

And now you know what she has in mind and you're not at all sure about this trip to London. The uncertainty of it all. Maddy's plan hardly contained a wealth of information and you hope she's put a lot more thought into it than first appears. However, with an eye on the prize, if she does pull this off it gives her the opportunity to move on with a clean slate, admittedly courtesy of James, but you can't have everything, and you push that detail into the back of your mind.

What happened this morning though does bring up the thorny subject of just how prepared you are to look after her. Okay, you hadn't slept well again only finally managing to nod off as it was starting to get light. But you did know she was planning on going to the gym and had decided to surprise her with the offer of joining her but she slipped right past you as you lay fast asleep, only waking to find her note later. It doesn't exactly bode well, does it?

In an attempt to do better, you've made a list of what you need and you're going to be kept busy tomorrow - today now that you glance at your watch, getting all the equipment you need and setting it up.

It's time to step up, you tell yourself. You've got to start to look like you know what you're doing and become the man she needs you to be. Because she's told you about Craig, and he sounds like a right bastard. That was a sobering conversation. Made it real and, you suspect, you haven't been told the half of it. You know the worst is yet to come.

<u>**Chapter 13**</u>

I forget it's Tuesday, and that Kourtney will be coming round so I'm surprised to hear a knock on the door at nine.

"I would've let myself in but didn't like to when I saw your car there, you all righ'?" she says, as she bustles in with her equipment, plonking it far enough inside so she can close the door.

"I'm fine, and you?"

"Yeah, okay." She certainly wastes no time getting out her polish and cloth and starting to straighten the sitting room, dusting as she goes. "No work today?"

"No, I've got to go away for a few days so I'm getting ready for that."

"Oh, where to? Anywhere nice?"

"London. Though it's not a holiday, it's on Ben business."

"Oh." She sounds curious but doesn't ask anything further. "Well I wish yer the best of luck with it then, and look forward to hearin' all abou' it," she says, and pauses long enough to give me a smile before vigorously plumping the cushions on the sofa.

I feel like I'm in the way so go through to the kitchen. Dan left for his shopping trip long ago and I clear up the breakfast things, then start cleaning the worktop before hearing Kourtney tutting behind me.

"That's what I'm here for."

"I know, but I can't be here and just watch you clean." She laughs.

"Oh, you'd be surprised at how many can." I'm sure, however, that's not me and I decide to pop out for a walk and put into action something I decided on in the night.

The sky, a study of unrelenting grey, hangs low and sombre, threatening rain and darkening moods. The lull before the storm, and like me, in something of a hiatus. There's no one about as I make my way up into the village and a while later I'm knocking on the door of a thatched cottage, my plan thwarted when there's no answer. Chris is not at home. I'm disappointed and knock again, just to make sure. He's definitely not there.

I'd hoped to be able to hide out at his place for a bit. I knew I'd feel safe there and I'm needing that today. Security. Comfort. But I'd also wanted to tell him what I'd told Diane. That bit about my background. Coming clean suddenly feels like the right thing to do so it's frustrating I'm unable to follow that decision through before I leave.

I turn and walk back down the path, then having nowhere else to go start the return journey home. I call in at the shop and buy a few goodies for lunch but there's no one in there to waste time chatting to and before too long I'm back at my own front door.

I can hear Kourtney upstairs but by the time I've put my purchases away she's back down and declares she's finished up there so at least I can make myself busy by going to pack.

Dan is back in time for lunch and he has several

bags. I contain my curiosity as I put the shop purchases together on the table but when we sit down to eat it's not long before his hand is diving into one of the smallest.

"There," he says, placing a rectangular box on the table, "welcome to the twenty-first century." It's a smart phone for me. We get the basics set up and it seems intuitive so I'm sure I'll get used to it, but I find myself rather reluctantly putting my old mobile away in a drawer.

I'm intrigued by his other bags. One has a pair of fluffy ears sticking out of it. I point at that one.

"Ears?"

"It's a rabbit," he says, as if that explains everything.

"Do we need one of those in London?" He looks at me patiently.

"It's for my sister, well the baby. She likes rabbits."

"Aww, that's sweet," I say, and I take a long look at this thoughtful man, who always seems to be thinking of others.

I'm genuinely interested in his other purchases too because, despite the way I earn my living, I've never used any equipment to do so and I'm keen to see what he's got that may be of use to me in the future. When I ask him about the other stuff though I don't get much by way of an answer and as he seems guarded about it I leave him in peace to continue to set up the phone onto which, he tells me, he is loading the apps he needs to be able to track me. Despite my interest he's definitely distracted so now is clearly not the time to show it, and I make myself scarce as he spends the rest of the afternoon organising his different gadgets and software things.

I book a room in a large and impersonal hotel that's located just outside the area of London I want to be and Dan, a little while later, books a separate room in the same hotel. That evening we leave, travelling down in his car, but he drops me at a railway station out of town and I take the train from then on. This gives me some time to myself in which to examine how I'm feeling now this is actually happening, something I haven't given much consideration to yet because I've been too busy getting ready. I am nervous about what I have to do over the next few days. But there's something more, I'm feeling a buzz of excitement about returning home and weirdly I realise I'm kind of looking forward to it.

By the time I've made my way to the hotel and checked in, Dan's already been there an hour or so and has spent that time setting up his stuff. We are a floor apart which suits me fine and we're in touch by phone and text. I've told him that's the only contact we're to have. You never know who's around, or watching, and I don't want anyone realising I'm not alone. However, as soon as I get into my room I have little to occupy me and, when not even the book I'm reading manages to distract my attention, I have to face the fact I miss not having him around so later that evening I take a calculated risk.

I call and ask if he fancies some sightseeing. He does, but if he's expecting me to take him on the well-trodden London tourist trail he's going to be sorely disappointed. I have other plans. It's late evening and the night is cold. I see Dan on the corner where we arranged to meet, the clouds of his breath highlighted by the streetlight he is under, and we walk off together quickly to get the blood moving and to warm us up. I know exactly where we are and as we travel along familiar streets I'm amazed by how little has changed. I'm wearing a beanie, heavy framed glasses, a scarf wound round so I can bury the lower part of my face in it, and my collar is up.

"Is this you under cover?" he asks, "I barely recognise you."

"Are you taking the piss?"

"Only a bit," and I sense the smile in his words.

"I knew I should have left you behind."

"Now, now, you know you're not to do that. I'm here to protect you."

"Yeah. Right." Like when we were in the car earlier I get the impression this is all still a game to him. Then we'd been talking through how I thought things were going to go over the next few days. I'd impressed on him that whatever happens under no circumstances was he to intervene.

Under. No. Circumstances.

He was going to be tempted, I knew that. But he was going to have to ignore that temptation and let me go. He'd agreed as readily as if I'd asked him if he fancied going away for a particularly dirty weekend once all this was over and I don't think he has the slightest idea what he's signed up for.

Despite the streets being quieter at this hour I keep my head low, feeling the need to hide myself the deeper into my old territory we get. It feels strange returning home. I'd thought about coming here, about revisiting at all. I'd pondered what may be brought up by the visit and whether I should avoid it but it felt strange to come back and not see this place. My anticipation rises the closer we get and I wonder if my old home will even still be here, or what changes might have been made to it. As we round the final corner though I see the precinct, the fish and chip shop dead centre. My old flat above. I slow, feel Dan falter by my side. Odd. He stops and I hang back with him, pull my scarf down from my face as I search his for explanation.

"What's the matter?"

"Nothing, I, just, er, guess that's where you lived?" His hands are deep in his pockets and he gesticulates in the direction of the chippy with his head. I don't believe I've ever told him specifically where I lived but perhaps I've given him enough of a description in the past for him to recognise the place. *Perhaps.*

"It is. That's my flat, right in the middle, above the chippy." I point it out and start to move again but he seems reluctant to follow. I turn back, perplexed. "What's going on?" He looks uncomfortable, like he'd rather be anywhere but here.

"Nothing," he says again, when it quite clearly is something. "I was just wondering if you needed me here, that's all. If I, er, shouldn't go and, um, get on with something else."

"Like what?"

"Scarle'? Scarle'! I thought that was you!" Bet appears as if from nowhere, which shows how distracted I am as that is not easy for a woman of her size. She waddles towards us, wrapping her large arms around me as I reply and hugging me tight to her massive bosom. I hug her back, the aroma of fried food not going unnoticed.

She stands, holding me at arm's length to take a good look. Finding that due to her considerable assets she's still unable to give me her full appraisal, she reluctantly lets go and stands back, finally nodding in satisfaction.

"Yer look great," she says, then to my astonishment, she addresses Dan. "You told me she was settled an' happy but not 'ow wonderful she was lookin'," and she nudges him in mock indignation. "It's good to see you again, and so soon too. I didn't think you'd come back at all let alone bring Scarle'. Daniel? Isn't it?" she adds as an afterthought, and holds her hand out.

He takes it. "Dan," he says, his voice quiet, "to friends." He swallows and looks like he has difficulty doing so as she pumps his arm enthusiastically.

"Come on, come on. Vince won't forgive me if I don't take you to see 'im." She leads the way, her backside jiggling ahead of us like a bag full of ferrets. Before we follow I catch Dan's eye. The look he gives me can only be described as helpless. He's been caught out and I am so filled with rage I can't trust myself to speak. Rage, and something I can't quite pinpoint immediately but then it comes to me, sorrow, like something buried deep down inside my heart has just broken.

He puts his hand on my arm to hold me back, to what end I don't know because there's nothing that can be said now that can possibly make this better. I pull my arm away and follow Bet.

I'm ashamed he has been here and seen this. Not because of where I grew up. There's nothing wrong with that. But I know he knows more, and that he has seen it all. I can tell in the way he just looked at me. In the way he is with Bet. He didn't just come here to see where I lived. He came to find out about me and he befriended Bet to that end. It horrifies me that he's done that, that he's looked into my past, that he knows the things I have done and the life I have led. Even as I think these things, tears prick the back of my eyes and I blink them away. I don't understand why he's not repulsed, why he ever came back to me after. Although of course he didn't, not like that, not like we were once.

And now I know why.

I playact my way through the next half hour. I am delighted to get the chance to see Vince and Bet again but the moment has been ruined by the knowledge I now have. Vince wraps me in his meaty arms and it's obvious he's also met Dan before. I order fish and chips for us both, though Bet and Vince won't hear of us paying, but I ask if we can go out back rather than sit in the window. It's late and quiet but there's no point making my presence obvious. It would only take the wrong person to walk past and word would be out. Bet and Vince are happy to shepherd us through the hatch in the counter and into the back room where I know they have a table set up, and as the shop's quiet they join us while they can. Whilst eating, I answer their questions about what I've been up to, although after the revelation about Dan's activities I don't enjoy my food as I usually would. I'd leave it but don't want to insult my friends. I enquire after their lives and catch up on what's been happening on the estate. Dan doesn't contribute much to the conversation, but then he wouldn't, it wasn't his life, and I leave him to ruminate on my mood because I never, not even once, so much as glance at him, meet his eye or acknowledge him in any way.

After a while the shop starts to get busy with those wanting to soak up the alcohol they've consumed, and Vince and Bet have to get back to work. I ask them to keep my visit to themselves, which I know they'll do, and once I finish eating I clear up. Amid promises to call in again, if I can, I leave, by the back door. Dan follows and we walk in silence.

He tries to stop me again, places his hand on my arm. "Maddy, I..." but I shrug it off and carry on. I can't speak to him, not now.

"Please stop. We need to talk." He has come to a halt. I walk on a couple more paces, turn and shake my head.

"Not here, my room, travel separately," I say, and turn and carry on, leaving him behind. I walk directly back to our hotel, and my room but once inside I can't settle and start pacing instead, wearing the carpet out as I march to and fro along the end of the bed.

He arrives a few minutes later. It feels longer, the fish and chips churning in my stomach.

After letting him in I walk across the room then turn back towards him. He looks uneasy, sensing my agitation. After all the build-up I have no idea where to start and instead of doing so I have the horrible feeling I'm going to cry, pain building behind my eyes. I rock on my feet and take some deep breaths as I try to quell the tears that are coming, but as I look down the view of my feet blurs and I have to use the heels of my hands to wipe my eyes. He's closer now, I can feel the heat of him, as his hand reaches out and cups my chin lifting my face so I'm looking at his, desperate and beseeching.

"I'm sorry," he says. *For what*? I think. *For investigating my past? For being caught?*

Or for what you found out?

I pull away from him as I struggle to find my voice. Eventually I manage, "How much do you know?"

"I think probably everything." I nod. It is as bad as I thought and the invasion of my privacy stings. I close my eyes in disbelief. All the worry I'd had about Tag telling him, all the efforts I'd gone to for that not to happen had been a waste of time. He'd gone and found out for himself.

"When?" I ask, because I need to know, although I've already guessed, "That day you went missing, just after we got together?" He nods.

"Why?"

He sighs and again reaches a hand out towards me but I take a step back to avoid it. "It sounds bad, but your file was so sparse on information, I just wanted to know everything about you, and I didn't think you'd tell me."

"There were reasons for that."

"I know. I know that now and I am sorry, Maddy. I thought I'd just find out a bit about where you came from. It seemed harmless at the time, but sounds worse now, when I say it out loud. I only wanted a bit of background on you, that's all."

"But you got more than you bargained for?"

"Yes."

"You got the details of the poverty I grew up in, the abandonment, the hunger, the caring I had to take on," he nods, "the abuse I suffered at the hands of the one person who should have pro-tected me? You got all that?" I hear the anger creeping into my voice as he nods again, pain etched across his face. "The being bartered for sex so she could get her booze and fags? I hope you got that, Daniel, as I would really hate for you to have missed out on any of the graphic detail."

"Maddy, please..." He reaches again but still I brush his hands away.

"You got all of this," my voice breaks, and I struggle to carry on, "and yet you still want to touch me?" I don't understand how he could bear to but then something unfathomable passes across his face. I see him swallow, I'm sure it's a delay-ing tactic before he tells me the unpalatable news that no, he doesn't want to, not anymore, not like that.

"I got all of this," he pauses for what seems an eternity, "and I never want to let you go."

He's closer now and this time I don't move, the relief his words bring palpable. He leans towards me, his lips brush mine, their touch soft then harder as I respond, kissing him back. His hand is on my waist drawing me close, our tongues probe, igniting a passion lain dormant for far too long, one I'd thought fully extinguished. And I'm so grateful it hasn't been, so thankful I'm still wanted, still desired. This wasn't how I thought the next little while was going to go, and some deep down dark part of me wishes I could be stronger, tells me I should still be angry with him, that I should turn him away for the trust he's broken, but it's too late, far too late for that. We both know how emotionally needy I am and given the merest encouragement how accepting, and like a breached dam there's no stopping us. Buttons pop and cloth tears as I rip his shirt open and love the feel of my hands on his skin. My top is pulled over my head, my bra slung to the floor and I relish the touch as my nipples graze his chest.

"Is this okay?" he murmurs, thoughtful given his evident desire, and yes, I tell him, yes, it's okay. I want this to obliterate what has gone before and hear his sharp intake of breath as I loosen his belt, free the top button of his jeans and feel his hand sliding into the top of mine as I lower his zip. Before I can reach further he pushes me and as I fall onto the bed he drags my jeans off, pulling me to the edge of the bed in the process.

Leaning over, his lips find mine briefly then travel down my body, lingering, tasting, sucking as they explore. His fingers tease the edge of my pants and I'm desperate for more but as I try to remove them he bats my hands away, then peels them off slowly himself and I feel his mouth on me at last, at long, long last, his tongue lithe and eager, seeking the climax that is so close already, so close, my eyes unfocused as my back arches, pleasure peaking like the crest of a waterfall, releasing and pulsing through me as I shudder and cry out.

With a hand on each side of my waist he slides me off the bed, lifting me onto his lap where he remains kneeling on the floor, I'm tender, still quivering as he does so. I kiss him then pull back, make eye contact and watch his face as I lift myself then bury him deep inside. I flex my hips, feel his heat rise and slowly grind against him, barely having to move as seconds later he groans, far less symphonically than with my own release, and holds me tight against him.

We're in touch by phone and text. I've told him that's the only contact we're to have.

That didn't last long and we spend the next few hours getting to explore each other all over again.

I lie awake later, waiting for darkness to fall but it doesn't, the window permanently bathed in yellow light. I get up and go to stare out across well-lit London, the pale haze that floats above all like a protective blanket keeping night at bay and I have a hankering to be home in the naturally lit

darkness of my cottage. I draw the curtains and return to bed, curling myself into the hollow of
Dan's body, his arms coming around me as I do.
I'm warm, it's dark and I fall asleep to the beat of
his heart.

Before it gets light, before the hotel starts to
move and breathe with staff and guests, I send him
back to his own room. We don't have the luxury
to chance jeopardising what we came here to do
and now we've found each other again, we can get
back to all of that later on. I miss him when he's
gone though, the bed too big without him.

Chapter 14

The next morning, and after a large breakfast to feed the butterflies taking flight in my stomach, I text Dan to let him know I'm leaving and I set off to find the old gang. I realise as I walk familiar streets that although a few years have passed not that much has changed. The roads are still non-stop traffic, though the fumes that tighten lungs and restrict the air passages of those that bustle along the pavements, are more obvious to me now. Locals still stop and chat and call out to friends and neighbours, each area its own village, of sorts. The shops I pass are still much the same as they were when I lived here, the corner shops open early, and late, the discount stores, the bookies, the fast food outlets, the air outside each permeated with the temptation of their wares. I don't think I've changed that much either. I'm still a girl wearing jeans, boots and a leather jacket, just as I was all those years ago.

But I do hear the noise. After the relative silence of the countryside; this is an assault, the constant hum, the rattle, the throng, the impatience of a city, intermittent car horns sounding off, sirens in the distance. That I notice.

I've deliberated for a long time how best to approach Craig. Whether to go in soft by tracking down one of his boys and entering his domain via them or whether to be more direct. I'm not sure there is much to be gained either way. He either accepts my return, or he does not, and as I have always tended to tackle things head on, plus I don't feel I have time on my side, I've gone for the direct approach. Of course, that might be harder than I expect. I'm assuming everything is just as it always was but all of that could have changed. The gang could meet up in a completely different place after all these years and although I've thought through a few alternatives as to what my next course of action would then be, I'm hoping none are necessary.

On the other side of the estate to where I lived was a sticky pub called The Pike and Eel. The tenants, held back by avaricious brewery landlords, had little incentive to increase their beer trade due to the knock-on hike in their rent so, having had any entrepreneurial spirit and enthusiasm for the pub business squashed out of them long ago, they turned their attention to other more lucrative sources of revenue and ran two sets of books accordingly.

Back in my day Don dealt with moving as much white powder out of the back door as the neighbourhood could absorb, while his wife, Maureen, managed the 'bed and breakfast' part of their enterprise, ironically breakfast being the one thing that was not on her menu of offerings. Before the ravages of time, her chain-smoking habit and the half bottle of whisky a day had taken its toll on her looks, Maureen took care of any occupiers of the rooms available, but as trade had started to dry up, two daughters arrived to inhabit the spare rooms upstairs that were in addition to the tenancy flat. At that time, Don and Maureen had no qualms about having Tag and his disciples hanging around the place and everyone scratched each other's back. Business for all parties had been brisk and now I sit and watch for a while from a café on the opposite corner to see what, if anything, has changed. The external appearance of the place certainly hasn't.

Beneath a second floor of dirty grey-green bricks the frontage wraps around the ninety-degree angle of the corner. The ground floor has a wood clad finish to it which is stained dark brown with diamond-paned windows through which a welcoming glow brightens the pub's appearance. The name is picked out in gold, stencilled across the top in large plain font.

I sit at a small table crammed in the corner of the café so I'm hidden from view but from my vantage point I can peer out and look across the street to see what's going on. The café has definitely changed hands since I was last here. Back then deep fat fryers cooked most things on the menu and a film of grease covered everything, while condensation ran down the windows, and black mould grew on the bottom sill from the constant damp. Now it has undergone something of a makeover as it looks like someone has tried to refurbish it into some trendy shabby chic coffee shop. The Formica tables and plastic chairs have gone and in their place are round wooden tables and stick-back chairs. Sadly, for the new owners at least, they didn't study their audience closely enough because the clientele hasn't changed to suit the surroundings. I'm the only woman in here and I'm sure that it wasn't the intention of those spending out on the makeover, and who probably had quaint ideas of dainty afternoon teas and delicate pastries, to be serving an all-day, belly-busting breakfast for less than a fiver. But when you've got bills to pay you adapt or die. At least they are still in business but the tomato shaped sauce bottles sit incongruously against the chintzy tablecloths.

I watch the comings and goings at the pub for a couple of hours while I drink coffee and buy food I don't need to justify my presence. I see Don come out to oversee a beer delivery which reassures me of one thing being the same. I wonder if Maureen is another constant, and still running the girls.

I'm bothered a couple of times by other customers wanting to come and join me at my table. I glare at them as I say, no, I don't want any company. One had the audacity to simply sit down, but soon got back up again.

My thoughts wander as I wait and ponder what Dan might be up to. It's going to be an intensely boring time for him, sitting in his hotel room monitoring where I am all the time. I have no big plans to be anywhere but here for the day. It's only if Craig has moved his base, which he might have done having ousted Tag from top spot, that I can see myself going anywhere else. But realistically, with all the benefits they no doubt still get working alongside Don and Maureen what are the chances of that happening?

I watch for two hours before someone I recognise arrives. At least I think I recognise him. Lee was probably about twelve when I last saw him and four years can see an awful lot of change at that age but he'd broken his leg as a child, it hadn't healed straight and, ever since, he'd walked with a limp. This is what I recognise and it saddens me that he is still involved in this life; he was a nice kid. I wonder how many others hadn't managed to break away and do something better with their lives.

There are various other comings and goings but no one else I can identify. That doesn't mean to say no one I know isn't already inside as there is a back entrance, one that's not for the public.

When I feel I can't put off my approach any longer I get up. After using the café's facilities, and managing to do so without touching any surface within them with bare skin, I cross the road. Nerves tighten my stomach and make me regret the vast amount I ate earlier as I push open the swing door to the public bar and walk in. I feel the slight tackiness of the tiled floor as soon as I go to take another step, my foot peeling away like tape from a roll. Another thing unchanged, as there had always been a consistent inability for whoever cleaned this place to do so successfully. Once inside the space feels small, the low ceiling simultaneously managing to make it both homely and claustrophobic as the windows inefficiently let in light through smoke-paned glass. The many lamps lighting the bar and mounted around the room are essential as it already feels like night is coming.

There are a few customers scattered at the bar or around the tables. I know I'm attracting curious glances but ignore those and walk straight up to the bar, behind which is Maureen, who looks more raddled than ever. A grey tangle of messy hair is piled haphazardly on her head. Thickly applied black eyeliner and lumpy mascara has already smudged while her trademark blood red lipstick bleeds into the lines around her mouth.

She screws up her eyes as she peers at me, then says, "Hey, ain't you Tag's gal?"

"I was, a long time ago. Hello, Maureen."

Her face breaks into a grin then she cackles, loosening the phlegm in her lungs which she clears with a hacking cough before she says, "My, ain't we all prim and proper."

I glance around, look at a room that has stagnated with time and, ignoring her comment, say, "Everything still seems to be the same here."

"Yeah, not much changes. What can I get yer?"

"Half a cider please." As she pours she reminisces in a way I wish she wouldn't, and as if I was only in here yesterday.

"Ah, I remember you an' me talkin' 'bout you 'elping me out upstairs." I take a swift gulp of my drink when she hands it to me. She turns away to the till with my money and adds, "'s not too late, yer know." You've got to give her credit for never missing an opportunity but I couldn't believe I'd seriously considered her offer once upon a time. Such were my aspirations in life.

"No, you're all right, Maureen. I've got a job." In an attempt to change the subject, I say, "How's the not smoking going?" When I was last here Maureen was forever trying to kick the habit, not because she wanted to but because she was so often in here and when the ban came in she found it tricky being a chain smoker when she could rarely get outside. She'd tried gum and patches, lozenges and sprays. She even went so far as hypnotherapy but came back proclaiming it to be a load of bollocks.

"I'm all into them e-cigarettes now," she says, and produces a vaping machine from under the bar, immediately putting it to her lips for a quick draw, a cloud of vapour filling the space in front of her face, "but it's a right fecking ball ache, I can tell yer." When the haze clears she squints across at me as if only then remembering I've returned. "What you 'ere for anyway?"

"I was in the area, thought I'd see who was about."

"Oh yeah." Suspicion is etched in each syllable. "Yer know Tag's not around no more, don'tcha?"

"Yes, I did hear that. Craig took over, did he?" She nods, then gesticulates with her head to the door that's standing open over the far side of the room. 'Snug' was printed in gold lettering above it. I nod to Maureen then pick up my glass, feel her watching me as I cross the room. I take a deep breath, letting it out slowly as I get to the door, and it's then that I spot Lee. He's waiting just the other side, on door duty, a promotion from the petty thievery he was involved in when I last met him. I down the contents of my glass and leave it on the nearest table before I take another step into the doorway. Lee raises a hand to stop me before looking at my face. When he does there's a double take, a recognition, then a slow smile. I think it's about the best welcome I can expect today. When I left, Lee was on the brink of becoming a teenager, and was a scrawny, scruffy kid used to dodging his stepdad's fists, and not always successfully. He'd been considerably shorter than me then. Now, I had to look up to meet his shifty eyes, the blinking a reminder he was constantly on edge.

"Scarle'?" he says, as though he's not quite sure it is me.

"Hi, Lee."

"Can't believe you remembered me name." I smile at him.

"I can't believe you're still here." I hope my disappointment is clear.

"Who's there?" comes loud and clear from behind him before he has a chance to answer. Lee widens his eyes at me then stands to one side revealing Craig only a few feet away. "Well, well, well. Look what's walked in." And then he smiles.

The problem with Craig is that he doesn't look like your average villain. What you want in a bad guy is for him to at least have the decency to look the part. He should have a beaten up face, a few scars, or at least a chip on his shoulder big enough for the bitterness to reveal itself in his features as the years pass. By contrast, Craig is handsome enough that he could have graced the pages of any glossy magazine, should he have wanted to. However, he didn't, and I see still doesn't, make the most of that, his weakness being his fashion sense, or rather lack of it. He's bigger than he was when I last saw him, considerably so, and less likely than ever to take any exercise yet he's clad in his signature uniform, a tracksuit, black, and could honestly have done with a larger size as it strains against the fleshy cargo inside. Spotless white trainers adorn feet that have never run a stride in their life. It's all labels and bling with Craig. He's all about the image, but lacks any sense of taste or style. Manicured hair is shaved up the sides, slicked back on top. A large, too large to be real, diamond stud in his ear. Rings adorn thick fingers like knuckledusters. He nods to Lee, who asks me to raise my arms. With a whispered apology he pats me down then stands back when he's sure I'm clear of weapons.

Craig holds my gaze for a moment or two, then he comes close, far too close, and reaches out to undo the top button on my shirt. I maintain eye contact as without a word he proceeds to undo them all until my shirt falls open and he can see I'm not wearing a wire. Even then he spins me round so he can check my back. Satisfied at last, he stands back.

"What d' you want?" is his less than welcoming first question.

"To buy you a drink," I say, as I make myself decent again.

"You've come all the way out of hidin' to buy me a drink?" He stands back and with a sweeping gesture with one arm directs me towards the bar. I hate taking the next step, it takes me out of the safe zone, out of the place where I could still turn and run, and directly into the centre of the wolf's lair, but I take it anyway, I have to, my legs strangely jellylike beneath me. I'm glad Craig can't feel the way my heart pounds in my chest or the rush of heat that follows, and I make sure my face gives away none of my fear.

The snug is essentially a dead end. There is no door out onto the street, no easy means of escape. Planned this way to deter the unwary from stumbling into what Craig would most likely call his 'office'; customers were not welcome in here.

I knew that there was in fact an escape, a back route out of the pub via the bar, because otherwise capture would be far too easy, should there ever be a raid. However, that involved negotiating the bar, which would, without doubt, have one of Craig's boys behind it. Should I attempt to exit that way, I wouldn't get far.

I know I'm walking right into a trap if this doesn't go well, each heartbeat telling me to run, but I have no other option. I ask Craig what he wants. Vodka, he tells me, neat. I order another half of cider and check round to see if there is anyone else I should get one in for. Other than Lee, who I doubt would be allowed to drink while on duty, there are only a couple of others present, neither of whom I recognise, but both are sitting at a table with a drink in front of them already.

"Go an' sit down," Craig says, indicating to the corner with his head. We sit, a low table between us. He stares at me for a long moment.

"Yer know Tag's locked up, don't yer?" he

says, as if he's only just realised my previous connection with this place. I nod.

"Yes, I heard he was."

"Devastated, he was, you know, when you left."

"I'm sure." I don't want to get into a relationship discussion with Craig, and it seems he doesn't either as he moves on easily.

"How did you know?"

"Know what?"

"That 'e was in prison." I hear the mistrust in Craig's voice, deep suspicion at my reappearance.

"I've kept my ear to the ground." I hope he doesn't pry any deeper as I have little more I can come up with if we keep going in this direction.

"So you'll know 'e was released a while ago then?"

"No, I did not know that," I say, as I feign surprise, "Where is he then?" and I glance round as though expecting him to pop up out of the woodwork at any moment.

"Back inside." He sits back in his chair as he gazes at me, "No idea what 'e did to be put away again, no one can get to 'im at the moment." I'm relieved to hear James has managed to keep Tag safely locked away in solitary as I'd asked.

"And do you want to get to him?" Realising my voice sounds accusatory, I take a breath and let it out slowly to relax.

His eyebrows rise, I assume at the tone. "No. 'e came sniffing round 'ere when 'e was released. But I told him, this is business, things change," and he spreads his arms wide as if there was nothing he could have done about it. Despite everything Tag has done there's a flare of anger deep in the pit of my stomach. Craig was meant to be his friend, his best friend. I make a noncommittal noise, then change the subject.

"How is business?"

"Good, what about you? Still in the game?"

I shrug. "Sort of. We move on as time passes, don't we? I'm into higher level stuff now. As I'm sure you are." I know damn well he's not, I can tell that already, that lack of ambition, the least effort for the most reward, that's Craig and I see him shift uncomfortably in his seat. "It's why I'm here. I need some help." At that he leans forward, his interest piqued. Before I say anything further he tells the guy behind the bar to bring more drinks and I switch to bourbon.

"I knew this weren't no social call. 'ow can I be of assistance?" His voice is rough like the jagged edges of the rocks in my glass.

"I need someone who can get into a safe for me."

"That ain't difficult, can't yer find someone to blow a safe yourself?"

"No, because I don't want someone to blow a safe. I need someone with some skill. The safe has to stay in situ, and look like it's never been touched. I want someone who can open the door." He asks me for the details and goes quiet as he thinks for a short time.

"I might know of someone, but it'll cost yer."

"That's the other thing. I don't have any

money." He fixes me with a stare like a hungry fox would give a chicken in a run.

"So what the fuck's in it for me?"

"I have a job in the offing I think would be of interest to you. It's too big for one person so I'm willing to share." He stares at me again as if weighing me up, as if deciding whether or not to trust me. But he knows me, and while he might not like me, he knows I'm good at what I do. That, I believe, is the decider. I wouldn't have come here with nothing decent to offer.

"Okay, I'll 'elp you out and you can owe me a favour. We'll come back to that. When do you need the safe doing?"

"Saturday night."

"Fuckin' 'ell, Scarle'. Yer don't leave a lot of time, do yer?" Exasperated he gets up, "I need to make a couple a calls."

He disappears through the hatch in the bar and presumably out of the back door. While he's gone I look around. The snug has been done up since I left but not recently. The paint job meant to freshen it already shows signs of wear, scuff marks and worn edges betray the passage of people. A leather corner sofa is new, to me at least. The bar is smaller than the main one next door and as I look at it I remember the many times I'd seen it before with Tag leaning up against it holding court, laughing and geeing everyone up. Craig, never far away, watching, serious. The atmosphere feels different now to what I remember. Stark, less welcoming. But that might be because there are so few people in here. I catch those that are sneaking crafty glances across at me, wondering who I am.

Craig is soon back and, after stopping to have a quiet word with the guy behind the bar, joins me again, dropping down onto the seat the other side of my low table. I'm not that comfortable. I'm sitting on a stool and have to force myself to sit up straight and stretch my back out. Before Craig has the chance to say anything I ask if he wants another drink.

"Sure," he says, then follows me back up to the bar. I feel better once I'm standing and on the move again. "I've got someone for yer," he adds once I've put my order in.

"Great. When do I get to meet them?" I'm surprised as I was expecting more friction. But perhaps my reappearance has intrigued Craig enough for him to take the chance.

"Tomorrow, at six, 'ere. We'll sort ou' the details then."

"Done, and thank you." Craig then does something I've always found disgusting, even when Tag did it. He spits on his hand and holds it out to me. I'm meant to do the same, I know that, and I do it, but after we shake on the deal it's all I can do not to wipe my hand down my jeans.

"I'll add something else," Craig then says, "this introduction is out of the goodness of my 'eart and just because I'm makin' it, it don't mean I trust you. In fact I don't. You 'aven't shown me what you've got for me yet and if you fuck me over on this and fuckin' disappear I will track you down, Scarle', and you'll regret it." He says this as if we were simply having a pleasant chat at the bar like two old friends delighted to have renewed their acquaintance. Yet the menace in his tone is unmistakable, I feel its chill down my spine and I'm glad I'm not planning to disappear on him, although perhaps one day he'll wish that I had.

"Don't worry, Craig. I'm going nowhere until I see this through." He lifts his chin in acknowledgement but still eyes me with reservation then turns to deal with someone who's wanting his attention.

The snug is filling up and it's no longer a male dominated environment which I'm pleased about, but while I want to leave now my business is complete, that is clearly not what's expected of me as Craig orders more drinks. I take mine and move along the bar to keep out of the way. He greets a couple of big blokes that arrive, bigger than him, and after getting drinks they take up their positions each side of the unused fireplace. They don't talk, they watch. Others keep arriving, some, I notice, slipping Craig wads of cash in the process, and one, lanky, his arm in a sling, does the same. Stands there, nervous. Craig looks at the notes in his hand, then back at the man in front of him. Lifts the bundle up to his face.

"What the fuck is this?" His target swallows, struggles to make eye contact.

The room goes quiet, all eyes on the action.

"It's all I could manage," he gesticulates towards his arm, ends feebly, "hospital." Craig beckons over the heavies by the fireplace with nothing more than a gesture of his head. They stand behind their prey who shrinks in their presence.

"Please, Craig. I'll do b.. b.. better this week." His plea goes unheeded.

"Liven 'im up, boys. But don't break 'is other arm, I don't want 'im any more fuckin' useless than 'e is already." He gets taken through the bar, and Craig glances over at me, checking out my reaction. The buzz of conversation starts up around me and I play it cool but hate what just happened, thankful when the heavies are back soon, their victim's punishment mercifully short.

That's changed. Craig's a bully, ruling by fear and doesn't even do his own dirty work; at least when Tag had an issue he'd deal with it himself.

I've obviously passed some sort of test because he calls me over and starts introducing me around. He tells everyone who I was to the gang and seems pleased with the connection, although, as expected, I feel the reaction to my being here is lukewarm. Some I know, and I'm not sure if it's my imagination but I'm not exactly greeted with enthusiasm which I guess, given the way I left, is hardly surprising; most I don't and then I'm generally treated with indifference, or perhaps it's suspicion.

A couple of young women come in and keep their distance, hanging by the door with drinks they bought through from the main bar. I wouldn't have taken a great deal of notice except one of them, her hair pulled back severely, keeps glancing over at us and I recognise that look. She and her friend whisper to each other and I pity her for her interest in Craig and sense her hostility towards me. Once upon a time, and if I'm being honest with myself, probably not that long ago, I'd have seen that as a challenge. My opportunity to assert my superiority as a woman. A chance to show that I could have any man I wanted by taking Craig out from under her just because I could. I'm glad I've become more self-aware and moved on, and I'm also delighted that I have Dan back. Properly back. I smile as I allow myself to briefly recall the delights of the previous night, then I reluctantly force myself back to the reality of now. She looks over again and I meet her eye; if I thought she'd listen I'd have a word, tell her he's not worth it, but I know it would be wasted.

Craig is telling some story from Tag's time when a lad arrives, no more than ten, skinny inside his scruffy clothes, I see him cast a beady eye at me and frown before disappearing into the crowd. He re-emerges at the end of the story, when all are laughing just as they should, and he jerks his head at Craig, takes him to one side and has a quiet word. He's only a kid, but one I notice Craig takes seriously, tilting his head to listen, and there's something, something about the way the lad's eyes flicker in my direction as he talks close to Craig's ear that unsettles me.

I've had more than enough to drink and slow right down, though I notice Craig doesn't. He's getting lairy with those he considers are mates and I try to step back a little and lean up against the bar, wondering if I can manoeuver my way out quietly. Unfortunately, he comes to join me, crossing his arms over his stomach, and we take a few moments and watch the actions of those in the room in front of us. One minute there is a gap between us, the next there isn't and I can feel his body in all the places it touches mine. I move ever so slightly to the side to open up the gap again. Moments later he's closed it. *Uh oh.*

I make an excuse, say I have to go to the ladies and once I'm out of the snug I head straight for the front door and leave. The cold air hits my face with its wintery blast and has the dual effect of initially sobering me with the shock then, as the fresh air takes effect, I feel my cheeks warm from the alcohol and realise I'm even more drunk than I'd like to be. It's not that late, just after eleven, but I've been drinking for hours and I'd prefer not to be where I am, when it's dark, I'm on the wrong side of merry, and alone. I start walking and force myself not to look behind. If Craig realised I was leaving, and I'm sure he did, there's every chance I'm being followed and that's okay. It's what I'd expect, because he'll want to know where I'm staying, however I want to look like I'm cool with it and I've nothing to hide.

The streets are still busy in places, less so in others, both have their dangers and as expected I have an itchy feeling like someone has eyes on my back. I'm passing under a railway bridge, the tarmac glossy under the streetlights from earlier rain, when a van skids to a stop next to me. Surprised, I glance over, the side door slides open, a bloke leaps out and, too late, I look for my escape as a bag is pulled over my head, my arms pinned to my sides and I'm lifted, another grabbing my legs before I'm hurled into the van.

I hit the other side wall head first, the thud causing my head to spin. I struggle to orientate myself, the van already moving, my arms pulled roughly behind my back and held tight, I feel the ratchet of a cable tie and lie still, helpless.

My heartbeat is through the roof and breathing shallow, but I quell my panic and force myself to calm, to take in what I can. The bag over my head smells musty, the cloth coarse like sacking on my skin. I think through what I know. I saw the van was white, no name, no artwork. As far as I can tell the inside is bare, the feel of cold metal through my jeans. My forehead thumps from where I landed. Due to the noise of the engine I hear nothing of those in here with me but I assume there are two of them. I also assume they are Craig's men. To what end? I don't know, but the vision of that lad muttering in Craig's ear comes to mind.

I feel every moment of the journey, my body at the mercy of the driver who swings wildly round corners and brakes fiercely. I move in tune with that heavy right foot of his, sliding through bends and shunting forward, my head eventually pressed up hard against the front wall. Fortunately, it's a short trip ending when we mount a kerb and come to an abrupt stop, the engine finally silent.

Relief that the vomit-inducing journey is over has barely registered before I hear the door roll open again, there's a blast of cold air, then hands take hold of my upper arms and I'm first slid across the floor then lifted out of the van and placed on my own two feet. I sway for a moment, giddy, then my head clears. I feel my phone being taken from my back jeans pocket.

Hands, which don't let go for a minute, push me into moving and I'm only taken a short distance before I realise I'm inside a building. I see light through the sacking, it's warmer than before and I'm shuffled into a room, a chair jammed into the back of my legs that the hands on my shoulders force me to sit on. Silence falls, then I hear the faint cry of a baby.

Not one word has been spoken since I was snatched and I sit and try to keep calm as I await what comes next. Part of the sacking is stuck to my face, I assume by blood, my eyebrow itchy and, unable to scratch it, I try to distract myself by wondering what Dan's doing, where his thoughts are. If he's realised what's happened and if so, if he's doing as he was told.

Under. No. Circumstances.

This is what I was anticipating when I gave that instruction. I hope his mind's focused now, I hope he remembers what I told him, because one wrong move and the whole plan is bolloxed.

I try not to consider what's going to happen to me, nausea already rising as fear roils the contents of my stomach. My head pounds. Too much alcohol, too little food. I could puke at any moment.

I decide to get things moving.

"Take this bag off, it stinks." There's a rustling nearby, I sense someone moving closer and the bag shifts as a hand grabs it, along with some hair which is pulled as the bag's removed causing me to yelp. The sacking tears away from the wound like Velcro, opening it up again, and I flinch then blink against the exposure to light.

Directly in front of me is one of the heavies, the bag in his hand.

"Ah, I thought it was you. I could smell your breath even inside that stinky sack," I smile, getting a slap across my face for my trouble, open palm, taste blood, my lip split all over again. My head spins and I shake it to try and focus.

Undaunted, I look round, search the room. "Where's your mate?" I spot him, over my shoulder, "Yup, there he is, fat boy."

"Shut the fuck up." I look up at my assailant, feeling a trickle of blood run from my eyebrow across the lid. My blink is sticky and wet. I hear a baby cry again and it's closer now. I look round the room. It's someone's sitting room. Colour scheme: angry red with accents of black. Too stark for my liking, cheap enough for Craig's. Black leather sofas to each side of me, leopard skin throws adding a feminine touch of trash.

I hear a baby again, look over at the door as it opens. Craig is at the entrance but turned away, his attention on those behind. A young girl, jigging to and fro, a baby held up to her shoulder, which she pats on its back. *Is Craig a family man now?* She barely looks of age, glances past him and gazes at me with curiosity but no surprise.

Craig's head turns towards me and I give him a lopsided grin.

"Don't think much of your hospitality, Craig."
It helps me, being cocky. That touch of bravado,
that putting on a front like I'm totally confident
and absolutely not about to throw up with nerves.
It steels me, and if it winds up my captors at the
same time then all the better. Plus, he knows I'm
tough and won't expect to find me a quivering
wreck.

He strides into the room and slams the door
loudly behind him, the baby's cries intensifying, a
flash of irritation crossing his face.

He's carrying something. A tool. My insides
clench as he places it gently on the mantelpiece
and turns to me, his eyes as black and dead as a
shark's.

"My boys been looking after yer, have they?"

"If they were meant to be they've done a shit
job." I keep my eyes on him. He grabs another
chair like the one I'm on and plants it in front of
me then sits. With my arms tied behind my back
and making my shoulders ache, I can't sit comfort-
ably and have to lean forward, which means bringing my head up to look at him. He doesn't appear
to care about the state of my face.

"Has something changed, Craig? Because I
thought we were getting on much better earlier."

His reply chills my blood.

"You were spotted. Last night."

"Oh? Who by?" I struggle to keep my voice
level.

"None of yer business." I try another tack.

"Why does it matter where I was last night anyway?

"I'm told you weren't alone." My worst fear realised.

"You were told wrong." The back of his hand connects with my cheek, teeth rattling, all those rings. Pain resonates and I blink away stars.

"Don't fuck with me." I flex my jaw, check it's still connected, bring my head up again, and fix him with a glare.

Can't do his own dirty work but doesn't mind hitting a girl. Says it all.

He leans in, his voice low and rough, "Who was 'e?"

"No idea what you're talking about." His hand connects again. I grunt. Hang my head as I wait for the pain to subside. Control my breathing. Tentatively check my teeth with my tongue. Wonder how far he's willing to go. I raise my head, silently telling him to bring it on.

He stands abruptly, wheels around and reaches to the mantelpiece, and the tool he placed there.

Bolt cutters. Small, but quite capable of inflicting significant damage.

My insides liquefy. Seems he's willing to go further than I was hoping.

He holds the handle in one hand, slams the head into the palm of the other, and feels its weight. Makes sure I'm watching. Then walks slowly around me until he's standing behind.

A pair of hands pin me by the shoulders into the seat. Fingers digging into flesh.

I clench my hands into fists burying my thumbs inside my fingers.

He grabs one hand and I try to wriggle it away

but he's too strong and holds it tight. He prises open my little finger. I gasp, a moan escaping as cold steel touches the skin. I feel the bite of the blades, the pinch as they tighten, and panicking I struggle to pull my hand away again. It's no use, I'm trapped and breathing heavily when he leans close to my ear.

"Last chance. Who was 'e?"

"No one." The blades tighten, there's the sting of blood drawn. I speak in a rush.

"A casual. That's all. A casual. A girl gets lonely." The pressure releases, slightly.

"My source says he recognised him." I'm keen to explain, keen to get my fingers back.

"There you go then. He must be local, I picked him up, shagged him and let him go again. That's it."

"That's it?" He releases my hand, I let out a shaky breath and he takes the seat in front of me again. Bolt cutters in hand.

I'm not going to repeat myself so remain silent and meet his eyes when he's back on a level with me. That was close but I've survived intact and that gives me strength.

"What's his name?"

"Don't know."

"You often fuck blokes you don't know the name of?"

"As often as I get the chance to." There's that look again, that stare, like he's trying to psych me out. It won't work, I learned all I know from the best and Craig is a poor imitation.

"I'm only going to say this once, Scarle'. I

didn't chase that useless fuckin' ex of yours away with his tail between his legs for you to turn up and think you can get one over on me. I'm gonna be keepin' an eye on you. Yer hear? An' if I find out you're pulling a fast one you'll be wishing I'd finished yer t'night." I nod, not going to dignify that with any other response, I'm not an amateur, and it's only what I'd expect from him, though this comment about Tag fuels the fire. I feel it flicker, ignite and start to burn. Tag may be history but he was my history and I'm protective about that, as Craig is going to find out.

Because until now, until this precise moment, I was doing James' bidding. But that's all changed tonight. Now it's personal. Now it's vengeance, and I'm going to love seeking it. Bringing down the one who took Tag's place and ostracised him my pleasure.

My fear is gone, blown away by the anger, my voice quiet, every syllable crystal. "Let me go." I give him the stare back; he holds it for a long moment and I can see I've pissed him right off. He's not used to this, this lack of fear in his presence, and I wonder if I've gone too far. He leans in, wraps his meaty hand around my jaw, which protests mightily, and pulls me closer.

"Might still do you tonight. You fuckin' irritate me." Yup, I have gone too far. But I can't stop now, he needs me and I have to remind him of that.

"You do that, you never get the pot of gold I have for you. Now let me go." He hesitates then does so, flinging me back in my chair in frustration, then stands. Speaks to the heavies.

"Take 'er back." He points to me, "You've used up yer only lifeline. I'll see you tomorrow."

"Looking forward to it already." He walks out without a second glance.

I stand, indicate to my tied hands, clenching my fists to force them to stop shaking. "You can cut this before you do anything else." I see the pair of them look at each other like they're not sure they should be doing that. "Just do it," I snap, and hold my hands away from my body. The larger of the two steps forward, pulls out a knife and slices through the cable, the relief instantaneous as I bring my hands in front, roll my shoulders and rub wrists already chafed by the tie. My little finger is bloody, the cut stinging. "Shall we go?" I say, taking the lead and heading for the door. They follow and I'm pleased to see the van still outside. I consider getting in the front but don't want to push my luck or, more importantly, be seen associating with any members of Craig's gang.

One of the heavies slides open the side door and both look as reluctant as I am to be getting back in the vomit-mobile. I hang on to the fact it wasn't a long journey and at least this time I'll be sitting upright.

A few minutes later we're bumping back up on a kerb again, the door slides open and I'm told to get out. The nearest of my travelling companions is unable to stop himself from giving me a hefty push out of the door which leaves me scrambling to keep my footing but I don't retaliate. My phone spins out after me hitting the pavement with a clatter, and I bend to retrieve it, amazed to see the screen's still intact. The van sets off again and I stand for a moment, relieved to feel cold air on my skin and to be alone. I pull my hair around my face as best I can, pull up my collar and head for the hotel entrance a short distance away. I note Craig's source had furnished him with where I was staying too.

I'm relieved to eventually step into the lobby and feel safe. The staff on reception are busy and no one so much as glances in my direction. I make my way to my room, to my bathroom, and throw up. Dry heaving once my stomach is empty and feeling much better for having done so. Shaking I sit on the bed, sip water, call Dan.

"What the fuck happened? Are you okay?" There's fear in his voice, and relief. "God, Maddy. I thought I'd lost you."

"I got taken, now I'm back, it's all fine." I play it down, no point doing otherwise and making him feel worse when he can't do anything about it.

"Did they hurt you?"

"Not much," I say, and I reach to feel the lump on my forehead rough with dried blood, the sticky mess around my eye. "Well done for not intervening." My smile is truncated by the damage to my lip as I hear his frustration on his exhaled breath.

"It was tough not to. I could see exactly where you were."

"That's useful, but you did the right thing," I reassure him.

"What did they want?"

"That's what we need to talk about. You were spotted with me the previous night. Someone told

Craig.”

“Who? Bet and Vince?” I shake my head, even though he can’t see that.

“Nah, they wouldn’t. Whoever it was said they’d seen you before. Any ideas?” I don’t want to bring it up but then can’t help but have a dig, “Someone from when you came down on your spying mission perhaps?” There’s an uncomfortable silence. “Well?”

“There was a boy, he wanted money to watch the car, sorry, I didn’t know.” That fits with the lad in the bar, I think.

“How could you know? How much did he fleece you for?”

“We agreed on a fiver but when I went back I gave him ten…” His voice tails off.

“And?” I have a feeling there’s more.

“And, a portion of fish and chips.”

“Thereby cementing you in his memory. Good one, Dan.” He sighs.

No good deed goes unpunished.

“What did you tell them?”

“That you were a one-night thing I spat out for breakfast.”

“Nice.”

“It seems to have done the trick, but you are going to have to stay completely hidden. If they see you again that’ll be it.”

“Understood.” I’m calmer now, my stomach settled. I’m keen to get to sleep but need to debrief first.

“How did the rest of your day go? It must have been quite boring for you.”

"It's not been the most exciting, until the end, and it was bloody freezing."

"You've been out?"

"Of course." He sounds like he's surprised I didn't know that. "How else would I have seen you get taken?"

"What? Wait. You saw that? In person?" I didn't realise he'd decided that was part of his role, and maybe I should have paid better attention to what he was planning. I'd assumed he'd track my movements from the comfort of his hotel room and leave it at that.

"Of course, I could see you'd been drinking," he continues, and I hope that's not admonishment I can feel coming across the ether.

"I couldn't help that, I needed to fit in."

"Of course, I was following you back here when I saw them take you. It happened so quickly."

"You could have blown the whole thing. What if Craig had sent someone after me? They'd have spotted you immediately." I'm alarmed by his actions which could have meant the whole day's efforts would have been wasted, and more importantly I shudder to think what Craig would have done to him should he have been captured.

"I didn't come down in the last shower, Maddy. You were followed. I followed them. Then the van arrived and the one following you on foot disappeared." He pauses for a moment, before saying, "you seem surprised by the lengths I've gone to today. You didn't just expect me to sit here watching a screen, did you? That's not proactive surveillance."

"I'm not sure what I expected. You've had so many holiday jobs, how would I know which ones you're proficient at." I think I have a point.

I hear him chuckle, "Get some sleep, Maddy." I need to, I know, it's the early hours and I'm shattered, but I have to shower first and get my face cleaned up and my finger. We say goodnight and I fish my first aid kit and Diane's potions out of my bag, thankful I had the foresight to bring them.

As I shower, washing the blood from my face and finger, I try not to think back to Dan's question on the way down here. The one he'd raised when I'd told him he was not to intervene, only observe. 'How long do I leave it until I do take some action then?' he'd asked. 'Two days, I'd told him. Two days. If I'm not back by then I'm not going to be coming back'. I shiver under the hot water, grateful to have survived so far.

Chapter 15

I will track you down Scarle', and you'll regret it, haunts my night, and wild unconnected dreams leave me ragged and exhausted by dawn. My head aches when I get up to drink more water and I take a couple of painkillers before lying back down again. Eventually I drift back into a more comfortable sleep and am woken hours later by the phone.

"I thought I'd better make sure you're okay. It's lunchtime," Dan says, and I hear concern in his voice. My headache has gone now and, thankful I'd had the foresight to hang the 'Do Not Disturb' sign on the door, I'm feeling better than earlier so assure him I will order some room service and pull myself together.

I look in the mirror and am startled. The skin on my forehead split when I hit the side of the van last night, hence the blood, so I'd cleaned it up when I got back and held the edges together with butterfly sutures. This has closed up nicely but the lump formed under it is prominent and purple. There's also a row of decorative bruises depicting Craig's rings down my cheek that I can do little about, and the ache under them is constant and made worse by movement. My lip, however, has already reduced in size due to Diane's magic, the mere thought of her sends a pang of homesickness through me. I peel the dressing off my finger now blackened with bruising, the edges of cut flesh proud and angry. I clean it again, coating it in antiseptic cream before redressing.

I order food and as I wait for its arrival, shower, and think through the events of the previous day. I thought it had gone well, right up until I left the pub anyway. I didn't appreciate Craig's threats, or the way he started cosying up to me by the end of the evening but maybe that had just been the drink. We'd never been friends before so it was unlikely he'd start trying to be so now, particularly when he'd made it crystal later on he didn't trust me.

I pull some clothes on just in time before a knock on the door announces my food is here.

Half an hour later I'm feeling considerably happier in body and soul than I was when I woke and, as long as I don't have to run anywhere for a while, I think I'll be fine. I rehang the 'Do not Disturb' sign on the door and call Dan. I've decided to stay in my room until it's time to go back to The Pike and Eel this evening. It's the safest place, but I most definitely need to keep away from him because we have no idea who might have been watching me since last night or who may have contacts with anyone on the staff in the hotel. It's time to be professional, besides we intend on being back in Crowthorne tomorrow and can surely wait until then to be together. Easier said than done. The hours crawl past. I doze, I watch rubbish TV, I read, I order room service, again. I ring Chris for a chat and realise a week has passed since that night in the pub with him and Dan. It feels like forever. I miss my friend and vow to spend some time with him as soon as this is over. I ring Diane to see how she is. She says she's fine and when I ask if there's any news from the village she laughs and says it's Thursday, I've only been away two nights, what news was I expecting in that time. I don't know, I say, it feels longer than that. I speak to Cubby and update him. I reluctantly do the same with James. He asks if I need any help yet and I get the feeling he's hoping I've rung because Dan has cocked up and I'm calling in the professionals. I don't, I say. Dan's doing perfectly well and I'm safe. I don't give him the graphic highlights of what's happened so far, just that everything's on track.

I resist the urge to call Dan again. But I do wonder what he's up to.

Once it's past five o'clock I get ready to go, although it doesn't take long. I don't go to any great lengths to cover the bruises on my face, let others make of them what they will. My finger is throbbing and I dose up on painkillers. I have limited clothes anyway and only brought one pair of jeans and a couple of tops with me, so I put on a fresh one of those and pull my boots back on. After checking in with Dan, I set off in the direction of The Pike and Eel again. I don't make any attempt to check to see if anyone is following me, as from now on I'm going to assume there is always someone watching, and behave accordingly.

Dan and I didn't discuss what he was going to do this evening, and I've left him to get on with his job. He's impressed me so far so I don't want to interfere.

Shortly before six I enter The Pike and Eel. Although I could do with a drop to settle my nerves I decide to put off having anything to drink for as long as possible so other than raising my hand in greeting to Maureen, just before she disappears behind a cloud of vapour, I don't linger but head straight for the snug. Lee is not on the door. Instead there's a beefy guy in a too tight suit, his collar straining around his thick neck, to pat me down before I'm allowed through.

The room is busier than it was at the time I'd arrived yesterday and it takes me a few moments to spot Craig through the crowd. He's sitting in the apex of the corner sofa. I've been concerned about how he was going to be the next time I saw him but unexpectedly, and as though nothing happened after hours last night, his face breaks into a smile when he sees me, and he beckons me through his people and pats the seat next to him. *Not a chance*, I think, and I pull up a chair so I can sit opposite him and with a table in between us.

"Undo your shirt," he says, ignoring my snub. I feel uncomfortable as I start to undo the buttons but try not to show this as although he watches me like the voyeur he is I refuse to be intimidated. He nods when he's satisfied I'm clean, and I quickly refasten my shirt without looking round to see who else was copping a look.

"Yer look a bit the worse for wear," he says, as though he's forgotten he's responsible for the damage.

"Nothing a few days won't heal," I say, like it's no bother, when I'm positively rattling, I've taken that many painkillers.

"What yer been up to today then? A spot of sightseein'?" I despise having to make small talk, and am unsettled by his Jekyll and Hyde changes in character, wondering at his mental stability.

Fortunately, I'm saved from having to reply when Craig is distracted by the arrival of someone behind me who must have entered via the bar. He gesticulates to bring them over and as I turn, a whiskery faced man pulls up a chair next to mine. He's hunched over, and scruffy, wearing baggy tracksuit trousers and an untucked thick red and black checked shirt, and gives off a whiff of fried onions as he sits. He's constantly twitching, his left leg jitters next to mine and he keeps his head low between raised shoulders, the dirty baseball cap he wears pulled down over his face. Craig introduces him as Cracker. *Seriously?* I think. But I keep a straight face, nod accordingly and hold my hand out to him. He doesn't look directly at me at all, seems surprised to see me reach out a hand and has to withdraw his from the depths of his pocket. When his hand meets mine it's hot and damp, and I rather wish I hadn't bothered. I turn in my chair to face him so we can run through the plans for Saturday night although I'm feeling far less confident with Craig's recommendation than I had been prior to this meeting. Cracker comes across as a mess.

"So, Cracker," I say, somewhat unenthusiastically, "has Craig told you what I want?"

"Yup." He continues to stare stoically ahead and I find it impossible to get a gauge on this man who won't even meet my eyes. I lean slightly forward to try to get in his line of vision. And then I see it.

As his head turns slightly towards me it reveals the other side of his face, the side that has at some point suffered a terrible injury. The skin pitted and rucked, deformed by scars that, like twisted ropes, distort his mouth and eye socket, his eyeball a pale blue and I wonder if he can see out of it at all. His hair is unkempt and I realise now he's grown it out so as to cover as much of his face as possible, likewise his scrappy beard. It's decidedly patchy on the damaged side of his face but I guess he feels it's better having it covering what it can. I don't blink, not wanting to look like it's even a thing. But there is an immediate issue. Cracker here is unlikely to go unnoticed, anywhere. If someone sees him he is easy to remember, and describe. You can imagine the question. Any distinguishing features? Well, yes, where do I start?

Craig has left it a minute, let the full effect of Cracker's ruined face sink in on me. Then he says, "Cracker don't blow safes no more, do yer, Cracker?"

Cracker shakes his head.

"Not since 'e got 'is timing wrong, ain't that right, Cracker?"

This is replied to with a nod. He is clearly a man of few words.

Okay, I think, I can see where this is going and I don't want to know anymore. I'd rather just deal with setting up Saturday night.

Ignoring Craig, I say to Cracker, "Can I get you

a drink?" He nods, "A beer?" I suggest and at a further nod I get up and go to the bar. So much for me not drinking, I desperately need something now so get a bourbon as well as the beer and a vodka for Craig too. As I'm waiting it occurs to me that perhaps Craig is setting me up and I don't know what to do about that. Though why would he? Other than to spite me. He wouldn't get a look in at the deal I'm offering if he does, I think, and after convincing myself that Craig would always put a large cash pay-out ahead of any petty revenge, I am reassured. Plus, I also know I'm running out of time to find another solution, if I want to meet my self-imposed deadline, and as I carry the drinks back across to the corner I decide I'm going to have to at least give Cracker the benefit of the doubt.

Fortunately, Craig then leaves us to it, to go and sort out some of his own business, and the noise level around us has built to a point where no one can listen in to what we say. As it is we can barely hear each other and I have to lean in close to conduct our business, the pungent smell coming off him strong enough to make me have to breathe through my mouth. Cracker and I discuss the arrangements for getting into Ben's safe, or rather I put forward how I think it would work and he grunts his approval, or not. He says little other than clarifying a few details of the safe itself and by the time he's finished his beer it seems he's got all the information he needs. He makes a move to go by standing, but before he leaves he leans down again, his mouth right next to my ear, and, as if he read my mind from earlier, he whispers, "It's al-righ', no one'll see me," and there's a glimmer of a smile as he winks with his good eye and then he's gone.

I sit back in my chair for a moment and think through all we discussed. I don't think we missed anything but despite his last words I'm not brimming with confidence.

Craig pops another drink in front of me. "Thanks," I say, "but I think I'll get off."

"Like that, is it?" He frowns at me and takes the seat Cracker recently occupied. "You get what you want from me and then bugger off?"

"After what you did to me last night, yes."

"That was business. I've gotta protect my own."

"Noted. And I've got to do the same." He doesn't react, so I finish, "I'll be back next week, after I've sorted this bit of business out."

"Can I trust you to come back? After all, you ran out on Tag, and you apparently loved him."

"That was personal, Craig. This is business. You can trust me to do what I say. Besides you made your intentions clear last night over what would happen if I didn't and I don't want you hunting me down, now do I?" I finish somewhat theatrically, but I want to make my point, that despite all the lip I had given out I had taken his threat seriously.

He shrugs, then shifts his chair closer, "Why don't yer give me a hint about the bit of business you're offering?" I watch him for a moment, then think it might be worth leaving him with a teaser.

"Okay," I nod, "it's all about art." I watch his face fall.

"Art?" he repeats doubtfully, as if questioning whether he'd heard me right. I'll guarantee he knows just about as much as I do on the subject.

"Yes," I say, in a matter of fact manner. "I've moved on, Craig. It would be ridiculous to still be doing the pick-pocketing and petty thievery we were involved in when we were kids, wouldn't it?" I say this in joking fashion but again there's that flash of discomfort which confirms to me where the bulk of his business still is.

"It would indeed," he agrees, then to clarify, "so we're stealin' some art?"

"Yes. Of course I'm assuming you have the ability to be able to pass that on?" And I watch his chest puff out as his ego rises. There's no way that's going to let him say no.

"Of course," he confirms emphatically. "How much is it worth?"

"Hundreds of thousands of pounds," I say, and his eyes light up. I'm not going to mention that one painting on its own is potentially worth a million. That might just blow his mind.

He signals for more drinks to be brought over. I want to go but he moves his chair even closer and asks me to stay a while.

"Why?" I say, confused, "You don't like me, you made that clear last night." I remember back to our earliest conversation, our ongoing competition for Tag's attention way back when.

"That was when Tag was around, I have nothing against you personally, you were just a distraction he didn't need, that's all."

"You must have been delighted when I left then." He looks sheepish.

"I was. We got back to bein' good friends again." His comment last night about Tag still rankles so I decide to probe that wound again.

"And yet you didn't act like a good friend, did you? You had usurped him by the time he came out of prison, and gave him no place to return to. That wasn't terribly friendly at all, was it?"

"That was just business," he says, and he shrugs and sits back. "What's it to you anyway? You'd already dumped 'im."

"I wanted to get away from the life I was leading, not necessarily from him, he was collateral in my decision." I didn't add that I'd only found out recently that it was him that I'd been running from after all, that would just confuse matters. I smile ruefully at Craig, "I guess neither of us were exactly there for him, were we?"

"No," he says, but he doesn't look as remorseful as I feel about that. He leans in, seems to have moved on. "Anyway, how about you and I get a bit friendlier? I could come and visit you at that hotel of yours." Fear trickles down my spine like a rivulet of water at these words, I don't want him anywhere near me, or my hotel.

He hesitates then reaches across and places his hand on my leg, sliding it far higher than it has any right being, "At least you know my name." His smile is laced with menace and his hand tightens on my leg. I feel a prickle across my scalp as goose bumps rise; there is no ambiguity over what he is after and I can't help but think back to what happened when I'd said no to Tag recently, what that led to, and my pulse quickens. Getting out of this could be difficult but I know I've not given him any encouragement to make him feel he has a chance so it's time to nip whatever this might be about to be in the bud.

"The thing is, Craig, last night you were on the verge of chopping my finger off, and I don't take that kind of treatment lightly. You say all that not liking each other is in the past, but for me it's not." And I remove his hand, placing it firmly back on his lap.

"Oh." He leans back and stares at me, a flash of anger in his eye. "You do know I'm doing you a favour, don't you?"

"Yes, but I can't imagine you would use that fact to leverage any additional 'friendliness', would you? This is business, for which you will be handsomely repaid." I hope I've made myself clear and I'm glad my voice is not portraying the fear I feel for this man. I finish, "Let's not ruin a perfectly fine business relationship, by doing something I'll at least regret, shall we? I must be going." I get up to leave, shrug my jacket on and try to play it cool when I feel anything but.

"You don't know what you're missing." He tries to make this sound casual but every word carries a threatening undertone.

"Tempting, but no," is my light but firm response and it seems this finally puts an end to his ambition and he moves on.

"Make sure yer return then, Scarle'. Don't forget what I said," are his parting words.

"How could I?" I raise my eyebrows at him, eager to leave, "I'll see you next week," and with that I walk away. The relief I feel as I leave the pub is immense and I wonder if the atmosphere had always felt that intense in there or if I was only now noticing it with the fresh eyes I could bring to the situation.

My hands shake as I struggle to do up my zip then I plunge them deep into my jacket pockets as I set off to get back to the hotel as quickly as I can. I scuttle along, jumping at shadows, feeling panic rising in me as I imagine every passing vehicle is about to stop. I couldn't have cared less if I was followed or not but I did hope Dan was out there somewhere watching over me. Having worked alone for years I've found I like that feeling, of having someone there as if we are partners in something together.

As soon as I get back to my room I open my case and start throwing everything I'd brought with me into it. I'm packed a couple of minutes later. I thought that would have allowed Dan enough time to get back too, so I call him. He'd just walked in through the door he tells me.

"I want to go home," I say.

"Yeah, we will, tomorrow."

"No, not tomorrow. Now. I want to go home now." It feels like a matter of urgency. I want to be in my home, with him, right now and I need to leave.

"Has something else happened?" His tone is

sharp.

"No," I lie, "nothing you need to worry about."

"Okay," he says, his voice guarded, "have you been drinking?" He asks this in a light-hearted fashion but I can hear the frown in his voice like he's trying to work out the reason for my sudden desire to leave.

"Yes, but I've only had a couple, three, at most," I say, having no idea of the exact number.

"You'll be missing out on a hotel breakfast," he teases.

"I don't care; I'll be as fat as a pig if I carry on eating those anyway. Dan, please. I need to get home."

"Okay then, we'll leave the same way as we got here. Only let me get outside first, will you? I want to make sure no one follows you from here." That was something I hadn't considered. I certainly didn't want Craig to find out where I lived. It was going to be bad enough that I'd be taking him to Crowthorne next week anyway, without him knowing that was where my actual home was.

Dan texts me once he's in position, by which time I have checked out and booked another room for the following week. Moments later I leave the hotel and walk off towards the underground. Before I enter Dan texts me the all clear and as I board the first train out of town I breathe a sigh of relief. I know every stage from then on will relax me further as I put more and more distance between me and Craig.

I've become tense over the last couple of days, I can feel it in my neck, my shoulders. It's difficult to believe that once that was where I considered home to be. That I felt comfortable in those streets and in that company. That earlier this week I'd looked forward to returning. It seems my new life has softened me because, despite the front I put on, I'm simply not cut out for it anymore.

I am delighted when I walk out of the station, several stops up the over-ground line and find Dan waiting there, his car warm and a safe haven for me. The grin I'm greeted with drops from his face when he gets his first proper look at mine. "You told me you weren't hurt," he says, anger in his tone. I nod in response.

"There's nothing you could have done about it, and I didn't want to worry you. Just take me home. But could we stop off for some food on the way?" He shakes his head at my insatiable appetite but, sure enough, a little while later he pulls into the services off the motorway, and I'm soon munching on a hot sausage roll content in the knowledge I have a donut waiting for my pudding. Dan has the same although he says it's only to keep me company. I promise myself that I will get back to the gym tomorrow, I need something to work the last few days of gluttony off and I don't believe even my shredded nerves are enough for the job.

I am ridiculously pleased when we drive back into the village, even more so when we turn down towards my cottage and I love feeling every lump and bump in my pot-holey road. We get in, dump our bags and head for bed.

"You're sure you want this," Dan teases as we make our way upstairs. He points back to the sofa.

"I could just as easily stay down here you know, it's very comfortable." I could cuff him for winding me up, and he's going to be disappointed if he's expecting me to beg for his attentions. I turn on the stairs and give him just the slightest sensation of what I have waiting for him and that puts an end to his nonsense.

I wake before Dan the next morning and enjoy spending a few minutes watching him. His tousled hair flops across his forehead and his face is relaxed and at peace; long eyelashes lie soft against his skin and full lips are gently parted as he breathes slow and deep. I don't plan on there being too much that is going to take me away from him, and this bed, today, other than a trip to the gym, and I might even get him to join me there. I have people to update, of course. Plans to check through and set up for tomorrow night and just the thought of that starts my nerves going again. I worry about what I said to Craig last night. Did I take it too far? Maybe I should have been 'friendlier' to him, although even the thought of that makes me shudder and again I'm amazed at the change in me. Only a short time ago, being 'friendly' in order to get what I want wouldn't have bothered me in the slightest. Now it seems a completely alien concept and I look back over at the pillow next to mine as I think this through, surprised all over again at the changes that could be brought by another person.

Dan wakes just as I'm considering getting up and continuing my fretting while making some tea. He reaches across the bed and pulls me towards him, his arms wrapping around me as he puts an end to my plans.

"Morning," I say as I study him.

"Morning," he says, "been awake long?"

"Long enough to wonder how you get your hair like that." I pause for a moment as I consider how much some people would pay to get those blond highlights. "Do you dye it?"

He laughs, "Of course I don't dye it. This is natural. A summer in Provence fruit picking before I started with Cubby is all that's responsible."

"Don't tell me, another holiday job?" His deep-throated chuckle is all the response I need. "How many jobs have you had, Dan?" It occurs to me that perhaps this phase in his life, taking over from Cubby, me, is nothing more than a fleeting thing for him and he'll be moving on before too long, and I'm surprised by how much this thought alarms me.

"I don't know," he says, apparently unaware of the concern this has caused in me. "A few?" he tries though it sounds lame.

"And do you think you've settled down at Watson and Grove?" I ask as casually as I can. He wriggles his body up closer to mine.

"Well I'm feeling settled right now, so yes I would say so," and as his lips find mine I know we're going to have a late start to the day.

Chapter 16

I'm still asleep, due to several hours of middle-of-the-night-worries, when Diane calls me at eight on the Saturday morning. There's no preamble. "Don't you think it's about time I met this man of yours? Bring him round for coffee. I've made brownies."

"Morning, Diane," I manage to croak back, "Will do," though I'm not sure she waited for a response. I turn my head, see a mass of tousled hair on the pillow opposite and reaching out I give him a nudge. "Diane wants to meet you," I say in response to his grunt. "She's made brownies. Don't eat them." That gets his attention and he rolls over towards me.

"Don't eat them? Why?"

"I'll check what's in them first. I ate some once that I'm convinced made me happy for the rest of the day."

"And that's a bad thing?" He grins and reaches out two hands to wrap around my ribcage, giving me a tickle. I giggle, then squeal, because I'm ticklish, ridiculously so. I grapple with his hands to try to push them away but then they still and pull me towards him and I know it's going to be a while before we get to Diane's.

"Is she going to give me the third degree?" he says, as we're walking towards her cottage later. I take his hand and glance over at him; he looks tense.

"Are you nervous?" I ask, somewhat surprised.

"Yes, a bit," he admits.

"She's not my parent," I clarify, in case he thinks I've made her some sort of substitute.

"No, but she's your friend, I want her to like me."

"Aww, that's cute," I tease. "However, in answer to your question, I have no idea whether she'll give you the third degree or not, I've never taken anyone to meet her before."

"Really?" His eyebrows are raised in question as if he doesn't quite believe me and I realise he probably doesn't know that my previous life at the gym was the nearest I got to having any sort of relationship since I moved here. "Then I'm honoured," he finishes, opening her gate for me with something of a flourish.

Cat is waiting on the windowsill when we arrive and I introduce him to Dan as Cat and he says, I can see that. "No, he's not *a* cat," I say, "he's called Cat," but before I get to explain Diane's view that he does not belong to her so he's not hers to name, Diane is at the back door to welcome us. I see her glance at our linked hands and a small smile comes to her lips like this pleases her. Things have moved on. But then she looks properly at me.

"What the hell has happened to you now?" Her welcoming smile is gone as she pulls me towards her and lifts my hair out of the way to better examine me, and I hide my hand and strapped up finger behind my back but she spots that too.

"I got into an altercation," I say and try to introduce Dan to her and while she flashes a smile towards him, distracted by my face, he initially gets cursory attention.

She tuts after unwrapping and checking on my finger, now shades of purple, the cut red raw and weeping, then says firmly, "Maddy, I don't know what it is you're dealing with there but I don't think you should go back to London. It's far too dangerous."

"I have to," I say as I place a hand on her arm to reassure her, "the worst is over. I'll be fine."

She mumbles to herself, clearly unhappy, before announcing she'll make me a special something up and drop it over. Then, as if remembering why we're there, her face brightens.

"Don't just stand there. Come in! Sit down," and she directs us to the chairs as if I'd never been in there before. The plate of brownies lurks in the middle of the table and with a look I flash a warning reminder to Dan not to take one.

Diane chats away as she makes, then brings over the coffees and we catch up on recent news which, given that we only spoke two days ago, doesn't take long. Diane pushes the plate of brownies in our direction, instructing us to help ourselves, and I raise my hand palm first towards her.

"What's in them?"

"Ooh, Maddy, you are suspicious. I know what you thought I'd put in them last time and I can assure you I would never add such a thing," she hesitates, "at least not without letting you know first."

She smiles broadly at us and winks. "No, no, I can assure you anything in my brownies is purely herbal and picked from my own garden."

"Hmm, that's what concerns me," and I try to frown at her but to be honest I'm so relieved to find her in what seems to be a good place that I push aside my misgivings and reach for a brownie. Dan does the same, and makes yummy sounding noises as he eats it. They are delicious, and more-ish, and I think I eat three in total, making the excuse I'd had no breakfast. Dan is encouraged into four by Diane who insists that at his age he can get away with it but if another one passes her lips it'll be on her hips forever.

We touch on the Ben business briefly when I tell her I should have news for her tomorrow, but other than that we have a fun, relaxed time and, as I suspected she would, Diane makes Dan feel right at home, she's skilled at that. There's no need for the third degree because she is far subtler. She makes you feel comfortable, she gets you chatting and the way she talks has you divulging all sorts of things you never intended to bring up. I know this, I've had to watch her in the past. But the important thing is that my great friend and Dan seem to hit it off, and this pleases me.

It's as we're walking home I realise I'm high. Not massively so, but enough to take the edge off, to feel a certain lightness of spirit. I look over at Dan and he meets my gaze.

"Hmm, I see what you mean," he says, his expression somewhat glazed. Then he smiles, "Fancy a massage?"

It's midnight, I'm in the city and while the clubs at the other end of the main street are just getting going, at the end I need to be all is quiet. I park a few streets away in a residential area and make my way towards the centre. I'd decided not to use the multi-storey this time. There was a show on at the nearby theatre earlier but that's long finished and now the car park's virtually empty. Mine would have stuck out like a clown at a wake had I left it there, so I've gone for the more discreet option.

Fortunately, after my afternoon spent entirely in the hands of Dan I'm now completely clear-headed and I jog into the centre which, following my dismal performance at the gym yesterday, won't do me any harm at all. I'm pleased when I finally reach the entrance to the access road and can take to the shadows.

I'd had a horrible thought in the early hours of the previous night that, because I didn't do what Craig wanted and play nice the other day he might have cancelled Cracker. My imagination has been working overtime on this point ever since and to such an extent that, other than the brownies, I've been unable to eat. Although I had to admit that their relaxing qualities were a great help in getting me through the day.

Dan kept reassuring me Craig wouldn't do such a thing and reminded me that he was wanting me to show up to repay the favour next week so what would be in it for him? I was sure he was right but once nerves had taken flight I knew they wouldn't fully dissipate until I saw Cracker. And I'm reminded again why I hate having to rely on someone else.

I pass quickly along the back of the shops until I get to the rear of Pritchards. There's no one else there and I worry anew about Cracker not turning up. However, all my fretting is in vain because I've only just got into position and checked my watch once, when Cracker surprises me, unfolding himself from his hiding place behind a stack of packaging outside the next unit. We greet each other in low voices. Even in the moonlight I can see he's in the same clothes as when I last saw him. I'm also hit with the realisation that it wasn't onions he smelt of last time, but body odour. I wonder briefly how long he has had that shirt on for, and decide that since I'm aware of the stench of him out here I'd better breathe through my mouth for the duration of our time together inside.

"Are you ready?" I whisper as we stand by the back door. He nods. "Got gloves?"

"Of course," he says, his tone scathing. He has a point, he is a professional and I'm showing myself up as a control freak. I'd even brought a spare pair, you know, just in case. But I can't help it, I'm not used to working with someone else, and having to relinquish control, as I'm finding, doesn't come easy. I pull out the keys and hold my breath as I try them in the lock. There is always the chance Ben has had the locks changed but no, the key turns smoothly and I'm able to push the door open. I hear the countdown of the alarm as I do so and flipping the key fob into my hand I click the off button. Easy, and all is silent. So far, so good.

I take out my pen torch and we travel through a small kitchen area and into a tiny connecting passage. I know the rough layout of the unit so confidently open the door to my right and walk directly into Ben's office. Once the door's closed Cracker flicks on the main light, which I was not expecting.

"What the hell are you doing?" I mutter, leaping to turn it off.

"I've covered the window," Cracker replies, as he turns it back on again. Ben's office is not salubriously placed. It looks out onto the access road, the glass toughened and covered by bars on the outside. Now I can see that cardboard packaging has been used to cover it and, effectively taped around the edges, no light can escape and alert someone who might just happen to be passing. It's unlikely, but stranger things have happened.

"Well done," I say to Cracker and curse myself for missing something so obvious.

"It'll be easier with a bit of light on the job," he says. This is the longest sentence he's ever spoken to me and it's only now I hear the Irish lilt to his words, but I don't comment as he's already on his knees in front of the safe and making his preparations.

Criminals on cop shows make picking locks look easy. A quick wiggle with a hair grip and they're in. In real life it isn't like that at all and it takes practice. Doing the same to a safe adds another dimension of complexity, and Cracker lays out a sophisticated set of tools before he starts work on the lock. While I'm keen to see how he does it I don't want to be a distraction to him so I stand by the desk and make sure I touch nothing else in the room.

This is the first time I've seen Cracker under bright light and as I watch I can't help but notice the full extent of the damage to his face. The scars that have puckered his eye so it's drawn down at the corner, the cruel twist they've given to his lip. It must have been an horrific accident, a life-altering moment. There's something else which catches my attention; his fingernails are spotless, which seems incongruous when set against the body odour issue. I ponder this as he does his thing. His hair is clean too, like it's been recently washed, like he showers, but then puts on the same clothes day after day. How odd, I'm not sure what to make of that.

In a matter of only a few minutes Cracker turns the three-pronged handle on the safe and, as I'm jerked out of my reverie about his personal hygiene, we hear the internal mechanism as the bolts slide back into the door and he pulls it open.

I smile, say, great, under my breath, and as I move nearer he gets up and goes to stand over the far side of the room. I'm reminded of the need to breathe through my mouth as I'm assailed by his odour as he passes.

I kneel in front of the safe, get out my phone, and take a photo of the inside before I touch anything. Then I set to work. There are some bundles of cash, which are tempting, but I move these to the side. Then there are loose papers which I take out and leaf through. The first ones I come to are to do with the business and of no interest to me but below these are a couple of folders. The first contains details of investment accounts and I take these out and photograph each sheet. I reluctantly admit that for this benefit alone it has been worth getting this new phone. The second folder is even more interesting. It contains the details of a couple of overseas accounts, both of which hold substantial sums of money. I don't know enough about finance to know if these are offshore accounts but whatever they are I bet they contain funds which Letitia knows nothing about.

Once I've taken photos of these accounts too I put the folders to one side and turn my attention to the remaining item. It's a sturdy box. I lift it out, it isn't heavy, but I place it on the floor beside me before I take off the lid. *Wow*, is my automatic reaction to the contents and I inhale a breath in surprise. Well, well, well. Inside the box is a duplicate of Ben's million-pound painting, the Ramboult, and I am fairly certain that it wouldn't therefore be the real thing that is hanging on the wall back at Pritchard Towers like Letitia thinks, because why would you keep the forgery in a safe?

I sit back on my heels for a moment and give this some thought. I ponder his need for a duplicate and can only assume he's hiding this original from Letitia in anticipation of an upcoming matrimonial battle during which he can announce that it turns out he only ever had a worthless fake after all. What a shame.

I'd hoped there'd be something in here to help in the fight back against Ben and I think I have that with the paperwork. This though, this is an added extra and far too tempting a proposition to ignore. I set the scene then pull out my phone for more photos. I look over at Cracker, "Won't be long."

"Take as much time as you like, as long as I'm far away by dawn I don't mind," and as he smiles I see the man he must have been before his injury. He should do that more often.

"I'll make sure of it," I say, turning back to the job in hand.

Chapter 17

I call Letitia early and ask if I can pop round. She tells me she barely got any sleep last night. She was fretting about Ben, and money, and the house, and getting a job and well, quite honestly, she went on for a bit before I got a word in. I hadn't got much sleep either, but for different reasons. By the time I leave, Dan has transferred all the photos over onto his tablet. He's also put a copy on a USB stick and gone out to get them printed off.

Letitia does a double take when she opens the door.

"What's happened to you?"

I far too flippantly, reply, "I walked into a door," completely forgetting she's heard this before. Her hands come up to cover her mouth.

"Oh my God! It's not Dan is it; he's not beating you?" Alarmed she's jumped to this conclusion, I'm quick in my response.

"No! Absolutely not!" I take a breath, tell her to calm down and go through to the kitchen.

"So what has happened then?"

"Only everyday life for me at the moment," I say. Then, seeing her horrified expression add, "I ran into some trouble in London, that's all."

"To do with this Ben stuff? I feel terrible," and for the first time she looks like she's realising that this is not all about her.

"It's more complicated than that, don't worry, my bruises are not solely down to you," and I give her a reassuring smile then tell her I'm in need of a coffee.

We have a quick catch up on her life while she makes it and I'm delighted to hear she has an interview for a job lined up for the following week. Then, once she's settled at her kitchen table and we are both nursing mugs of coffee, I spin the tablet I've brought round to her and let her skim through the photos.

"You said you didn't know anything about his finances. But do you recognise any of these investments or accounts now?"

She shakes her head and I leave her to absorb the details for a minute or two. Her eyes widen as she remains focused on the screen.

"Wow," she says, but without her old exuberance, and once she's been through them all. She sits back. "I can't believe he has all this and I never knew a thing. I feel so stupid." I reassure her she is far from that. Ben is just particularly adept at squirreling away his fortune.

"So," I say as I smile at her, "now you know you can have the house and leave him far from destitute, shall the bargaining begin?"

"Why not? Let's strike while the iron is hot." She calls him there and then and tells him she has been thinking and has decided she would be happy with the house as her divorce settlement and wants him to put it into her name now. I hear his guffaw of laughter followed by the expected no. She's cool and doesn't push that any further, instead she tells him she's received some rather fascinating post she thinks he'll be interested in and suggests they meet.

"At the house?" he asks.

"No, neutral territory, the pub." They agree on four this afternoon and after making another couple of calls, I say that I think our work is done for the morning and I shall see her later.

I call in to see Chris next, as I have a job for him, a specific task perfectly suited to his particular set of skills and crucial to the success of this afternoon's meeting. Once we get past his alarm at the state of my face he assures me he'll deal with the matter as soon as he's dressed. Currently he's in a pair of superhero pyjama bottoms and a faded Black Sabbath tee shirt.

I walk home, hands buried in my jacket pocket, one clutching my phone while Dan's tablet is held up under my armpit. About half way down the high street, I hear a car slow then draw up level with me; alert to the consequences the last time this happened I cautiously glance over, relaxing a little when I see who it is. The passenger side window slides open so I turn and peer in, leaning on the lower sill as I do so. "You do know it's illegal to kerb crawl, don't you?"

"Funny," says James. "Get in."

As I do so, rather reluctantly, I say, "We're meeting tomorrow, can't this wait until then?"

"No." He drives off, turning round at the end of the road before heading back in the direction of Oakton.

"Have you been following me again?"

He glances across, "No, I was coming to your cottage but spotted you walking."

"Uh ha." I don't believe him. "Are you wanting an update on how last week went?"

"No, though I see you played down your meeting with Craig when you told me about it," he says, lifting his chin to indicate my face, "as I suspected Danny boy didn't manage to protect you after all."

"Dan did fine. He did exactly what I needed him to do."

"So what's with the bruises?"

"It's a hazard of the job. If anyone's to blame for me getting into this state, it's you."

He has his eyes fixed on the road ahead. "You should have taken up my offer of protection."

Yes, I think, *and then I wouldn't have got what I needed from Craig*. He just doesn't get it.

I change tack. "What do you want to talk about then?"

"Something more personal."

To my dismay I realise we're about to have the conversation I never wanted to have. The one that follows on from me rebuffing him in my kitchen but I expected it at some point so have made certain provision for. We pull into the layby just outside Oakton. It's a deep one, an island of bushes and trees screening much of it from sight of the road and he stops. Then after turning off the engine he twists towards me in his seat and gets straight to it.

"I think I made my feelings clear in your kitchen. I wondered if you'd given that any consideration." This was going to be awkward. I'd hoped that, because of how I'd reacted he would have forgotten all about that and it would never be brought up again.

"I thought I made my feelings clear in my kitchen too."

"Yes, yes you did," he says, and he touches his lip briefly as though it's still tender. "But I think we both recognise there's an attraction between us and I thought you might have reflected on that further?" I swallow, my throat dry. It wasn't like I hadn't. He had most definitely occupied some of my peripheral thoughts, if I was being honest some of them less peripheral. It wasn't like I wasn't attracted to him, I was. But that's not enough, that's an instinctive response, an animal reaction, and just because you feel it, it doesn't mean you should act on it. So while I could freely admit to myself I'd spent some time thinking about his potential as a lover, and would have totally gone there, once, that was before Dan and I were most definitely back on and I knew we were a better fit. Dan was light-hearted and made me laugh, he brought fun into my life. How could I seriously consider pairing up with a policeman? That idea was ludicrous. I hadn't realised I was staring down at my hands until I felt his fingers take hold of my chin then lift my head to meet his eyes again. The echo of Craig causes the faint tinkle of alarm. His eyebrows rise, a silent nudge.

"No, no I haven't."

"Liar." He leans closer, reaches his hand over and places it between my thighs as though planting his stake in the ground of my territory. "You want me as much as I want you. You know you do." I try to keep it civil and clear, speaking in words of only one syllable.

"I said no." I see his expression darken, his hand moving higher as fear slithers snakelike down my back.

"You can't say no to me. I hold all the cards."

"What do you mean?"

"I mean that amnesty I offered, your future freedom, it's all in my hands." He tilts his head, "If you're not cooperative it could make it hard to grant after all." He feigns sorrow at the unfortunate decision he might have to make. I lean closer still, my lips near his.

"And when you say cooperative?"

"I mean sex, Maddy. You and me having a filthy old time of it." He says this like he's offering up the most fun afternoon imaginable and I don't know what it is about me that makes him feel like he can, but I've heard enough.

"Okay then, if that's how it has to be," he smiles, self-satisfied, going in for the kiss. My hand comes up, blocks his mouth, and his expression clouds with confusion. Then I tell him what's what, right up in his face, my teeth gritted. "No, no, no. It's not that easy. You want to fuck me; you're going to have to take it." I watch his expression change, his eyebrows rise. But I'm not finished yet, "Think you can do that, James? Think you're up to it? Not every man is, you know. Tag was, but I'm not so sure about you. I don't think you have what it takes to rape a woman. And that's what you're going to have to do if you want to get inside me." He goes to speak but I don't let him.

"You're going to have to beat me. You think you can do that? You think you can knock me senseless, that you can pin me down? That you can force yourself into me?" I pause, let my words sink in. His face tightens, he removes his hand, draws back. "No? I didn't think so. A step too far, even for you." I don't want to hear another word from him so open the door and get out only too well aware of my vulnerability alone with him like this, but as I look up I see Dan's car drive into the layby; he slows, hangs back, watching but not interfering. Relief sweeps through me, my determination to see this through bolstered.

I lean down to peer back in through the door at him, "Don't contact me again unless it's about business, James. If you do, this will go to your superiors," and I bring my phone out of my pocket, holding it towards him. It's still recording.

He curses, jerks his head away in frustration, then shoves the car into gear and I only just have time to slam the door before he drives off, exiting the layby at speed.

I take a couple of deep breaths, and turn to Dan who has remained in his car and smile, one weight having lifted from my shoulders.

Once in the car I hug him, not wanting to let him go until I feel my shaking subside. Eventually I pull away. I know he'll have questions but I raise mine first.

"How did you know to come?"

"I got back and expected to find you there. Contacted Letitia who told me you'd left ages ago, checked on the tracker and found you in this layby.

I doubted it was anything to do with Craig so I was concerned. Did I do the right thing?"

"You absolutely did, I've never been so pleased to see anyone." I give him a run down on the confrontation with James, feeling his anger rise as I do so. "I knew it," he mutters, and I reassure him I've dealt with it. I spare him the grisly details and hope he never gets to hear the recording. I then try to distract him as we spend the next few hours girding ourselves for what the afternoon will bring.

At four o'clock we are waiting. I sense the nerves in Letitia, her understandable fear for the confrontation to come. I empathise, I want to get this over with too. I need to deal with Ben then get myself back to London. That return is what I'm most nervous about.

At this time in the afternoon on a Sunday the pub is quiet. Josh is behind the bar, with a lady called Lucy, he's training her up in the art of pulling a decent pint and Dan is enjoying a quiet chat with them over a drink. I didn't want him to come but he'd insisted, said he'd stay in the background. I'm getting to like that, the security he brings me, the reassurance that he's around, though I know deep down I'm anxious about how long that is likely to be for.

Letitia and I wait quietly. We've placed a circular table the other side of the fireplace and sit at it, waiting. With nerves silencing us, I contemplate what's left of the fire, the glowing embers burning orange and red. It needs attention or it will soon go out so I get up and throw another couple of logs into the fire basket.

Ben walks through the door shortly after four; he looks round, spots where Letitia is and comes straight over. I know from the conversation he had with Letitia that he was at work today and I wonder if he noticed anything amiss in his office, or any lingering smell.

It isn't until he gets past the fire breast that he sees Letitia is not alone and I'm gratified my presence startles him, although he recovers well.

"I wasn't expecting you here," Ben says, ignoring his wife, "since when have you two been friends? No, don't answer that. I bet it was ever since you went tittle-tattling to her about my business, wasn't it?" And the way he cocks his thumb at Letitia rather than address her puts my back right up.

I assume that was a rhetorical question so don't answer, merely telling him to sit instead. He looks mutinous as he does so, then glances at Letitia. "What's this about?"

"I want the house."

"And I told you earlier, once I'd stopped laughing, you're not getting it. I hope you haven't dragged me over for that. Nothing has changed." Letitia, cool as a cucumber, takes a photo out of the envelope she holds on her lap and slides it across the table to him. He turns it round, looks carefully at it and becomes terribly still for what seems like an age.

"Where did you get this?"

"It was put through my door, anonymously."

He pushes it away. "I have no idea what it is, it's clearly fraudulent." But I can almost see his brain whirring as he tries to work out how we got our hands on this evidence.

"Really?" says Letitia, puzzled, "but it's in your name, look," and she runs her finger along the relevant section on the photo as if maybe he had missed it. "And it appears to have been sent to the office address, which immediately looks suspiciously like you are trying to hide something from me, plus I couldn't help but notice there are an awful lot of zeros on the balance." She holds it up and points at the total as if perhaps he hadn't spotted that bit either. He remains stony faced. "Okay," she says, "well I guess I'd better just hand it in to the police then. Maybe it's one of those identity theft cons, you wouldn't want to be defrauded by one of those," she adds, then looks across at me as if seeking agreement.

"It could absolutely be identity theft," I say, helpfully. "The police will know exactly what to do with it."

"All right! All right!" he says, "Okay, yes, it is an account of mine. It wasn't that I was keeping it a secret from you, it's just that it dates from prior to our marriage. It was an inheritance. I'm assuming you wouldn't expect any part of that on our divorce, would you?"

"No, you're right. I don't think I would. But now that I know you have enough to get by on, I do want the house." She is adamant and I like this firm and business-like Letitia. "Otherwise, I will come after the rest," and she waves the photo in front of him.

He sighs and says, "Okay, you can have the house in the divorce."

"No, not in the divorce, I want it now." I'm delighted she's sticking to her guns, I know if it's left, then by the time the divorce is all sorted out his solicitors will have everything tied up in knots and she won't get so much as a fraction of what's due to her. By my reckoning, and with the knowledge of what he has stashed away, I still think he's getting away lightly.

I lean forward. "While we're on the subject of property. There's something else for you to consider."

And at that point Diane walks round from the bar. Ben's mouth drops a little but then he's quick to round on me.

"What is this? An ambush?" he says with a smile like it's something to laugh off but I'm completely serious when I say,

"Something like that," as Diane takes her seat. "Now, recently you threatened my friend here with a huge increase in her rent. We've already discussed your reasons for doing that, Ben, and I don't think they are fair. What do you think, Diane?"

"I don't think they're fair at all," she says, bristling with indignation. "I've paid you enough rent over the years to have bought the cottage outright and now you're taking the anger you have with someone else out on me, it's simply not on."

I hold out my hands, palms uppermost, "You see, Ben. Diane doesn't think it's fair either and she made an excellent point there. She has already paid you enough rent over the years to have bought the cottage outright. So what do you think you should do about that, Ben?"

He looks bewildered, like he doesn't know what we're expecting of him, or can't believe it. "I don't know. As far as I can see it's simple, I rent the property out and the tenant pays the market rent on it. It's business."

"Well, firstly, it's not a market rent, it's well above that now, and secondly, it's not business, it's personal. You've made it so." This is a surprise, and welcome, interjection from Letitia.

Looking partially defeated, he says, "So what are you wanting me to do? Lower the rent again?"

"I think we can do better than that, don't you?" I say, and indicate for Diane to proceed.

"I want you to transfer the cottage into my name," she says firmly, and pulling herself up to her full height in the chair as she does so.

"Are you kidding me? I'm not doing that."

"Letitia?" I say, and she slides another photo across the table to him. His eyes roll as he reaches for it but again he becomes quiet as he takes in its contents. I know it is a copy of what I suspect is an offshore account. One I daresay the taxman would be very interested in.

"How did you get this?" He asks me rather than his wife and I hold my hands up and refer to the anonymous delivery line last used by Letitia. He folds up the photo and showing frustration pushes it into his jacket pocket.

"Oh you can keep that one, we have copies," I

say with a smile. "So here's the plan, Ben. Tomorrow you are going to go to your solicitor and arrange for both of these properties to be transferred into their new owners' names. I understand, with the power of everything being online nowadays, you should be able to get that done within a couple of days. Letitia and Diane will be around and available whenever it is necessary to sign whatever you need them to in order for that to happen, won't you, ladies?" They both voice their agreement. "So shall we say Wednesday for you to deliver proof of the transfers?"

"I have no idea if I can get it done in that time." I can feel his anger threatening to boil over as he says this.

"Oh, do make it happen, Ben, I'm sure you can, I have every faith in you. And just think you might even get a discount from the solicitors for a two for one deal." He glares at me and starts to rise. "Don't go yet. There is someone else who wants a word first." And I look up to see Kourtney join our little gathering.

"Oh for fuck's sake," he mutters under his breath then continues to get up. "I'm not staying around for this."

"I think you'll want to," says Kourtney. "At least stop long enough to read a little somethin' that Chris 'as written about you." He stares across the table at her and if looks could kill she would be lying dead on the floor right about now. She takes some pieces of paper out of the folder she has with her and passes them round the table. "This," she says, as she places the final copy in front of Ben, "is the piece that will be landing on the desk of the editor of the local rag in the morning." We fall silent as we absorb the contents of Chris's article. It exposes the world of dodgy dealing and backhanders that have been used to assist local businessmen to amass the fortunes they have and climb the ladders as far as they do. Chris has cleverly not specifically named Ben, no doubt for fear of being sued, but he has used the copies of the paperwork I obtained from the safe and clearly spent a happy few hours concocting a piece that does refer to those with ambition enough to seek mayoral office, and I'm certain this will raise enough suspicion to cause Ben a significant dip in popularity. Certainly anyone who knows him will definitely know exactly who this has been written about.

Ben looks horrified. "You can't do this? It'll ruin my reputation."

"Like you ruined mine, you mean," says Kourtney, a fierce glint in her eye. He pauses for a moment as if only just realising for the first time what he did. Then he makes it worse, a whole lot worse.

"That's not the same, you're just a cleaner. This is my whole business," and he waves the paper he's now holding in his clenched fist in her direction.

"I'm just a what?" Fury adds colour to Kourtney's cheeks.

"You know what I mean," says Ben dismissively, which is only going to inflame the irate Kourtney further.

"Oh, he writes very well doesn't he?" says Diane, defusing the situation just a tad, and Letitia and I agree wholeheartedly and I know Chris will have loved putting this together. Kourtney stands.

"You know what?" She turns to the rest of us. "I don't think I am going to give him an option. Let him see what it feels like." I don't blame her but that wasn't exactly the plan.

"Think carefully about what you want out of this, Kourtney," I say, not wanting her to take her eye off the ball. She clenches and unclenches the fist that is closest to me.

"There's an option?" Ben asks hopefully, looking up at her. Kourtney expels her breath with frustration and she grumbles with irritation as she reaches back into her folder and passes around another set of sheets.

This is the first time I have had the chance to see either of them and I am seriously impressed, Chris has come through big time for Kourtney here.

Ben doesn't look any more pleased when he finishes reading this one. It is framed as a letter of apology to Kourtney and an admission to everyone else that local businessman and mayoral candidate Ben Pritchard, made a mistake in accusing Kourtney of stealing. It goes on to say that he appreciates the harm this has done to her business and that he is writing this open letter to the paper to make it very clear to everyone how wrong he has been.

It's a hard thing for a man with his ego to admit to but I have no sympathy for him. He did wrong and he now has a choice to make.

"So?" Kourtney asks, "which is it to be?"

He's holding one of the articles in each hand and looking back and forth between the two, a rock and a hard place. We give him a few moments' quiet to consider his options.

"The apology," he mutters.

"Sorry, I didn't catch that," Diane says, leaning forward and turning her head as if hard of hearing.

"The apology," he repeats, louder. Then he flings both papers onto the table and gets up. "Is that it? Are we done now?" he asks to no one in particular, "there isn't some other poor pathetic person you wish to drag out of the woodwork that I'm supposed to have wronged?"

"Nope," I say, looking round the table as though to check in with everyone else. I'm met with a chorus of nos. I stand and look Ben in the eye. "I think you can go now." He hesitates as if he'd like to say more but then turns and walks swiftly away and out of the main door.

After celebratory hugs with all three women, I follow as far as the bar, planning on getting in a drink for everyone, and I ask Lucy for a bottle of something fizzy as I wrap my arm around Dan's waist and he squeezes me back as he lays a kiss on my temple. I'm smiling inside and out as the door bursts open and a furious Ben marches back through it. As Dan tries to put himself between him and me, Ben points a threatening finger at me and apparently he's remembered what it was he wanted to say.

"I don't understand where you fit into all of

this, but when I find out, you will regret crossing me."

"Bring it on, Ben," I say, easing alongside Dan and standing to face him, "I have so much more from where that came from." He looks like he could throttle me but turns again and storms out with plenty to think about.

Chapter 18

Dan and I are due to go to the gym first thing Monday morning. That's what we agreed last night. However, I wake to the sound of rain pounding on the roof, a lighter pattering as it drives against the windows, and it's all too tempting to bury myself back under the duvet for a little longer. Particularly as these are the last few minutes I get to enjoy having Dan in bed with me for the next couple of days. Eventually though I force myself to get up, and wake Dan in the process.

Although I enjoy getting my workout done and dusted early in the morning I'm not convinced Dan appreciates getting up this much earlier than he's used to so, in an effort to be thoughtful, I lean over and, whispering close to his ear, suggest he stays where he is if he wants to. He's told me that his body is simply not awake enough to function properly at this time of the morning and while I'm hoping he acclimatises to the early start, because I enjoy having him there with me, I think that outcome is unlikely. This morning, however, despite me giving him a free pass to stay tucked up under the covers, he throws the duvet back and sits up, swinging his legs off the side of the bed, before yawning loudly. I suspect once this situation blows over he will revert to fitting in his workout around his job and therefore in Hartleigh. Which means he'll be going to my old gym. Given this reminder, I briefly wonder how things are there, whether there is still the same attendance by the same faces, on the same timetable. I suspect so, people do love their routines.

It's one of those dreary grey mornings today, where daylight struggles to break through against the onslaught of rain, and we have to make a dash for Dan's car to avoid a soaking. The gym session this morning is all about reducing my stress levels and by the time I leave, having given my body a decent workout, I do feel calmer. However, on the journey home I am tempted to pop in to Diane's to see if she has any of those brownies left, but then resist.

The rain has stopped by the time we're driving to Hartleigh to attend the offices of Watson and Grove together. As we enter the town I see Sidney's shop is being gutted. There's a skip parked like a car on the road, a couple of flashing lights on the outside corners in warning, and as we pass I see two blokes carrying out one half of the counter then chucking the whole thing in.

Dan and I have organised a meeting with Cubby and James to have a catch up on what has already happened as well as running through the plans we have in place for this week. If I'm being truthful with myself I recognise the fact I initially dismissed Dan's involvement. Firstly, because I've always worked alone so didn't want, or think I needed, anyone else along for the ride, and secondly, and I'm embarrassed to admit it but, I didn't see what the point of his input would be or if he would be of any use out in the field. I'm pleased to find I've revised my thinking and have appreciated his efforts. He seems to have a good sense of when to hold back and when to take action, as was proven yesterday, so for the first time I've properly included him in my plans and he knows exactly what's going on.

As I'm thinking through what I need to say to the others on the way there, I realise I've started saying 'we' not 'I', which feels like another positive step forward. We're getting to be a team, to be properly working together, planning together and it's good having someone else in my corner. It's like it was when I was with Tag, only different, and better. I feel we're more equal partners, each pulling our weight in the areas we're strongest in, and, although I've enjoyed working alone since Tag, I'm finding letting someone else in is not so bad either.

This time as we walk from the Market Square Dan takes my hand in his, giving it a little squeeze as he threads his fingers through mine. He answers my smile with one of his own when I glance across at him. For some ridiculous reason this simple act of his feels like it's cementing our stop-start romance which has not had the smoothest of passages to date. Our times together have been sporadic and, for the most part, since we got back together, we've been unable to show we even know each other let alone have any public displays of affection. At times I've wondered if what we have is even real and can't wait to get the situation with Craig dealt with so we can get back to attempting to be a proper couple, whatever that may mean as it's not something I've done before.

As we approach the offices Dan tightens his hand around mine, and it feels supportive like he knows without being told: I'm not looking forward to seeing James again.

When we get to Cubby's office, James is already there and as we walk through the door I see him clock our linked hands. His jaw clenches and he looks away. I've been concerned about how he'd be with me, but also worried that Dan may not hold his anger in check. While Dan doesn't acknowledge him at all I keep my greeting formal; he glowers in response but I ignore that and turn to Cubby.

He comes out from behind his desk and, separating myself from Dan, I enjoy being enveloped in one of his hugs. I know things move on but I will miss having this man in my life and know that once this is all over, and Cubby has properly retired, I need to make sure I still keep seeing him. We have been through too much to simply stop spending time with each other. When he lets me go he takes a second look at my face.

"I know you don't like me to interfere in your business, Maddy, but isn't this going too far?" Concern accentuates the lines on his brow and I place my hand on his arm.

"It's alright. Hopefully the worst is over."

"Hopefully?" I give him my best reassuring smile.

Dan and James continue to studiously ignore each other and although Cubby must sense the prickling tension in the room, catching my eye at one point with a meaningful glance, he says nothing as we help ourselves to coffee from the tray already on the desk and take our seats. I run over the events of the last week, or at least those I'm willing to share, and explain where we are now. I tell them that a favour is owed by me to Craig for him providing the malodorous Cracker to help me with some personal business I had to attend to, but I don't elaborate on that, or even name Cracker. I know Dan will have brought Cubby up to speed but as far as I'm concerned James doesn't need to know the details. I no longer trust him and I'd hate to get Cracker into trouble.

Now is the time for me to repay that favour, I tell them. That is the point I want to get across at this meeting and what I want to deal with this week. I'm not interested in allowing this to become a long running thing. A debt owed that's going to hang over me for ages. And I don't think Craig is interested in that either. He probably suspects I'll simply disappear again if we leave it too long and then he'll never get repaid.

Plus, there is the little matter of all that stuff about him tracking me down, and me regretting it and so on and I doubt he'll forget to carry that threat through.

I tell them I've dropped enough hints to Craig to raise his interest and I'm hoping I will have enticed him sufficiently so that by the time I get back to London he's keen and eager to go through with the raid on Letitia's house.

Once we get to this point we have a quick break for more coffee and as that is being organised

James can't help himself.

"You managed to lose her then," comes his rather unnecessary comment directed straight at Dan.

Not giving Dan a moment to respond I say, "He's doing fine, thanks, James. Perhaps you should concentrate on the job you have to do rather than sniping at Dan."

"And, now you've got your girlfriend defending you, aww." He smirks and, seeing the flash of anger that crosses Dan's face, I realise I've not done him any favours by weakening him in James's eyes, so refrain from any further comment.

Cubby fortunately calls us to order and we press on with business. I run through the plan for the next few days and there's not much to it as far as anyone here is concerned. We've decided Wednesday night is the best time to carry out the raid. So the alarm is off and the house easier to access, Letitia will remain at home and, not wanting her to be alone and scared Dan will stay with her, playing the part of some new boyfriend. He will travel back from London early evening on Wednesday so as to be in place in plenty of time. James will have his team primed and ready to go. Dan will confirm when the gang is on its way by tracking me, as well as being able to carry out progress reports as necessary along the way and James can step in and catch everyone red-handed.

And there's the issue.

Everyone.

There is one major sticking point which I don't

bring up, and that is how I'm going to extricate myself and not get arrested along with everyone else. Dan had noticed the hole in my planning and mentioned it previously and although I said I was sorting it, snapping at him in the process I seem to recall, I'm still no closer to working it out. I'm not sure how I can manage to escape without raising Craig's suspicions that I'm the one responsible for the trap. My plan therefore, if you can call it that, is to wing it on the day. I'll see how things pan out and try to be in a place where, when the police strike it looks perfectly natural for me to be able to do a runner. Failing that I am prepared, if necessary, to take my punishment along with everyone else and hope a lighter sentence can be wangled in a way that won't raise any doubts with Craig and cause repercussions in the future.

This outcome is not mentioned in this meeting by anyone else, for which I'm relieved, and I certainly don't want to bring it up myself so I bury my head in the sand over the issue, confident in the certain knowledge that some resolution will somehow present itself.

The meeting winds up a short while later. James walks out with scarcely a goodbye, having barely contributed anyway, taking his ill-concealed temper and the awkward atmosphere with him.

"What was going on there?" Cubby asks.

"I had a run in with him." I admit, "I'm afraid it's done our working relationship no good at all."

"I can see that." He smiles then wishes us luck, tells us to take care of each other, and we get big hugs as he says how much he's looking forward to getting some fishing in next week when he gets back to his retirement, and we smile and joke and I feel pleasantly light-hearted as though this is not in fact happening to us at all but to someone else entirely.

That feeling evaporates as soon as we leave the offices and find James waiting. He's on the corner between us and the car and there's no way to avoid him.

"I want a word." We stop. He glances at Dan.

"If you have anything to say you can do so in front of him." I'm fed up of his attitude towards Dan. James looks uncomfortable and clears his throat.

"Okay. I only wanted to apologise for any misunderstanding yesterday."

"Misunderstanding?" Dan blurts out, taking a step towards him. I place my hand on his arm, knowing he's simmering.

"There was no misunderstanding, James. The recording makes that clear." I see the tick, the mental flinch of his reaction.

"I was hoping you might agree to keep that to yourself." Given how terse and unhelpful he was while in the meeting I don't see why I should do him any favours, but still.

"We have a deal already in place," I say. "I do my bit, you do yours and no one gets to hear it. It's as simple as that. You mess with me though, well, then all bets are off." He nods, suitably chastened.

"We're done," Dan adds and starts to walk away.

"We'll see you Wednesday," I say, and follow Dan back to the car.

There's a tension that descends between us as we head back to Crowthorne, and no conversation.

I know why, and I'm embarrassed by my behaviour. I like the fact that Dan has always shown me enough respect to leave me to deal with my own issues, knowing I'm quite capable of doing so. To my shame I haven't granted him the same courtesy.

"I'm sorry," I say. "I shouldn't have defended you earlier."

"So why did you?" He grips the steering wheel firmly. "Do you think I'm so feeble that I need you to stand up for me?"

"No, I'm, well, I'm just so used to dealing with everything, I guess. I jumped in."

"It's bad enough that he believes I'm the weak link in this chain, without you thinking it as well."

"I don't think that!" My voice is raised and I lower it before I continue, "I've said I'm sorry. I won't do it again."

"Okay then," he finishes and that appears to be the end of the matter but we have nothing further to say to each other for the rest of the journey, which is awkward. I assume he simply needs time to calm down so when we get back I give him space by going to pack then I spend some time out in the garden.

The horses are back in the field. I haven't seen them for a few days so go to lean on the wall in the hope they will come closer. In due course they do, the grey coming right up to me for some attention.

His lips nibble along the flat of my hand as though searching for food and I touch the exquisite velvety softness of the skin around his nose. His soft brown eyes regard me steadily as I reach further and stroke down his cheek. He tires quicker than I do though and soon wanders off again, dropping his head to graze.

I go back inside, Dan's in the kitchen.

"That's nice to see," he says.

"What is?"

"That smile, it's the first time you've looked that relaxed in a while."

"Oh, don't forget the brownie day, I think I was smiley then." He chuckles, draws me to him and I hug him back, happy to remain in his arms forever. It appears I'm forgiven.

Dan's returned to his usual self when he and I travel to London but this time I feel none of the excitement I felt last week. Then I'd thought I was returning home and that I'd find myself, and it, largely unchanged, but now I know where my home is and every mile that takes me away from it increases the ache in my heart. Now fully aware I've changed, my constant worry is whether I'm even up to the job anymore which fills me with trepidation for what's to come. I text Dan when I arrive and find we're on the same floor this time. Even closer temptation.

I lie awake later unable to sleep as I run through the different permutations of all possible conversations I try to imagine myself having with Craig. When I eventually sleep my dreams are vivid, and of flying, of enjoying the thrill of taking off, of launching myself skyward, of experiencing the brief exhilaration of escape only to feel something grab my heels and draw me back towards earth at the last moment. I wake exhausted and fractious and decide it's just as well I'm alone with the mood I'm in.

Chapter 19

I'm due to meet Craig today. I said I'd be back and I wonder if he has had any concerns about whether I'll reappear or not. His not so subtle threat, *I will track you down Scarle', and you'll regret it*, has not strayed far from my mind but I find myself lingering on the way, gazing in shop windows, though I see nothing of their contents, in a bid to put off that which can't be avoided. With no idea as to if he'll be there when I get to The Pike and Eel mid-afternoon. We didn't exchange numbers, it's less of a problem for me nowadays but for him, well you never know who might be listening. That was always Tag's philosophy and Craig's doesn't seem to be any different.

I'd seen his phone, nothing more than a burner, and I realise my attitude is changing as I move further from my illegal activities. I've found it useful to have access to Dan's laptop recently and although I will hate to admit it to him I am getting used to my new phone. It has proven its worth more than once.

I stop and exchange a few words with Maureen on the way in and buy myself a cider. She looks much the same as she looked last week and I find myself wondering if she ever takes her makeup off, or if she simply tops it up each morning. It would be interesting, though potentially horrifying, to see her without it.

As she places my drink on the bar she says, "I

told Don you was back, I know 'e'd like to see yer, 'old on," and before I can say anything to stop her she disappears through the door I know leads to the cellar and I, along with the rest of the customers, are treated to her dulcet tones yelling for him. I feel distinctly uncomfortable with her pulling Don away from whatever he is doing to come and say hello, though, as I'm sure he's not all that keen, but when he walks through from the back his face lights up and he does indeed look delighted to see me.

"Hey, Scarle', Reenie told me you was back." He pulls a pint for a guy who has just walked in, which gives me a moment to study him. The years haven't made much difference other than a few extra grey hairs. Wiry, that's how I would describe him. If he was an animal he'd be a rat, there is just something about him. His attitude. A fighter, and dirty with it. Once the customer has settled up Don returns to me. "So, how's it goin'? I 'ear you got a bit o' business with Craig?" I hope that is the extent of his knowledge.

"A bit, yeah. How are things with you? Business good?"

"Oh, yer know, mustn't grumble. The bastard landlord 'as always got 'is hand out but we make do. I've go' a bit on and Reenie does well, with the girls like."

I nod and take a sip of my cider; they had always been an enterprising couple. I am searching, trying to come up with something else to say, stalling by drinking, when he continues the conversation without me.

"She told me she'd offered you a job up there," and he jerks his head towards the ceiling, then he grins. "Shame yer turned 'er down, I always get a bit of a freebie with 'er girls, and yer know..." he looks me up and down, licks his lips, "I wouldn't mind..." and he leaves that hanging there. I have no words. I'm not even sure how I'm meant to respond to that, it's all I can do to suppress the shudder. Fortunately, I'm saved from having to do so by a shout.

"Scarle'!" I look over at the door to the snug. There's Craig and with a movement of his head, he orders me towards him. I never thought I'd be relieved to see him, and I guess I shouldn't be, out of the frying pan and all that.

"Sorry, have to go," I say to a leering Don and I hurry across the room.

When I enter the snug I see that Lee is back on duty and he's the one who pats me down. I'd like to have a proper catch-up with him at some point but doubt we'll get the chance. Without Craig asking I undo the buttons on my shirt to let him check me over, then when he's satisfied he gestures to a table and tells me to sit before taking the chair opposite. I wonder which version of Craig I get to see today.

"Cracker see you all right?"

"Yes, thanks. He did a good job."

"Ripe, ain't 'e," he adds with a smirk.

"Yes, why is that?"

"'e 'as no sense of smell. Never 'as 'ad."

"Single?"

"Of course." I bet he thinks it's his face that's

putting off the ladies, it isn't, despite the damage done I remember his lopsided grin and that cheeky wink. "Business?" He says. I nod, dive right in.

"Seventy, thirty." His eyes widen.

"You've got to be 'aving a laugh!"

"No." I've never remained more serious.

"I assume I'm puttin' up the manpower?" I nod. "And the vehicles?" He assesses me for a long moment and my guts clench, the knot in them now a permanent feature. "An' you're wantin' seventy, nah, you're the one owing the favour." Like I need the reminder. He shakes his head having reached the conclusion of his consideration. I study him a moment. He seems in a good mood, so I push my luck.

"Cracker would have cost you, what, a grand? Two? Nothing more. You stand to make fifty times that, minimum, for a few hours' work and bugger all expense." I lean towards him. "I know I owe the favour, Craig, but I'm not about to be ripped off."

I sit back in my seat. I could have sweetened the deal, told him about the million-pound painting but I don't want to oversell it, or appear desperate. He'd be suspicious if I simply rolled over too. But I watch, see greed light up his eyes, imagine the cogs turning somewhere behind them. I don't think he was expecting such a rich pay-out so to get this done I take a chance and up the ante.

"Tell you what, so as not to prolong this, I'll drop to sixty, final offer. You don't like it, I'll go elsewhere," I say, and get up to leave. He raises a hand, indicates I should sit. When I do, he spits in his palm, holds it out and we shake on it.

Easy.

Craig and I spend the next couple of hours working out a plan. Or rather, we spend the next couple of hours with me talking him into going with my plan. We don't drink, we keep it serious, we ignore all comings and goings around us.

He asks a lot of questions. As he should. He wants to know how I know about the art. I make no secret of it, I say I know Letitia, though change her name to Theodora, it being suitably swanky. She works out at a gym I used to go to and I don't like her. She's a real snobby cow, I say. Posh. I know he'll hate that. Always mouthing off about everything she has, everything she does. So is this what? he asks. Vengeance? No, I shrug, I have nothing to get back at her about. She simply shows off about the art too much, about what they paid for the latest piece, about what the collection is worth. Asking for trouble. I have to be careful here. I don't want Craig to realise how well I know Theodora, or just how close I live to her. That won't do at all so I tread carefully, hoping to satisfy him while saying little.

Craig baulks at my timing.

"Wednesday," I say.

"What is it with you and short timelines?"

"I like to repay favours quickly," is my simple answer but then I give him more. The point being that Theodora has recently broken up with her husband and he has left the marital home. As the art is technically his there's every chance he could come back and move some or all of it. Therefore, we need to act fast.

I impress upon him that, as I see it, the only thing he needs to organise besides the personnel, which I know he has readily available, is the transport. I suggest SUVs. They won't stand out in the countryside and two, possibly three, depending on how many of his crew he intends on bringing along, would be enough as well as giving ample room in the back for the paintings.

He eventually comes round to my way of thinking and we agree on Wednesday night. It's the safest time for us, the quietest time. I ask casually if he needs me to come along seeing as how he has plenty of others to take. Hoping he says no, I'm not surprised when he says he does. I don't mention it again.

Our business is eventually concluded and by now it's early evening. He offers me a drink which I accept. I'm going to have to be sociable, to be one of the gang. I've prepared myself for that. He knows I'm staying in an hotel, and supposedly alone, so it might appear odd if I don't hang around for a while and it is only for one more night, I reason to myself.

Don appears. I think back to how he was in Tag's day. He was often on the bar in here, then became the life and soul of the party after hours. He loved nothing more than a lock-in though always with an eye on his margins and gave little away. I remember him being a little handy with some of the girls too. Never me though. I now know that was because of Tag, not because he didn't want to. I keep catching him looking over and it creeps me out. Other than buying my share I do everything possible to keep my distance and I try to ignore the almost tangible feel of his eyes on me.

The evening drags on and I sip long drinks slowly, wanting to keep a clear head. There's music playing somewhere adding to the decibel level and it's difficult to talk so I keep in the background, happy to watch. I see Craig going about his business. He's in a good place tonight, his mood influencing the whole vibe of the place. I see him chatting to various members of his crew, pointing me out, talking close to their ears and, I assume, recruiting them for the job. Rallying the troops, he talks to several; *the more the merrier*, I think, like the Pied Piper leading the rats to their doom.

Lee is still on the door so I venture over and try to engage him in conversation. Careful not to be overheard, I ask if he's happy doing what he's doing, if he's ever thought of leaving.

"I did once," he says. "Got myself a proper job, in a supermarket." And he looks proud as he recalls that memory.

"So what went wrong?" I ask.

"Craig," and he jerks his chin in that direction. "'e don't like people leaving. Made trouble for me and got me sacked." *What a shit*, I think. Even more reason for tomorrow to work. Maybe, just maybe, if I can get Craig out of the way for a while there's an opportunity for Lee to break away again.

The evening drags and once it's past midnight

I want to leave, mainly because I need a decent sleep but also because being stuck in this bar for the whole evening has been boring, totally and utterly boring. But, I realise, probably nowhere near as boring as it has been for Dan, or as cold. I go over to tell Craig I'm off and as I do his arm snakes around my waist and he pulls me to him, all buoyant good humour. I treat it as a friendly gesture, lean in close to say goodbye and feel his hot breath on my cheek as he asks me to stay longer, to stay the night. Comes right out with it. Like he didn't hear what I said the other day. I don't mix business and pleasure, I tell him now, smiling and disentangling myself from his grasp as I step away. He reaches for me again but I hold my hands up as though warding him off and give him just enough of a warning in my look to prevent him from furthering his advances.

"You can't hold me off forever," he says in a way that sends a chill down my spine. *I can have a damned good try*, I think, as I keep it friendly by smiling but simply repeat my goodbye and walk out of the door. Again, I feel like he's coming after me and I try to appear cool, to not run or look panicked, but I'm relieved the moment I'm outside the pub and from then on, although alert to any potential repetition of being snatched from the street, my anxiety eases with every step I take away from the place. I don't search for him but dearly hope Dan is watching somewhere because that thought alone makes me feel safe.

I walk quickly, gathering pace, head down, my hands deep in the pockets of my jacket as I stride out, keen to get off these streets and into the safer environment of the hotel. Acutely aware of the people around me, even at this late hour, I realise I cannot wait to get back home to my quiet life in the country. I no longer belong here.

I burst in through the front doors of the hotel as though seeking sanctuary, which attracts the attention of the night staff on reception but as they glance over at me I merely smile and say goodnight in reassurance that all is well as I make my way towards the lifts.

By the time Dan calls I'm already in bed. I ask how he's faring before I update him on the events of the evening.

"Surveillance is nowhere near as interesting as you think it's going to be," he says, and I hear him yawn, realising he's already bored with this stint at another job.

"It's nearly finished," I reassure him, before confirming that Craig is fully on board with our plan, that we've agreed the way forward and that all systems are go. We're all business as we run over the plans for tomorrow.

"Another twenty-four hours," I say. "Twenty-four little hours and all this will be over."

"And the things we'll do to celebrate," he finishes, and as he makes me smile I roll my eyes at his salacious tone, sincerely hoping I'm going to be around to celebrate with him.

Another positive for my new phone is discovered when Dan sends me the link to the front cover of the local rag. Such convenience! The paper has done us proud and it makes me think that perhaps the editor is not a fan of Ben. His picture is prominent and they've chosen the one from his mayoral campaign, which he must be spitting feathers about. There's a terrific photo of Kourtney too which I was not expecting and when I read the article it's all there. Local estate agent and mayoral candidate falsely accuses cleaner of theft, the grovelling apology. They've even given a little plug for Kourtney's business and I'm hoping that at least some of her old clients will return off the back of that.

I call Kourtney for a quick chat and she tells me she's thrilled, she's already had a call from one client who had cancelled full of profuse apologies and desperate to have her back. How fickle folk are. I call Chris next, congratulate him on his fine work, again, and we have a brief catch-up. He asks where I am and when I tell him London, he says we must meet up for a steak when I return. Deffo, I say. I can't wait to get back to normality.

I check in with Diane and Letitia too, getting updates on their property transfers. It seems Ben is on the case, or at least his solicitors are. Both women attended their offices on Monday to sign the relevant transfer documents. Only time will tell as to whether Ben comes through with the confirmations today or not. Both are primed to let me know if he does.

I pop out a bit before noon, telling Dan first, of course. I want to see Bet and Vince before I leave, and catch them before the lunchtime rush. When I get there it's still quiet. Vince hands me a portion of chips without me asking and I liberally sprinkle them with salt before nibbling on them as we talk. They are a hot and crisp distraction for my stomach to feast on, managing to quell the queasy feeling I get whenever I think of what's to come.

Vince is busy with the fryers as I go to leave and calls out his goodbyes but Bet insists on a hug. She chokes as she tells me to call in again, whenever I'm passing, she says, but when she lets me go she looks at me and there's a sadness in her eyes. She knows this is it, even before I do.

I get to the corner and look behind me. I focus on the flat, the memories it evokes, and I know. I know this is over, this part of my life. I won't be coming back, I'm certain of that now, and, with that, I turn and walk away.

At two that afternoon I make a mistake.

A big one.

Dan and I had been having a bit of banter by phone. I'd been teasing him, flirtatiously winding him up about only being a few doors away, enticing him with the thought of what we could be doing given the whole afternoon of waiting that stretched before us. I don't know why I did it given we couldn't satisfy our desires. Bored, and needing to fill the time? Anxious, and desperate for frivolous distraction? Who knows? Whatever the reason I'm giddy when I end the call. Stupidly so.

Grinning, I hear a knock.

Preoccupied, I think it's him, rising to my baiting.

Foolish, I take no precautions…

…and answer.

The moment the catch is released the door's kicked in and I'm grabbed by Craig.

"Not one fuckin' sound," he warns, thrusting a finger towards my face. He drags me by my upper arm into the room as without another word he takes my phone out of my hand and throws it onto the bed. I feel a surge of nausea for what he's about to do to me. A leftover from Tag, the penalty I paid for saying no. I'd said no to Craig too, and now fear the consequences. He tells me to get my boots on. I reach to pick up my jacket.

"Leave it!" his voice staccato sounds.

Moments later we're walking to the lifts, we wait and when I hear the ding I pray for other occupants but the doors slide open to reveal an empty box.

"What's going on, Craig?" I say once he's punched the button for the ground floor. "This wasn't the plan."

"I'm goin' off script," is all he says. As we walk out of the lifts he puts his arm around me like we're a couple. As we go past the reception desk I catch the eye of one of the staff. I'm not sure how to alert her to the fact that I'm in trouble but clearly my glare makes no impact as I'm greeted by a smile, a 'have a nice day' cliché called out as we pass. I'm taken straight out of the front doors, and told to get in the waiting car. Craig gets in beside me and the moment the door closes we're on the move. I doubt much more than a minute has passed since Craig knocked on my door and all I can think of is Dan sitting on his bed and staring at the surveillance equipment, all of which tells him I'm safely in my room.

"Where are we going?" He looks across at me, his face giving nothing away.

"We're doing the job now." I have no idea why he's changed the time, other than because of his natural caution, and my stomach churns with anxiety, the chips threatening to make a reappearance.

We're going early and I have no way of letting anyone know. All the planning to no avail.

Letitia's going to be alone and terrified.

The police won't be waiting.

Craig will get away with the art.

And it's all my fault.

I think that about sums it up.

A few minutes later we're dropped off outside The Pike and Eel. Craig doesn't leave me for a second, and I wonder if something has happened to trigger the change of plan or if this is just what he does.

Craig was providing the vehicles to travel in. We'd discussed using a couple of SUV's which would provide enough seating plus a large enough space to stack the art. However, parked up outside the pub is a small, white lorry and we head towards that. I see Lee leaning up against the wall. He pushes himself off when we come into view, gives a whistle and I count at least ten faces I recognise from last night, and a couple more I don't, leave the building and climb into the back of the van. None acknowledge me. Lee closes the doors then walks up to us.

"Sure I can't come along, boss?" he says, keen and looking for approval, as my heart lurches. I don't want him involved in this. I want him to stay behind, to be safe, to always be the sweet kid I once knew.

Craig acts like he's giving it some thought, but it's nothing more than a cruel twisted taunt to show his control, toying with him just because he can. "No, I need you to keep an eye on things here." His manner is brusque and although I see Lee's face fall I'm pleased, and later, Lee will be too.

"Come on," Craig says, taking my arm once more and leading me round to the cab. I climb up onto the double seat and Craig joins me, shoving me along until he has enough room, his bonhomie of last night gone. There's not a lot of room, our thighs pressed together and I try to edge as far across as possible to create a gap. I look over at the driver already in place. He's the guy in the too tight suit only now he's in a dark sweatshirt over jeans, much like all those who got in the back. He doesn't so much as glance my way. I'm not intro-duced, and I don't ask.

We set off, the lorry bouncing on its suspension as it drops off the kerb. I see Don has come out to see us off and I'm glad that whatever happens to-day at least I'll never have to see that creep again.

Craig seems in no mood to talk so I remain quiet and try to work out how to alert someone. We hit the motorway, the miles passing at an alarming rate. I see a sign for the services.

"I need the toilet," I say, and see his annoyance in the twitch of his mouth but have no sympathy. "Your fault, Craig, you hustled me out with no time to prepare." He tells the driver and we take the next exit ramp, find our way through to the lorry park and stop. He lets me out of the cab then walks with me towards the buildings. There are people about, plenty of them, but all are on their own agenda. Without making it obvious, there's no chance of attracting anyone's attention.

I concentrate instead on there being other women in the toilets I can approach for help. I intend on asking to use their mobiles, failing that I'll give them Dan's number to call, or James's. That's one good thing to have come out of my criminal past, the ability to remember numbers. I'm ready to put this plan into action as soon as I get through the door then all my hopes are dashed when Craig walks right through it with me.

"You can't follow me in here!" I say, looking back at him then around at the startled women in there already.

Craig holds his hands up, and shines his brightest smile on the room. "I'm sorry, ladies," he says, then pointing at me, adds, "this one's a flight risk, it's only out of the goodness of my 'eart she's not in cuffs," and as he pours on the charm to all present I scowl as I feel any sympathy I might have been able to use slip away from the faces around me.

I freeze, embarrassed.

Someone tuts.

Craig gently places his hand between my shoulder blades and gives me a push towards the nearest vacant cubicle. I curse him under my breath as I do my business and have a quick scout round the space at the same time in the hope someone may have helpfully left behind something I can write with. The paper is available, obviously, but unsurprisingly there's nothing I can use to scribble on it. I leave the cubicle in something of a sulk and try to ignore the inquisitive glances I feel burning into me. By comparison Craig is positively chirpy on the way back to the truck like this has brightened his day. I tell him he's a shit to which he responds,

"I'm not lettin' you out of my sight, Scarle'. Not till this business is done. I don't trust you."

And there it is.

I knew it already of course. He'd told me the night I nearly lost my finger and it seems nothing has changed since.

I don't blame him. In his shoes I wouldn't trust me either, but it's not exactly going to help with the predicament I find myself in. I briefly wonder if he'd trust me more if I'd spent last night in his bed as he'd wanted.

I notice that since we've been gone the van has

been liveried up. What looks like magnetic sign-age has been attached to both sides declaring the details of a removal company though I notice there is no such information on the back. I'm guessing you wouldn't want a following vehicle to have too long a look at the details.

Craig holds the door of the van open for me like he's being a gentleman and makes a sweeping gesture to get me up into the cab as though my carriage awaits. Once we're settled again we're off and as he lapses into silence once more I try a different tack.

"I don't know why you're not following my plan, Craig. The van will be spotted, you know. At this time of day, it'll be reported by the neighbours."

"But you said the 'usband 'as just left," he says as he turns slightly in his seat to continue, "so it would be perfectly reasonable for a van to turn up to get 'is stuff. Don't yer think?"

I pretend to ponder this a moment already knowing that yes, sadly for me, it was perfectly reasonable, and I end up uttering a pathetic, "I guess so."

"And it would do that in daylight, not in the middle of the night. Wouldn't it?" I nod reluctantly and he continues, dismissive of any perceived threat from the neighbours, "By the time any nosey bastard 'as got on the net to check us out, we'll be long gone."

He turns back to look out of the window as he finishes. I have nothing else and, not wanting him to think I'm not still on board with this venture, I sit in tense silence instead which leaves me with plenty of time to worry about what is going to happen when we get to our destination. Letitia is going to be terrified with us all piling into the house. I know that. Though maybe she'll be out. There's always that, and I hang on to that glimmer of hope. But how would we get in then? Hold that thought, I can guess the answer. Having come this far I can't see Craig being put off by a locked door or two.

My stomach growls. The driver doesn't bat an eyelid but it's loud enough for Craig to look at me, raise an eyebrow.

"I'm hungry," I say, in the hope of slowing the journey further. "Any chance we could stop for some food."

"We're not out for a fuckin' day trip," he snaps. "What d'yer want? A fuckin' picnic?" He shakes his head in despair, then can't help but ask, "You always bin this demanding?"

I bristle, offended by the insinuation. "No. But then I'm not usually dragged along unprepared because someone's changed their mind." He doesn't react. "What about your boys?" and I indicate towards the back with my thumb. "Some of them might need a break."

"This ain't a school outin'. And they're not kids." His voice rises; "none of 'em need a break, okay?" I raise my hands in a calming motion. Then can't help myself from asking something that's been on my mind.

"Was that your baby, the other night?" He nods.

"Congratulations," I try, somewhat tentatively, because he doesn't appear to be that pleased about it. He glances at me out of the corner of his eye.

"Barely got a wink of sleep last night. Little bugger's teething." Which explains the change in his demeanour, but not the fact he wanted to sleep with me when he's got someone waiting at home. Faithless sod.

"That must be tough." I try empathy, but then my curious nature gets the better of me. "And yet you wanted me to stay last night?"

He gives me a look like, so?

I ponder if Tag was the same. Maybe he had me but also anyone else he wanted.

I'd never considered that before and find I don't care for the thought now.

I turn my attention back to praying for a miracle. Failing that for engine trouble, a puncture, a crash, anything to slow down our progress. Anything to give Dan a chance to realise something's wrong.

A crash.

I look over at the driver. The steering wheel. And wonder if I could.

It would be easy enough to cause, but I consider the likely damage, the chances of survival, of me, of the boys in the back, of the innocents around us. The ensuing carnage. A mental shake bringing me to my senses. *That was dark*, I think, *truly dark*.

The truck slows and I look ahead at vehicles bunching, crawling to a stop. A notorious roundabout coming up. Every minute counts when passing through this time-sensitive spot. Rush hour traffic clogging the system like thick blood oozing through a fat-laden artery. It will slow our progress by five minutes, maybe ten, but no more. I gaze at the cars around us, frustrated by how close help is at hand, yet how far.

We come to a complete standstill, then nudge forward in short increments. The engine of the car next to us cuts out then springs to life with each new start, annoying my frayed nerves.

I know this journey but have done nothing to help the driver. Not that he's asked for it. He's relying on the sat nav on the phone he has attached to the dashboard and, while I've recognised the landmarks we've passed, I've taken little notice of the surroundings as I've wracked my brains for some sort of solution. Now I despair over the fact that Dan is still sitting in his hotel room unaware I've even gone. Unless, I think, he tries to contact me and, getting no answer, comes to my room. It's a remote chance that he will do that though, I rationalise, we had no plans to talk further and in fact he knew that after I was outrageously flirty with him I was going to try and get some sleep ahead of tonight, so even if he does come to find me gone it won't be until much, much later. Far too late to be of any use.

Okay, I think, trying to be sensible. I can't come up with anything to stop this burglary from going ahead. So I turn my attention ahead and start to wonder if I can do anything to alert the police once we get there. I know Letitia still has a land line, perhaps I could get to that while we're in the house. It would be easy to call 999. Even if it gets cut off I know the police investigate calls like that. However, images of a police car cruising casually past the house sometime later in the day come to mind. I doubt it's going to raise the instant response I want unless I get to stay on the line, and the chances of me getting to do that undiscovered are slim. Perhaps I could leave a note, get whoever finds it to call DI James Lambert and tell him where we're going. That might even be Letitia after we've gone. They're going to leave her behind, so she could raise the alarm. This lifts my spirits momentarily before I consider that, in order for that to happen, they will have to leave her in a condition to be able to do that, and this thought causes me to shiver. I must do everything I can to protect her, that is essential. It's one thing losing the paintings but, putting aside my earlier alarmingly dark thought process for a moment, to have someone injured or worse, because of a plan I've put into action, I can't bear to consider. All these thoughts and more tumble and turn through the maze of my brain as we cover mile after mile and I can't see a clear way out.

As we draw closer Craig hands me a plain black sweatshirt, like the rest of them are wearing, latex gloves, a black baseball cap, and a snood, a practical one. It's a tube of lightweight black fabric you wear round your neck which does the job of a scarf and in bad weather can be drawn up over your face. Together with the baseball cap it will do an effective job of disguising who we are.

After what seems like the shortest journey ever from London we are all too soon cruising into

Crowthorne. We turn down the side road that leads to Letitia's and slow right down as the driver and Craig look for which driveway to turn into. In an attempt to be part of the team I point it out to them, then my heart falls as I see Letitia's car parked up. Our driver swings the vehicle round in the drive so as to be facing the right way for a speedy getaway, if needed. Although I argue internally that the lorry in itself is nowhere near as well equipped for such a getaway as my SUV's would have been.

The Pritchards' property is surrounded by tall trees, and despite the feeble excuse of an argument I made earlier it is highly unlikely that, now we are on the drive, any of the neighbours will notice us. No one overlooks this place. No one can easily see in because of the dense foliage. Craig pulls up his snood and peers out of the windscreen, craning his neck to look up at the property before adding the baseball cap. I follow his lead with the disguise.

"Nice pad," he murmurs, then springs the door handle.

While the driver walks to the rear of the truck to let the others out, Craig goes straight to the front door and rings the doorbell, like any legitimate caller. I'm shocked to see Diane standing there when the door opens, glad my face is covered so no one sees the surprise and confusion this causes. She's wearing an apron, her hands clasped together in front of it.

Her greeting of, "Can I help—" is cut off as Craig pushes her straight back into the house.

"Do you mind!" is her outraged reaction as she stops and forcibly removes his hands from her body.

"Who are you?" he demands as he continues to hustle her through the hall and into the kitchen, telling me to keep up.

"The housekeeper," she answers, bristling and appearing as though it'll take more than a bunch of hoodlums bursting into the house to faze her, which I'm relieved by although still confused by her presence.

Craig tells me to stay with her while he returns to the hall and I turn to see him quietly directing his boys to search each room in turn and take down all the art they find. I turn to Diane who's standing by the island. Pulling the snood down to my chin I whisper, "What are you doing here?" But before she can utter a word she glances over my shoulder and I know Craig is back in the room. I hastily cover my face before I turn to him.

I can see a few paintings have already being stacked in the hall, along with a pile of packaging brought in from the truck. Two of his team have started wrapping rudimentary packing around each of the frames, as we'd discussed when planning. At least he'd taken notice of some of what I'd said. I can hear the sound of tape being stripped from a roll to hold the cardboard in place securely. I can't see that any have been taken out to the van yet, but it won't be long.

The dogs who had accompanied Diane to the door, barking, are now milling around the kitchen, apparently having no issues with the intruders at all. Useless creatures. They lope across to greet Craig like he's a long lost friend, and one who's come with biscuits which I see him take out of his pockets as he makes a fuss of them. I'd told him there were dogs but didn't expect him to come quite so prepared.

Bizarrely, he's talking to them in a voice I've heard others use, but only on their pets, or babies. "Who's a good boy then. Yes, who's a good boy. Do you want some?" he says to the second dog who's butting in on his cuddles with the first. "Do you? Do you?" he says as he hands out doggie treats like Smarties, and they can't get enough of their new best friend. Bewildered by this latest erratic mood swing in the many-sided Craig, I take a moment to refocus, a movement outside catching my eye. As Craig is distracted I glance out of the window, surprised to see Joe there, hoeing a border, while Gaz is tinkering with the ride-on. They don't appear to be aware of anything going on in the house and hope surges as I wonder if I can somehow alert them. I glance over at Craig the dog-whisperer, still acting stupid with his furry friends, then look back disappointed to see both Gaz and Joe disappearing out of view around the end of the house. Another opportunity dashed.

All these surprises have made me completely forget about my land line idea and now I look longingly at the phone in its holder in the corner of the kitchen worktop. Unfortunately, Craig is between me and it. Frustrated, I glance back at Diane and she gives me a warm smile as though to reassure me but which vanishes as Craig straightens up from fussing the dogs.

"Dogs always love me, don't know what it is?

But they can never get enough," he smirks, and although I can't see it I know he's grinning under his snood.

"Maybe it's the biscuits," I mutter somewhat sarcastically.

Ignoring me he turns his attention back to business, wanders over to the doorway and silently gesticulates to someone we can't see. I take the opportunity to ease my way back towards the corner, and the phone. He turns, I stop. He has a cable tie in his hand.

He walks towards Diane, indicates towards the fridge with a jerk of his head, lifting a hand to encourage her in that direction, and takes his eye off me.

My heart pounds as I reach behind me, sweat pinpricks my skin as I lift the phone from its holder, glance quickly at the keypad, and dial 999. I slide the handset further into the corner, behind the biscuit barrel. The line open.

Diane is silent and docile, watching me as she distracts him fully into tying her wrists, first together and then to the handle of the fridge. A small smile is on her lips, then:

"Honestly, is it absolutely necessary to tie me up? I'm hardly going to cause trouble with all these men here, am I?"

"Shut it! Or I'll gag you as well," is Craig's response, and I send her a warning look, a barely perceptible shake of the head. I appreciate her efforts in giving the emergency services something to listen to but don't want her to rile Craig and get a punch in the mouth for her trouble.

She's only seen dog-loving Craig, and has no idea who she's dealing with.

One of the boys comes through from the hall to tell him they've finished going through the ground floor, and I'm relieved when he leaves Diane and crosses back to the doorway.

Considering I brought this opportunity to Craig, he's well and truly taken over, his men, his command, I guess, but, under different circumstances, I could have been well and truly pissed off. However, on this occasion this suits me well. Because maybe, just maybe, there is the merest glimmer that the police have now been alerted that all is not well at Pritchard Towers. It won't exactly be like James's lot, the cavalry riding in over the hill to the rescue, but at least it's something. For that reason, I'll be keeping quiet and out of the way all in an attempt to fade into the background, just in case there's the slightest chance I get to slink away after all.

Sadly, it appears I've not been forgotten.

"You," he says, pointing, "Are coming with me." I obey, meeting him at the door. I see the two large gilt-framed oil paintings from Ben's office next in line for wrapping. The Ramboult, already disappearing under a sheet of cardboard. All hands to the pumps to catch up on getting everything packaged up and in the truck.

Craig assesses what's left, assigns four to carry on, and gathers the others at the foot of the stairs ready to tackle the first floor.

We've only been in the house ten minutes or so and there's barely been any noise made so far. I'm

impressed by how stealthy Craig's crew are, however I'm still surprised, and more than a little perplexed that we haven't seen anything of Letitia,
because I think Craig has made a mistake here.
Left up to me I'd have asked Diane who else was
in the house when we first entered. Searched it
quickly, just to be sure. He didn't. For all he knows
Letitia could be hunkered down in an upstairs
room and on the phone to the police right now. But
this is Craig's show, not mine, so what do I care.

We get to the top of the stairs and he directs his
boys down one end of the landing while we start
on the other. I wonder if she is out after all, perhaps she has walked to the shop? If so she's lucky
and I'll be relieved if that is the case, thankful
she's not involved in this mess and pleased she's
okay, that is right up until the moment I turn the
handle on her bedroom door and push it open.
Then everything stops.

Time.

The world.

My heart.

Because there is Letitia. In bed. Naked. And not
alone.

Dan is with her.

They spring apart like atoms in the big bang,
and while she clasps the duvet close to cover her
modesty Dan keeps on moving across the bed like
he's going to come towards me. And I don't want
that. I don't want him anywhere near so hold my
hand up to stop him. I don't understand. He's
meant to be in a hotel room in London watching
over me but he's not. He's here. In bed. With her.

"What the fuck's going on?" I yell, breaking
the quiet the whole crew has maintained right up
until this point.

The only response I get is a demand from Craig.
"Who's this?"

I point at Letitia first. "That bitch owns the
house, and he *was* my boyfriend." I don't wait for
or care about Craig's reaction but pull my snood
down and round on Letitia first as Dan starts edg-
ing off the bed again.

"What do you think you're doing? Eh? You
think you can just wait until my back is turned and
move in on him do you? You cheap slut." I look
down at the floor and, spying one of Dan's shoes,
I pick it up and hurl it at her; she ducks and it
misses, but I see she's rattled and clutches the duvet to her that bit tighter. Like that's going to save
her. My voice rises and I sense others gathering in
the doorway behind, keen to find out what's going
on. "Ben's barely been gone five minutes and you
can't keep your hands to yourself. I would have
thought better of you after what he did to you, yet
here you are helping yourself to someone else's
man." The other shoe follows in the same direction and Letitia looks terrified at the rage spewing
towards her, and so she ought.

"Come on," says Craig, and he pulls at my arm,
which I wrench out of his grasp.

"Don't you pull me away; I'm going nowhere
until I've dealt with this bitch. And I'll sort you in
a minute," I add, thrusting a finger in Dan's direction which brings him to a stop again.

"I'm not gettin' in the middle of a domestic,

Scarle'. Yer can sort it out later. Come now, or we'll leave yer behind."

"Just. Go," I order, through clenched teeth, without so much as a glance in his direction, then dismissing him with a wave of my hand, add, "So much for your loyalty, Craig. Tag would never have left me behind."

"I don't want to leave yer! I'm telling yer to come with me now." He sounds exasperated.

"Not until I've dealt with this."

Then Letitia foolishly tells me to, "Calm down." And I turn back to the bed.

"Calm down! Calm down! I don't know how you've got the nerve. After everything I've done for you I don't fucking believe you, you fucking ungrateful whore."

"Everything you've done for me! You're bloody robbing me," she shrieks.

As if this reminds him why we're here I see Craig turn and lift the nearest painting from the wall.

"If you think that duvet is going to protect you, you can think again," I shout and attempt to grab the painting from Craig to use as my next weapon. He holds on tight, and we're grappling with it one minute, the next he twists ripping it from my grasp accompanied by my howl of rage. He shakes his head, shouts good luck, presumably at the pair of them, and I don't acknowledge him leaving.

Fury boils through my blood at the betrayal and I'm lost as to what to do next, except knowing I want it to be violent. My hands are on my head and, rocking, I look desperately between Dan and

Letitia.

Dan is moving closer now; one hand stretched out towards me while the other clutches a pillow to his groin. I've caught them naked together, the very thought makes me want to vomit. I feel my stomach clench, the acid churning inside. He's making hushing noises like I'm a wounded animal he's trying to approach.

"It's not what it looks like, Maddy," he says softly.

"Seriously! You're going with that. It's not what it looks like! You're naked and in bed together. It's exactly what it looks like." And the act of saying these words out loud causes the tears to flow. I can't stop them. They run hot down my cheeks and I wipe them away with hands shaking from shock. The pain inside unfurls and I have to hold back the scream I want to emit, it coming out as a groan instead, and I'm rocking on my feet and he's coming closer, and closer, and closer. His hand remains outstretched and I smack it away. He stills, tries again, speaks quietly.

"It was all part of the plan," he says, "remember? So that Letitia wasn't alone?" and in the silence that follows I hear the van leaving, its tyres rolling over the gravel drive. My throat is sore from screaming, a weakness floods through me but Dan catches me, his arms wrap around and he's holding me tight as I quiver, a wreck as it all comes back to me. The plan. I remember now, vividly. But it wasn't meant to be like this, not like this, not so visceral. Not so naked. I hated seeing him with her, hated it. Even if it was all part of the plan it was a step further, much, much further than I was ever expecting.

As I regain my senses I realise the worst. I've failed. The van has left, the art is lost and I am in deep trouble.

Dan doesn't seem as concerned about this as I am. I feel the devastation of my failure wash over me in huge waves as he sits me on the bed then dresses quickly before leading me from the room and downstairs. We're in the kitchen, Diane calming me as I sit on one of the barstools, and she rubs my back, big circular movements that are gradually relaxing me, lowering my heart rate, slowing my breathing. Letitia joins us a few minutes later, respectably dressed. She gets a bottle of brandy out of a cupboard and pours large measures for all present. Joe and Gaz walk in and she keeps pouring.

I pick up my glass, notice my hand shaking and try to stop it by bringing both hands to the job. I feel such a fool, and tears come to my eyes again.

"I'm so sorry, Letitia," I say, my voice croaky after the strain I've put it through.

"Hey," she says, coming round to my side of the island to give me a hug, "don't worry. It's all over now." I'm thankful she's so understanding, I said some terrible things to her.

"Let's call the police. They may still find the van," I say to Dan, only now realising what I should be doing.

"Don't worry," he says, smiling at me, "it's all in hand." I don't know what he means by that. Has he called them or not? They could have removed the signs on the van by now, and changed the number plates for all I know. The police won't know what vehicle they're looking for should they even attempt to catch up with them. I know the original plan had been to return to north London, so at least I know the direction they are going in, I can tell the police that, Craig said he had a lock up there but hadn't let on where that was. But when I rattle all this off to Dan he tells me it's all right and repeats it's all in hand before hugging me to him as I take another swig of brandy.

Within ten minutes there are three police cars in the drive. To my surprise James climbs out of one, walks into the house and straight into the kitchen.

He nods at Dan then looks at me. "We got them," he says. "It's over."

The relief is almost overwhelming and I let out a long shuddering breath, placing my hands on my knees to brace myself. I feel like I've been spinning plates for so long and for this to finally be done releases everything.

"How?" I don't understand how they have managed this when Craig jumped the gun. In fact, there's a whole lot I don't understand. I look at Dan, as if for the first time. "You?"

"Your man here did well," and James reaches out to shake Dan's hand with something that looks remarkably like respect.

He studies me closely, asking, "You okay?" I manage a nod and nothing more. "You did all right, Maddy, and don't worry, I'll keep to my end of the bargain. Now though, I need to go and over-see my men, but we'll talk soon, all right?" I murmur a vague response and with that he leaves.

I'm left with many questions to ask but before I get the chance there's another arrival.

Ben.

He appears at the front door, looking round at the police activity in bewilderment but he's allowed to pass by the officer checking people in and out as long as he only goes through to the kitchen.

"What's happened?" he demands.

Not in the mood to tell him the full story Letitia says, "It's the art, we've been raided," her voice betraying her weariness. "It's all gone."

"All of it! You've lost all of it!"

With not one word of concern for her or any of the rest of us, who he studiously ignores, he turns on his heels and heads back out to the hall, where we hear him remonstrating with someone who's not allowing him to pass but, after a robust discussion, it goes quiet and we assume he's been taken to his office. Dan and I exchange looks. Ben's back moments later, his pallor evident despite the orange of a recent tan.

"It's gone! My painting has gone."

"I told you. They've all gone." Letitia's patience is wearing thin.

"You know what I mean. That one was special."

"Only in terms of its monetary value, Ben. Turns out that's the only thing you care about. Anyway it's all insured." I like the fact she's not telling him it's also already in the safe hands of the police, along with the rest. Making him sweat just that little bit longer. "Why are you here anyway?" she asks. "You don't live here anymore, remember."

Reminded of the reason for his visit, he reaches into his inside jacket pocket. "I came to deliver this, as agreed. It's Wednesday," he says as he drops an envelope onto the table, then looks over at Diane, saying, "seeing as you're here as well, you might as well have yours. It'll save me a trip." A second envelope lands in front of Diane and without waiting to watch them opened, Ben walks straight back out of the house. Letitia and Diane look at each other as each picks up their envelope and opens it. Inside is a letter of confirmation from Ben's solicitor, attached, a copy of the updated title deeds from HM Land Registry.

"I think this calls for another round," says Letitia, a gleeful tone to her voice.

"Hear, hear," says Diane, as she reaches for the bottle then comes across to give me a hug. "Thank you," she whispers, then she stands abruptly. "Hey, look who's arrived." I turn to see Chris and Kourtney giving their names to the policeman at the door and I'm baffled by their appearance.

For the next little while there is too much going on to find out all the facts. We're separated and have to give initial statements to the police, then once Dan and I have done ours he wants to take me home. I resist, keen to stay with the others and find out more, but he insists. Diane backs him up, and, unable to fight the pair of them, I finally agree. I've been living on my nerves for weeks and am utterly exhausted.

"How did you know I'd gone?" I get to eventually ask Dan later. We're curled up together on my sofa having snacked on what we could scavenge from the fridge.

"I tagged you with more bugs than you knew about."

"Oh, sneaky. Not just my jacket then?" He shakes his head, then shrugs before he leans in to explain.

"Following the phone was a start but realistically that was the most likely thing they'd separate you from if they were suspicious at all. The next thing was the jacket, but it's a loose item of clothing you take on and off depending on whether you are inside or out. It's easily left behind." He gives me a cheeky grin before continuing and judging by the amount of enjoyment this is giving him I dread what's coming next. "I then presumed you were no longer living the lifestyle where you removed your trousers regularly," and as I gasp he flinches, dramatically protecting himself from the elbow I nudge into his ribs, "So I hid a tracker in the waistband of your jeans, thinking they were the most likely piece of clothing you'd keep on."

James was right, he'd done well, and he'd saved me. He had taught me a valuable lesson too. That I didn't need to go it alone, not anymore, and I realise I'm okay with that, with relinquishing control, life is turning out to be better with two.

"Bed?" he says, having given me barely a taster

of what he'd done.

"Oh, no, not yet. Not until you tell me everything. Come on, spill."

<u>**Chapter 21**</u>

You know the moment she starts moving. And you know she shouldn't be.

You race out of your room, your phone clasped in your hand so you can see where she is in the hotel. It wouldn't do to bump into her. You run to the stairwell and follow the lift, leaping down the floors as quickly as you can without breaking your neck, arriving in the foyer just in time to see her leave through the front door. She's not alone, which causes both relief she's not off on some private mission and alarm she's being taken against her will. A man has his arm around her like they're more than friends. You haven't seen Craig, but the bloke fits the description she gave you of him. You watch as they get in a car and drive away, and you don't know if you've done the right thing by letting that happen.

Decisions, decisions.

You run back to your room and watch the screens, adrenaline spiking through your veins while you try to decide what to do.

Under. No. Circumstances.

That's what she said.

But what about now?

What's changed?

Anything? Or, nothing?

Should you intervene? Or let this play out? It may be that Craig has jumped the gun which will require some action on your part, or that Maddy's been taken for a far more sinister reason and she needs your help. But get this wrong and you're the one who's cocked up the whole plan.

You watch your screens and try to decide.

You watch your screens and try to think clearly.

You watch your screens and try not to panic.

That's not going to help anyone.

But you can't help thinking that this is it, this is the pivotal moment, and you're woefully out of your depth.

You watch your screens, and follow Maddy along the streets until she's back at The Pike and Eel. She stops for a bit and you wonder if that's it, if that's where she's staying. Then she's moving again, too fast for her to be on foot, so you know she's in a vehicle. And that makes your mind up.

Grabbing all the equipment you need, you run.

You dash to your car, your hands shaking as you plug in your phone, setting it to track her as you get ready to follow. Once on the road you breathe easier, you're on your way, you're taking action. It feels good.

Soon you know they are heading for Crowthorne. Craig has gone early for reasons of his own, but you know that nothing has been pre-pared for their arrival, not at this time. Letitia doesn't know, James doesn't know. This theft is going to go down in broad daylight rather than in the planned dead of night and you are the only one who can do anything to help Maddy pull this off. If that's even possible anymore. No, you tell your-self firmly, pushing that defeated thought from your mind, you can do this, she needs you and this is the moment for you to step up.

Maddy is not the only one who can put a plan together you think, although yours is having to be made up on the run. Still, you give it your best effort. You make calls. You alert those who need to know. You ask others for help and they are only too willing. You like that. Maddy engenders that love, that loyalty, and you doubt she realises it.

The phone's burning red hot with the calls being taken and made, the discussions, the plans. You're working hands free, of course, no good getting stopped now, although you're still risking that with the speed you're moving at.

And, all the time the plans are being made you're closing in on her at an unexpected rate. While this is helpful, you don't understand why until the moment you pass her. You'd assumed she was in the car she was taken from the hotel in but realise she's not when you overtake a white removal van, her tracker clearly showing her inside. You wonder if she saw your car, if she realises you are close by, if she knows you are coming to her rescue, a knight in a battered Mini. Her knight. And you realise your imagination is working overtime and tell yourself to shut up. You are having to give it some welly to get ahead, to get back before them, your foot is to the floor and you can feel the car struggling with the strain you're putting it under. The engine under pressure, the cogs, the wheels whirling, as sparks fly and pistons explode upwards to produce the power needed, and you pray it all holds together for this journey. This one journey.

You screech into Crowthorne. You doubt you're more than a few minutes ahead of the van and you want time to brief everyone. You turn into the gravel drive far too fast, wheels spinning, stones flying as you head for the garage, the door's open and you don't hesitate to dive inside, park and jump out. Joe's waiting, says he'll close the door. You keep moving but exchange a quick word with him and Gaz, both are okay, both know their role in what is about to play out.

Diane has the front door open already and ushers you in. You hope you're not exposing her too much, but she insisted on helping when you called, said that seeing her will make Maddy realise the game is on and all is not lost.

Letitia is on the stairs, she leads the way, and for the first time you realise how awkward this is going to be. As you head towards her bedroom she turns towards you and looks as uncomfortable as you feel.

This had felt okay when it was going to be in the middle of the night. That had been the plan. They would have been playing the parts of a couple having been disturbed from their sleep then. They would have had pyjamas on or suchlike, it wouldn't have all been quite so exposed. Now it's a completely different game.

Couples found in bed together in the afternoon are unlikely to have clothes on. Fact. And it would look suspicious if they did. So, you both start to strip off. You fling clothes across the floor like they've been thrown there in the throes of passion, the action resurrecting the briefest flash memory of your first night back with Maddy in London, then you flush that from your mind as your body stirs at the thought.

You turn your back on Letitia, allow her to slide between the sheets with some privacy and then as you prepare to do the same, exposing as little of yourself to her as possible, you hear tyres on the drive and know the plan is about to spring into action.

This is unusual, she says, as she gives a nervous laugh. You glance across and see she's pulled the duvet right up but she flashes her eyes at you, which you find disconcerting.

Ignoring that action, you look back at the window. You're tempted to go to see what's happening, check on how many of them there are, watch what they're doing, but you don't, you stay put and you strain your ears for any indication that someone is about to enter this room so that you and Letitia can appear to be doing what comes naturally.

It's extraordinarily quiet. And you look at Letitia, who now seems to be concentrating on the matter in hand, and you raise your eyebrows in question to see if she can hear anything but she shakes her head.

Seconds tick by, your heart is thumping, blood pumping and you try to anticipate the opportune moment.

Then you hear it. A squeak. Letitia gasps, it's the hinges on the door of the next room, she says. Come on. And wrapping her hand round the back of your neck she pulls you on top of her.

She's surprisingly strong.

You hear the door open behind you, the gasp, and you ping away from Letitia like you're opposing magnets. Maddy is glaring at you, fury erupting and you have to admit her acting skills are excellent. "What the fuck's going on?" she yells. You glance at Craig, handsome bastard, she never told you that, and he's taking it all in, asking who you are.

That bitch owns the house, and he was my boyfriend, she yells. She's going for it, you're impressed, and you like the sound of that, boyfriend, she's never said that out loud before and you choose to ignore the past tense.

She turns on Letitia, saying, what do you think you're doing? Eh? You think you can just wait until my back is turned and move in on him? You cheap slut. Then to your surprise she picks up one of your shoes and throws it at Letitia, who ducks and it misses, but you can see Letitia's rattled and she clutches the duvet to her that bit tighter. Ben's barely gone and you can't keep your hands to yourself. I would have thought better of you after what he did to you and yet here you are helping yourself to someone else's man. Your other shoe follows in the same direction and Letitia is looking terrified at the rage she is facing, which is not surprising as you're finding it alarming yourself.

Come on, says Craig, and he pulls at Maddy's arm, but she wrenches it out of his grasp.

Don't you pull me away; I'm going nowhere until I've dealt with this bitch. And I'll sort you in a minute, she adds, thrusting a finger in your direction. She's worrying you, anger you were expecting but this is off the scale, either she's a worthy Oscar winner or there's something else and you watch her closely as she starts arguing with Craig.

I'm not getting in the middle of a domestic, Scarle', he says, you can sort it out later. Come now, or we're leaving you behind.

Just. Go, she replies, So much for your loyalty, Craig. Tag would never have left me. And even under these circumstances you can't help but feel the palest green tinge of jealousy that he even gets a mention.

I don't want to leave yer! I'm telling yer to come with me now. He sounds exasperated.

Not until I've dealt with this.

Then Letitia shouts out, calm down. You turn towards the bed wishing she hadn't interrupted as Maddy's attention is drawn back and, as you expect, she retaliates. And it's then you know this is not an act, this is absolute and gut wrenching pain you're witnessing. And you're not sure how to stop it.

Calm down! Calm down! I don't know how you've got the nerve. After everything I've done for you I can't believe this.

She grapples with Craig over a painting and you're happy he wins the battle as it was only ever going to be hurled at Letitia otherwise. Then Craig throws his hands up in despair, he's done with it, you can tell. He shouts good luck at all those left behind and no one acknowledges him leaving.

Job done.

You move closer now, needing to stop her, needing to sooth her, stretching one hand out towards her while the other clutches a pillow to cover yourself, more for Letitia's benefit than anyone else's. Hush, you say, over and over. Trying to calm her as you attempt to move nearer.

It's not what it looks like, Maddy, you say, and you keep your voice low and calm to try and placate her. But she's not ready for that yet, not nearly ready.

Seriously! You're going with that. It's not what it looks like! You were naked and in bed together. And she's crying with fury, tears streaking her face, and when she wipes them away you notice her hands are shaking.

It was all part of the plan, you say, remember, and you hope she does, and you remain calm, wanting to be that rock she's going to need to cling to soon and in the silence that follows you hear the van leaving, its tyres rolling over the gravel drive. You have hold of her now, and you're home, for that's what she is to you and your arms wrap around her tight, her body wracked with sobs and you remain quiet and allow her to cry herself out.

<u>**Chapter 22**</u>

We gather a couple of days later. Following a day of relentless icy rain driven by a chill wind that hinted at the winter to come. We are pleased to claim the space in front of the roaring fire at the Snipe and Partridge. Letitia and I are on the squishy leather sofa on one side. Chris, Kourtney and Josh are opposite us on the other. Diane and Joe have taken an armchair each to close off the rectangle. I'm pleased everyone agreed to come, including Josh, a late addition due to him being able to arrange cover in the form of the new barmaid, Lucy. Now he and Kourtney are properly dating he felt he couldn't be working every evening, although I do notice him keep checking in at the bar to make sure everything is running smoothly.

I wanted us to all take the time to meet and for me to buy a few drinks to say thank you. I'd been round to each of them individually yesterday to let them know how much I'd appreciated their help. Even Gaz had a visit although he'd simply waved away any thanks I offered. Happy to help, he'd said. It was good to get to misbehave for a good cause. Because that is what he'd done, he and Joe. When I'd seen them disappear off round the corner of the house they had surreptitiously been making their way round to the far side of the truck whereupon they had managed to flatten all the tyres on that side of the vehicle without being spotted. This had alarmed me; what if they had been seen? All those blokes, they wouldn't have stood a chance. Joe had grinned at me mischievously when I'd mentioned this. Said he hadn't had as much fun in ages. And it had made a difference, it had slowed the escape down considerably.

The second delay had been deliberately caused by Chris and Kourtney, I learned later, and was all in the timing. Chris, because he's a good man, was giving Kourtney some driving practice in his car. Sadly, her driving wasn't going as well as she'd hoped and she'd become stuck trying to get out of the lane down which Letitia's house was located. What with it being a junction, and uphill, she'd stalled several times, effectively blocking the road to all exiting traffic.

You can imagine.

It had become hairy for them then and they'd flipped the door locks on as both Craig and the beefy driver exited the lorry. As if the blocked road wasn't enough it seems the pair had just discovered the flat tyres too and there'd been a lot of arm waving and gesticulating between them. But then, as Chris watched anxiously in the rear view mirror, it looked like they'd decided to drive on regardless and were approaching the stalled car with some menace just as the police arrived. The rest is history.

The police case had been helped hugely by the additional efforts made by Joe and Gaz who had taken it upon themselves to photograph the truck, and those coming back and forth carrying paintings, from their hiding place in the shrubbery at the end of the drive.

As each piece of the picture slotted into place I had become more and more impressed with Dan. He told me it was a plan cobbled together in the sheer panic of the situation but the important thing is he did it, and he pulled it off.

Although he denied it, saying it was just down to luck, and my extreme reaction, he'd even come up with the solution to the problem of me getting caught and arrested along with all the others. Get them to leave me behind. Simple. All the best plans are.

"When are you going to put Ben out of his misery?" I ask Letitia.

"Oh, about the paintings being safe? I'm not sure I am," she says with some relish, "Although, unfortunately, I'll have to eventually. He left a message earlier wanting to know the crime number the police had given me but I thought I'd let him stew for the weekend first, at least spin it out as long as I could."

"You are a wicked woman, Letitia," I say, fully supportive of her approach.

Diane raises her glass in my direction. "I'm betting we don't know the half of what you've gone through on our behalf, Maddy, but I do know we all love you for it and I for one shall never doubt you again." The others raise their glasses too which makes me blush with embarrassment.

"You didn't so much doubt me as not know what I was capable of, Diane, and there's no reason you should have known that. But thank you, I'm just glad we all got the outcome we wanted."

And we raise our glasses to toast again.

Dan arrives straight from work. This was his first proper full day back, which at least meant he had a short week to start him off, but I am concerned as to how well he is going to settle down into what I imagine is a fairly steady work life. Especially after all this excitement. This last couple of weeks has shown him to be far from the conservative prude I initially thought him to be, and I love him all the more following everything we've been through together. It can't have been easy for him, coming into my world, and yet he has taken it on, and risen above and beyond anything I expected of him. However, this increases my worry over him settling, the concern only strengthened by the number of jobs he's had in the past. Why would this one be any different to all the others?

He comes through to join us and collapses onto the sofa between me and Letitia. Fortunately, it's big enough for us not to be squashed up together. However, something about the possibility of Letitia touching him unsettles me, so I squeeze over to ensure that doesn't happen. Ridiculous, I know, but I can't help the way I feel.

He kisses me, a peck on the cheek, not some embarrassing over the top public display of affection. I like it. We check in with each other quietly, then he turns to the group.

"You are not going to believe what happened today," he says, somewhat dramatically.

"What happened today, Dan?" chorus most of the group, although Chris adds, "in the exciting world of insurance." For which he gets a nod of approval from Dan, he'll take that.

"Ben Pritchard put in an insurance claim."

"So?" says Letitia, "He'll withdraw it as soon as he knows the paintings are in safe keeping with the police."

"Ah, no, you don't get it," continues Dan. "Quite apart from the fact he has, shall we say, enhanced, the value of several of the pieces. He has also claimed for the Ramboult." Then he pauses, as though waiting for the penny to drop.

"Which he knows full well he has the original of in his safe," I finish.

"Indeed," Dan says, nodding his head. "That is called fraud, and I don't think the authorities are going to look on it very favourably."

"I certainly don't think it's the sort of behaviour that's becoming in a mayoral candidate," says Diane, "Wouldn't it be terrible if the papers got hold of it," and a wicked glint comes to her eye as she smiles.

If only someone had a photo of the original painting propped up by the open door to Ben's safe, I think.

Chris pulls himself out of the depths of the sofa to go and get in another round and I follow him as I need a trip to the ladies. We've not had much time to chat recently and I miss him. Plus, I want to tell him all I told Diane, about my past, about everything. I want him to know. No more secrets.

"Hey," I say, stopping briefly beside him at the bar where he's waiting for Lucy to become free. "How are you doing?"

"All the better for seeing you more relaxed and

happy than I ever have before," he says, and I smile. He's right. Having faced my past and now put that firmly behind me, secure in the knowledge no charges are going to be made against me now, or for anything I've done before, feels like I have a whole new future stretching ahead of me.

"I am feeling good, Chris, although I'm missing you. Can we get together for a chat soon; I want to hear all about where you are with your book?"

"Absolutely," he grins, "Although from all that's been going on I think it should be you writing a book, not me." I laugh.

"I need to fill you in on all of that too."

"I shall look forward to it, Madeleine, I've missed you too. Steak and fudge cake?"

"Got it," I grin, "just let me know when," and leaning in I give him a kiss on the cheek before I continue on my way to the toilets. When I come out he's still at the bar and I pause for a moment to watch him. I had noticed he'd taken on the role of chief drinks deliverer this evening, and now I think I know why. Lucy. She's lovely, and I like the way she's listening attentively to what he's saying. She laughs lightly then holds up a hand to him as she turns to serve another customer who has just come to the bar, empty beer glass in hand. I see the way Chris's eyes follow her and I know he's smitten. I smile to myself, because that makes my heart sing.

"I'll take those, shall I?" I say. "It doesn't look like we're going to get them any time soon otherwise," and I reach for the tray of drinks he seems to have forgotten about and give him a knowing smile as I lift and carry it away.

"What?" he says, spinning round to watch me. Like he doesn't know.

Everyone's happy and chatting around us. I've ordered food which should be arriving soon, which is just as well as I think we could all do with something other than alcohol in our stomachs.

A little warm and woozy I cosy into Dan, enjoying the solidity of him.

"I have something to ask you," I say.

"And I have something to ask you," he replies. Which spikes my interest.

"You first."

"Okay, well we have a family gathering on Sunday, I wondered if you would like to come."

"I would, thank you." A real family, I look forward to seeing how that works. Though an alarming thought occurs to me. "What if they don't like me?" He smiles.

"I love you. My family will love you." His confidence in the certainty of that astounds me. "Go on then," he continues, "what were you going to ask me?"

"Ah, yes. I was wondering if you would like to move in. Like in a proper way, rather than camping out. Like in a giving up your flat kind of a way," I try to clarify, losing confidence as I speak.

"I get it, Maddy, and yes, I'd like to do that," he says quickly, putting me out of my misery, my big goofy grin matching his.

Probably carried away with all the good stuff going on and a tad sentimental, I feel like I need to tell him something, something meaningful, so getting close enough so no one else can hear I say, "You know, Dan, the best days of my life started the day I met you."

He looks surprised and I feel foolish, like I've gone too far, and exposed too much. "Thank you," he says, "I feel the same and I think I'm going to have to make an honest woman of you before too long." He grins at me and I smile again, relieved I haven't frightened him off, and that he's also put himself and his thoughts on the line. It's early days, I know that, but I'm glad he seems as committed to this relationship as I am.

"Hold on," I say, "You're going to have your work cut out making me a law abiding one first." I laugh when I hear his chuckle, as wrapping his arms around me he pulls me close and I settle in, home at last.

The End

Thank you for reading. If you are able to leave a few words as a review on the retail site of your choice, Goodreads, BookBub or any place of your choosing, then you will feel the warmth of my thanks in the form of a virtual hug. It really does matter as it helps inform other readers as to whether they should pick up this book, or not.

Now follows the beginning of the first novel in the A Shade Darker series.

A Killer Strikes

1: Behold a Pale Horse…

Death is no stranger. I have known it. Tasted it. Seen its violent colours. Its abrupt finality. Yet still, I didn't see it coming.

Three days the sheets have hung there. Rain has fallen solidly since yesterday. I ride past the Jacksons' place once again, look over, and there they remain, sodden, clinging to the line, like limp blue sails. It's unlike Jan to have left them out. She runs a tight ship, one that puts mine to shame.

I trawl my memory to see if I can recall her telling me they were going away. She usually would do, as I feed the cats. The faintest whisper of alarm creeps over me; I might have forgotten, and the cats, being a fancy, flat-faced, fluffy breed, and completely ill-equipped to provide for themselves, could even now be fading away from starvation. But I come up blank. I always put stuff like that on the calendar. Always. And there's nothing written on it, I checked earlier.

The cars are in the drive. Another sign they've gone nowhere. We last saw them on Boxing Day, but maybe they'd holed up over what remained of the Christmas period. Hibernated away like a sleuth of bears, to watch endless box sets on TV, while they ate their way through multiple snacks and leftover selection boxes. That, I could understand, almost, if it were only John and Jan at home, although it is out of character even for them, but the girls are of an age where they are unlikely to tolerate too much time with the old-ies. For instance the eldest, Jenny, has her own car and would surely have wanted to see the New Year in with friends. Yet there it is, in the drive alongside those of her parents and, like them, as far as I can tell, appears not to have moved for several days, the gravel still dry underneath. It makes little sense. Even if they were ill, there would surely have been some signs of life. That thought alone is enough to make me uneasy.

I'm now well past the Jacksons' place, Number 9, and nearly out of the village, so I turn my attention back to Macca. She is one occupant of my livery yard, her owner an Australian. I push her forward into a trot, a pace we keep up for the next hour, to build fitness. Throughout the ride I keep my collar turned against the wind, my face tucked down low to protect myself from the bitter sting of rain coming in on a slant. I slow to a walk for the last half mile to cool Macca down before we get back to the yard.

As I dismount, my eager terrier Scout greets me as though I've been gone for a week. I lean down to scrabble her ears. It's a shame, but I've lost her down one too many rabbit holes, so she can no longer accompany me when I ride out. It isn't worth the worry to come to her rescue so often and I can't bear the thought that one day I might never find her. Now she has to make do with the free run of the stables and adjoining paddocks, scarcely a hardship. As I stand straight again, I roll my shoulders to release the tension built up as I cowered from the elements throughout the ride.

After I put Macca away, I'm kept busy the rest of the morning. Although some owners have shaken off their New Year celebrations and arrived to deal with their own horses, not all have been so keen to brave the filthy weather, so I still have two more liveries to exercise. I've also given Harry and Pip the day off, something I always regret, but know they'll appreciate. This means I still have several more stables to muck out, and the yard duties to do. I'm nowhere near finished when my growling stomach tells me it's lunchtime and, as I've been on the go since six, I need the break.

I cross to the house, Scout at my heels. She sniffs around her food bowl for any surprise treats and curls up in her bed for a snooze. I peel myself out of my wet outerwear, spread my long riding coat over the dryer, and lever my boots off. Then, as the Jacksons have not been far from my mind since the first ride out, when I enter the kitchen from the utility room I glance up at the row of keys to check I still have one for Number 9. I find it buried on the end hook, and my fingers, stiff with cold, struggle to free it from those that rest on top.

'Can I help with whatever it is you're looking for?' interrupts my thoughts and I glance over my shoulder to see my husband, Seb, in the doorway. I finally get the key off the hook and lay it on the windowsill, my intention to pop round to check on the place after lunch. Seb walks further into the kitchen, looking warm and toasty in his thick sweater, the pink pages of his paper folded and held in one hand; the other in his pocket. Clearly, he's had an easier morning than I have, but I know he'll have done something about lunch. I'm not disappointed as he spins the dial on the microwave to heat the soup.

'Thanks, but all sorted. It was the key to Number 9 I wanted,' I say, as he envelops me in a hug, my head tucking neatly under his chin.

Heat radiates off him and I soak as much in as I can, cramming my icy hands up under his armpits, before he grumbles, 'You're freezing.' Stoically, he continues to enclose me in his arms and holds me tight to encourage the heat transfer, one hand wandering lower until it rests on my bottom.

'I know, fortunately I have you around to warm me up,' I say, and with the growling of my empty stomach overriding my need for his warmth, I pull away to run my hands under the tap before I take two large rolls out of the bread bin, split and butter them. "I'm going to go round after lunch, as I'm worried. There's been no sign of them for days.'

'Go round where?' The start of the conversation is already forgotten.

'Number 9.'

'On New Year's Day?' Incredulity is etched into every word. 'They'll have been to a party and are sleeping it off.' I pause. I hadn't considered that. As I think about it, I realise not everyone lives like me with a need for early nights caused by pre-dawn starts. Some people even go out past midnight.

'But the sheets are out. Something's wrong.'

'The what?' His eyes narrow with confusion. I knew that wouldn't make sense to anyone but me. He makes the tea, and I split the soup between our bowls as I explain further.

'Jan has sheets out on the line. She must have hung them out during those bright couple of days after Christmas, but they're still there and it's raining.'

'So, what, you're going to take them in?'

'The sheets? No, well, I might do while I'm there, in case they're ill. Although, you'd think one of them would have been able to have done that.' I mull over this thought as I take the seat opposite Seb and trust the first spoonful of steaming soup rather tentatively to my mouth.

Seb goes quiet and stares into his bowl, deep in thought. He looks over at me with that awkwardly apologetic expression he has when he thinks I won't like what he's about to say. 'You're not going to like this but I don't think you should go round there today.' I meet the eyes of my ever-so-reasonable husband and shrug, because he's right, I don't like it. Knowing me only too well, he peers over his glasses at me, realises he's left them on, and as he hates any outward sign of his advancing years removes them, placing them on the table before he continues in his conciliatory manner. 'They're probably having a quiet family New Year's Day. That *is* what normal people do, you know. Not everyone's like you with dozens of animals to look after so barely gets so much as a lie-in.' His eyes crease pleasantly at the corners as he warms to his theme. 'Some people actually spend the whole day in their pyjamas. They have, what do you call them...?' and he points the half-eaten roll he's holding in my direction as he looks at me, perplexed, as if I would have the answer. I see the look of satisfaction land on his face as he remembers, '... duvet days. Yes. That's what they have. Duvet days.' He dunks his bread, happy he's solved the mystery.

'Hmm, one of those sounds great.' I fantasise for mere seconds on this before I remember I have no patience for such indulgence. I'd manage, maybe, one film under the covers before guilt would drive me back out into the yard.

'That life could be yours, you know?' Seb says, and his eyebrows arch as if it's merely a suggestion when we both know it's not. 'And I wouldn't mind the opportunity to spend a day or two under the duvet with you.' He gives me a cheeky grin, which I can't help but respond to with a smile, but as I continue eating, I return to the problem occupying so much of my thoughts. Much as I hate to admit it, he's probably right. Today might not be the best day to pop in, in case Seb is correct and they are in the middle of a family day, which I'd hate to interrupt. I consider phoning instead, but dismiss that option for the same reasons.

My friends having a duvet day doesn't explain the sheets, though. However, while that continues to puzzle, I realise I've already got plenty to fill my afternoon so, relieved not to have another thing to fit into it, I decide to put off my visit until the next day and change the subject.

'When you haven't been thinking about getting me under a duvet today, what have you been up to?'

'Oh you know, the usual.' I don't know, actually, but as I murmur something to encourage some conversation, he inclines his head towards his newspaper. 'Checking my portfolio, researching potential investments, that sort of thing.'

That sort of thing.

Seb, (called Sebastian by everyone other than me) and I are a case of opposites attracting. As such, we agreed early in our relationship that we would each stick to what we did best. Because he, unbelievably, doesn't like horses, and I don't have the slightest interest in whatever it is he does for a living. Crucially though, we support each other in whatever way we can, and while I'm painfully aware that he does far more for me than I ever do in return, this makes our marriage work.

When he isn't doing his work from home, he works in the City. Something to do with high yield investments and hedge funds. Stuff which I don't fully understand, even though he's explained it to me. Because I have no interest in it, I don't 'get it' as he has said on more than one occasion. A bit like how he'd react should I try to explain the ins and outs of snaffles and pelhams, I imagine. I can see it now, the glazed look forming across his features as he tries not to yawn with boredom.

I leave him to what I suspect will become a doze in front of the wood burner for a good part of the afternoon and wrap up warmly before I venture back outside. Scout jumps up the minute she sees me put on my boots. She's a scruffy brown terrier of indeterminate origin and, as my most faithful of companions, would never let me go to work unaccompanied, however cosy her bed.

A Killer Strikes can be found wherever you buy your books.

<u>**Get exclusive content by signing up to the**</u>

<u>**Georgia Rose Newsletter**</u>

You have got this far so thank you for reading *Loving Vengeance*. I really enjoy interacting with my readers and love to build that relationship via my newsletter. If you sign up to that (via my website), you will receive some exclusive content.

Thank you.

<u>**Acknowledgements**</u>

Ideas and inspiration for writing fiction come from many places and I'd like to thank Steve Cowley (my most favourite boss from a time when I was still gainfully employed) for inadvertently giving me the solution to a problem in this story, and Debra Cartledge for confirming it was possible. I like the facts in my fiction to be accurate so a big thank you goes to an undercover source of mine who provided me with all the police information I needed.

As always a huge thank you is due to my beta (test) readers. This time Claire Millington, Kathy Sapsed and Katherine Winters were exposed to my work at a horribly rough stage as I like early feedback and I thank them for their candour and for telling me what they really thought (even though I know it's difficult!); it informs my way forward.

After working together on *Parallel Lies* I was delighted that my editor, Mark Barry, agreed to take on this project as well. I have not made it easy for him as the manuscript has been back and forth and I know he is a busy man. I thank him for his words of wisdom and warning, and for telling me when mine are simply not good enough but most especially I thank him for his friendship and for the bucketloads of enthusiasm he shows for my work. May *Loving Vengeance* find many readers that feel the same way! And may Mark get back to writing his own stuff in the very near future… we are waiting, somewhat impatiently.

There are countless punctuation and grammar rules and I consider myself truly blessed, and mightily relieved, to have met Julia Gibbs who knows them all! A great big thank you goes to her for her diligence in proof reading my work so that the final product is as polished as it can be. Any errors that remain are mine and mine alone.

I feel fortunate to have been introduced (by Mark!) to the wonderfully patient Simon Emery who has designed this fabulous cover. I thank him for his expertise and I am delighted with the end result, a perfect sequel to *Parallel Lies*. What a pretty pair these covers make!

My thanks as always goes to the incredibly generous online community of authors, readers, bloggers and reviewers. Much to my surprise, finding all of you has been one of the most enjoyable aspects of becoming an independent author and I thank you for your friendship, knowledge and support.

I thank everyone on my mailing list for signing up to find out more. I love hearing from you and particularly thank all those who have taken on the challenge of being on my ARC (Advance Reader Copy) team. Your early help and support means a great deal. Let's hope you like what you have just read.

Last, but by no means least, is the thank you that goes to my growing family. They have to put up with the actual process of me trying to get a book out and while my grown up children have now largely escaped most of that, my husband has not. So, Russell, thank you once again for putting up with me through all the times when my thoughts are focused on my fictional world and on getting the work done. x

<u>Contact details</u>

Thank you for reading this far. I'm always interested to hear from readers with any feedback, thoughts or observations they are willing to make. If you'd like to get in touch, or you want to hear about what's coming next I can be found in all of these places:

My website at www.georgiarosebooks.com where you will also have the opportunity to follow my blog or sign up to my newsletter.

I'm on Twitter @GeorgiaRoseBook

On Facebook or you can 'like' the Georgia Rose - Author page.

I'm easy to find on BookBub and Goodreads too, as well as Instagram and Pinterest (although I have absolutely no idea what I'm meant to be doing on those sites!)

Finally, if you have enjoyed reading this, please tell ~~someone~~ *everyone* you know and, whatever you think of it, if you are able to, would you please consider leaving a review? Of whatever rating! You might not think your opinion matters, but I can assure you it does. It helps the book gain visibility and it informs other readers whether or not to purchase it, so if you could take a minute or two to leave a few words on the retail site of your choice and/or Goodreads and BookBub that would be hugely appreciated.

Now, if you're sitting there holding a beautiful paperback in your hand and you're thinking that request doesn't include me... well please think again. It doesn't matter how or where you bought your paperback, all the sites will still accept a review from you.

Thank you.

<u>OTHER BOOKS BY GEORGIA ROSE</u>

A Single Step (Book 1 of The Grayson Trilogy)

Before the Dawn (Book 2 of The Grayson Trilogy)

Thicker than Water (Book 3 of The Grayson Trilogy)

The Joker (A Grayson Trilogy Short Story)

Parallel Lies

Loving Vengeance

www.ingramcontent.com/pod-product-compliance
Lightning Source LLC
Chambersburg PA
CBHW032046050726

47590CB00001B/145